I0631672

A R D Publications©

©2012 A. R. DEAN

ALL RIGHTS RESERVED

Published by A.R, Dean

Third Edition – October, 2016

Please be advised that this book contains content of an adult nature and is not suitable for children.

Dedications

To Deb,

Thank you for being my editor in chief! I never would have finished this project if you hadn't been there reading it and encouraging me along the way.

To the many authors that have penned your words and influenced my life by making them available to read – Thank you. Please don't stop writing.

Acknowledgements

Special thanks to J. Hill @ DiversifiedBeat for all your hard work creating this awesome cover; you are a Godsend!

Also special thanks to Stacey L Garcia for the great photos you took for the cover and website.

Bloodline

Immersed in You

A.R. Dean

Table of Contents

ONE

TWO

THREE

FOUR

FIVE

SIX

SEVEN

EIGHT

NINE

TEN

ELEVEN

TWELVE

THIRTEEN

FOURTEEN

FIFTEEN

SIXTEEN

SEVENTEEN

EIGHTEEN

NINETEEN

TWENTY

TWENTY–ONE

TWENTY-TWO

TWENTY-THREE

TWENTY-FOUR

TWENTY-FIVE

TWENTY-SIX

ONE

Early summer rays played lightly across my shoulders coloring the exposed skin a warm shade of bronze. Above the clearest of skies boasted a spectacular, rich azure that stretched in all directions far to the horizon. There were no clouds today; nothing to indicate where ocean left off and sky began. There was only the blue above me perfectly reflected in the ocean of glass below.

Leaning into the wind it wrapped around my body, gently caressing, and whipping my hair behind me. I was speeding across the smooth, flat surface of the open water racing toward the distant shore. Beneath me the boat glided effortlessly, without so much as a bump. Like a sea of diamonds the water sparkled as the sun reached its surface and broke into a million pieces giving the appearance of quicksilver, shiny and iridescent.

Ahead a flock of gulls hovered above the water, dipping down to catch shrimp that were popping on the surface, chased by an unseen predator. A feeling of pure bliss encapsulated me.

Glancing to my left, I caught the gaze of the captain of the boat. Tall, dark, and handsome he was smiling at me and I smiled back. I was happy, so utterly happy, and then the buzzing noise started, growing louder and louder…

I awoke disoriented, fragments of my dream still drifting through my brain. Lying there in bed, I pushed through the fog trying to remember where I was and determine the source of the sound – the sound that had awakened me from my – oh so wonderful – boat ride.

With a sudden start the realization came. The noise was my alarm clock and it was time to get up and get ready for work. Turning quickly on my side I hit the button that would silence the alarm then fell back into the comfort of my pillows.

I closed my eyes again and replayed the scene in my mind. The dream had been so vivid – so real. I wondered how my mind could create a situation that I had never even experienced. I smiled to myself as I thought about the captain until the snooze on my clock forced me back to reality. I grimaced. Only a few minutes ago I had been in heaven without a care in the world. *Life can be such a bitch!*

The room was cool and dark, illuminated only by the faint glow emitting from my clock. It was four-thirty a.m. Only a few hours ago I had dragged my weary body into the bed.

I yawned, gathering my shoulder length, brown hair away from my face as I did. For a few more moments I lay quietly collecting my thoughts in preparation for the day ahead.

Today was Wednesday, and the last shift I would have to work for the week. Tomorrow I would be able to sleep in, but now I had to get up and start moving.

Even though I didn't have to be at work until six-forty five I was slow moving in the morning and liked to sit on the back porch and enjoy the tranquility as I drank my first cup of coffee. I would start my second cup as I hopped into the shower and be well into my third cup when I started the drive to the hospital where I worked.

Sitting up with a groan, I made my way to the kitchen for that first cup.

For a woman of thirty-six, I feel that I've done well for myself. I own my own home, drive a decent car and pay my bills on time. Known as Kat to the closest of my friends, Kate or Katy when my mother is fond of me, I almost never go by my birth name of Katherine. The proper title is reserved for less enjoyable times. Like when my husband wants to discuss the national debt – our debt – well mostly his, ours by a marriage license.

I had been married once before although the marriage was so short I didn't count it. I was only sixteen years old and still in high school. It was the typical story of the girl that gets pregnant and ends up married to the baby's father. In less than a year the two of us had decided to go our separate ways, doing the best we could to raise our baby girl. Somehow we managed to maintain the friendship we had started out with.

Our daughter, Callie, moved in with her dad once she was out of school so that she could be close to where she was attending college.

I had no children with my second husband nor did I ever plan to. It had been difficult enough trying to raise one child while working twelve hour shifts. My days began at four-thirty a.m. and ended at eight p.m., then there was dinner, a shower and an attempt to squeeze in six hours of sleep before it started all over the next morning.

I had worked as a nurse in the hospital since I was twenty, mostly on the medical /surgical floors but five years ago had decided I needed a change. I opted to transfer to the emergency department. It was a fast paced unit that kept me constantly moving. As busy as I was however, the hospital was small, so there were very few major traumas. The more serious injuries were diverted to larger facilities in the area.

With my mug in hand I stepped out into the darkness of the back porch. I was fortunate enough to live on a small piece of wooded property. The property behind the house was undeveloped forest land.

The night canopy was exquisitely black accentuating the brilliance of the stars. Two larger, brighter bodies occupied the southeastern sky, planets I

13

assumed, maybe Venus or Mercury. To the south both big and little dipper were displayed. The moon was merely a silver sliver that would soon disappear altogether in another night or two.

Looking out across the yard I could barely make out the outlines of structures and other objects. Near the tree line something light colored moved along the ground. I watched for a moment before deciding it was the small cottontail I'd seen many times before.

In the distance the rattle of tree frogs started growing ever louder and closer as their song reached a crescendo then died down again. A nearby splash told me that a frog had jumped into the pond.

It was cool this morning and the air was dry, unusual for July. I was glad for a break from the humidity that normally plagued the Gulf coast area in which I lived. A light breeze stirred in the trees. This was me, this was what I loved; peace and tranquility the surrounding darkness afforded. This was my time. Before long the sun would be up and the hustle of everyday life would be in full swing. For now I was leaning back in my chair, enjoying my coffee.

Returning inside I poured a second cup of coffee and headed to the bathroom stopping along the way to straighten the bed. Only my side had been slept in. The other side remained empty and untouched reminding me that my husband, Dan, was away on business.

Dan and I had married nearly eight years ago. We had met while working in the med/surg unit in the hospital. After two years of an on again – off again relationship we decided to marry. I had thought at the time that we would work through our differences. Unfortunately I had been wrong.

What I did discover was that outside of the hospital we had little in common and it didn't take long for the romance and intimacy of our relationship to dwindle. My efforts to bridge the gap and become involved in things that Dan was interested in had proven ineffective. With my transfer to the E.R. we had even less to talk about.

Within a month of my transfer Dan took a job outside of the hospital selling medical equipment. His new job required a lot of travel and he was often away overnight.

Even when he was home he seemed distant and disinterested. When we had sex it was almost always on Dan's terms. If I approached him he was usually too tired or had too many things on his mind. His latest excuse was stress on the job. Due to Dan's frequent refusals I had started to develop a complex.

Stopping in front of the bathroom mirror I yawned and stretched the full length of my five-foot-five-inch frame. Removing my night clothes I stood looking; my eyes resting on the imperfections of my body.

I was not fat but I was not as slim as I used to be either, my weight increasing over the past few years. After perusing a few moments longer I sighed. *I can't expect him to like what he sees when I don't even like what he sees. Time to get back to the gym!* With new resolve I headed to the shower.

Angie looked up and smiled to see Kat walking in. She was glad they were on the same schedule today. With any luck they would have some time to catch up on the latest gossip and fill each other in on what was going on in their lives.

The two had met there at the hospital and become close friends over the years. In the past when Angie had been going through difficult times it was Kat that had been there for her. When other people were giving her unwanted and unsolicited advice it was Kat that was there just listening. Truly it had been Kat's support that had given Angie the lift she needed to help her over some of life's major bumps.

I looked up from my phone as I walked into the department. I had made it a habit to send Dan a text message each morning as I arrived at work just to say good morning and tell him I loved him. Today I added an extra "be safe driving in" to my message.

I was hoping that maybe we could get out for dinner since I didn't have to work the next morning. It was too early though for a reply since Dan wouldn't be up for another hour. I slid my phone into my pocket as I reached the time clock then turned to talk to Angie.

Angie had been with me on the med/surge floor and we worked well together. We had known each other long enough that we could anticipate what the other would need or want before we asked. Along with the physicians in the E.R., mostly interns and residents, we had an awesome team.

Saint Frances was a teaching hospital so there was always a group of new doctors hanging around. It was fun to watch how they responded in an emergency. Having them around all the time we were able to get to know them and never had to go looking for a doctor when we needed an order.

Because it was a small hospital, everyone knew everyone. In the last sixteen years I had become friends with many people in many different departments. Angie however was my closest friend. She had come to the hospital five years after I started here. Prior to that she had been deeply involved in charity organizations; going into poverty stricken, third world countries, providing what medical assistance she could.

Her family came from old money so she really never had to work for a living. Her desire to be a nurse came from truly caring about those that could not help themselves. Her husband, David, had been a journalist so for a time she went everywhere he went and found something to do wherever they happened to be.

When the couple decided they wanted to have a baby they began trying in earnest but after three miscarriages were forced to turn to a professional for help. Eventually after numerous medications and doctor appointments she was able to get through the first trimester. The two of them decided it would be best if Angie settled at home in the States to carry and deliver the baby.

David was killed in a freak accident while on assignment never getting to see his son who was born a month later. His death almost destroyed Angie and she found a reason to live only in the small boy that she labored more than twenty hours to have.

It wasn't until Justin, as her son was called, was six months old that it became evident that something was terribly wrong. Over time he was diagnosed with severe autism and could never truly respond to Angie's attempts to give him affection. When he was seven he had to be placed in an institution because he had started cutting himself and beating his head against a wall. A regular child care facility could no longer care for him.

Justin died when he was eight leaving his mother with still more heartache. As if that was not enough the next year her mother who had suffered from early onset Alzheimer's passed away. Her father, who was almost twenty years older than her mother, died shortly after, grieving over the loss of his wife.

Angie's grief only fueled her determination to not let someone else suffer the way she had, if at all possible. Her job consumed her as she went about tending to the wounds of others. She worked tons of overtime not wanting to allow herself time to dwell on her own misfortunes.

I often thought she had never fully gone through the grieving process but maybe this was how Angie grieved. Moving through her everyday tasks she often seemed stoic, but when she cried I was the shoulder she cried on. It was for this reason that Angie had asked me to accept medical power of attorney for her should she become incapacitated. I had agreed and the paperwork had been drawn up and signed. I earnestly hoped I would never have to use it.

The day turned out to be somewhat slow, patients trickling in here and there; a baby with a bladder infection, an older man with chest pain and the usual drug seekers making the rounds through the local emergency departments. Luckily Angie and I had a lot to catch up on so it helped the day to pass.

I pushed back in my chair and stretched my hands above my head, yawning. It was on slow days like this one that I really wished I had the money to just stay home.

"God, what I'd do if I could win the lottery." I said as I righted myself in my chair.

"You have to play to win." Angie said grinning at me. The lotto was something I spoke about all the time but I'd actually only played once or twice. "Besides, what would you do if you won?"

"I don't know….Stay home…..Get out of debt…..Change my life in general I guess."

"Money isn't everything you know. You'd just get bored at home once you ran out of projects. There's only so much you can do." Then thoughtfully she added, "What would you want to change about your life really – that you could actually change with money?" I thought about her question for a moment and realized that no amount of money could buy the changes I wanted. Angie had a way of making me look at things from a different angle. I sighed.

"I guess you're right, what I really would like is a do-over. You know, to be able to go back to where I made that first life changing mistake and start over again."

"And what exactly would you '*do-over*' if you could?"

"Well first of all I would not have had a baby when I was so young. I think I would have been a better parent if I'd been older and maybe Callie and I would be getting along better now."

I thought about the strained relationship I had with my daughter. Things had been good until she hit puberty then an all-out war started between us. It didn't help when I re-married. For some reason she just never liked Dan and there was always tension in the house.

I believe part of the problem was that she had wanted me to get back together with her dad. Of course Dan hadn't helped matters either. Instead of being the adult he chose to act like an adolescent as well and I was often stuck in the middle, acting as mediator between the two.

"Don't sweat the small stuff Kat," Angie said knowingly. "Callie will grow up and come around again. You did the best you could under the circumstances."

"I just can't help but think that if I'd been older and she could have grown up with both parents in the same home she wouldn't have lashed out so."

"Maybe not as extremely as she did, but we've all been there before; don't you remember how it was when you were a teenager – dying to get away from your parents?"

I remembered it all too well, that was the problem. My mother and I just couldn't seem to reconcile our differences even after all this time. I loved her – she was my mom, but I was better off loving her from a distance. The truth was I was not close to any of my siblings either and I was afraid that somehow I had caused Callie to feel the same way about me as I did my mom. The whole thing was starting to depress me so I decided to change the focus to Angie instead.

"I didn't realize you went through a rebellious period. You always seemed so close to your mom."

"Yes," she laughed, "I was absolutely horrid to my mother. When I think of some of the things I did to her…no wonder she didn't want to have any more children."

"Did you want any brothers or sisters?"

"Oh yes, I begged my mom to have another baby. I hated being the only child. I was so overprotected that I never really had friends. I thought I would have a friend if she'd just have another baby." Angie looked thoughtful.

"I guess that's why I wanted to get so far away from them for a while. I needed to be out from under their umbrella. As soon as I was old enough I joined the Peace

Corps and found I really enjoyed the work as much as the freedom."

"Callie had wanted a baby brother too and I have to admit that there were a few years when Callie was younger that I desperately wanted to have another baby. At the time I'd felt as though I'd die if I couldn't have another one."

I paused for a moment reflecting. "The feelings had been so intense. I really struggled hard to push past them and focus on life. I had one child. That should have been enough. I just couldn't see trying to raise another one on my own. I didn't need another mouth to feed.

After I married Dan I was afraid another child would only make him resent Callie more than he did, especially if I'd had another girl and by then she was older and I just wasn't sure about starting from scratch again."

Around ten I received a text from Dan telling me he was not going to make it in today and something about his boss wanting him to contact another possible client before coming back. Disappointed I turned to Angie with my hurt. Angie suggested we go out for dinner and happy hour. I jumped on the offer.

When evening shift came on Dean, the lab manager came around to draw some labs. I was surprised to see him on the floor. Dean had started as a phlebotomist the same time I had started and worked his way up through the ranks to be the manager.

"No vampires today so they had to send Dracula himself out huh"? I asked when I saw him.

"You got it" he replied.

Dean was a very attractive man about five, maybe six years younger than me with sandy brown hair and hazel eyes. Standing about five foot ten inches, he had a slender, athletic build and wore a soul patch and long sideburns beneath his longer, wavy hair.

During a brief stint in which I worked in the clinics, I had spent many hours with him in the lab. I had always been good in microbiology and loved hanging out with him.

For a time I had thought that maybe he liked me, but he was a very private person, not showing his feeling except when it came to the lab. In the lab he came alive, bubbling with excitement and the desire to share his knowledge with others. I wondered why he hadn't become a teacher as much as he loved doing it.

It was a learning experience with him and it never ceased to amaze me how he could figure things out. Constantly he was analyzing stuff backward and forward until it made sense. Together we had spent hours looking through microscopes and hovering over petri dishes.

Where I had been good in microbiology Dean had excelled in it. In just a few years he had earned the reputation of being the "go to" person if you had questions about an infectious disease. If it could be grown in a petri dish or affected the blood in any way he could normally figure it out. On the side he was working to further his education.

It had been a while since I'd spent any time with him and I was glad to see him. After he collected the few labs that had been ordered on patients, he came back to the nurses' station. "Come by and see me sometime when you're not busy".

"I will," I replied.

Just before shift change my manager, Jackie, approached trying to fill the schedule for Thursday night shift. She was in need of two nurses. One nurse was on vacation and another was out sick with little chance of recovering by the next evening. Angie looked up "I'll work if you will."

Night shift was the last thing I wanted to do at the moment but Angie egged me on. "Just think of the extra money we'll make. It will be fun one time. Besides Dan probably won't be home and you've nothing else to do."

When I remained reluctant to agree Jackie offered us both double adjunct pay. That was enough to push me over the edge. Maybe it would be fun to pull a night shift with Angie.

"Sign me up," I said.

TWO

I met Angie at nine that evening in the bar at Jack's Grille, a small restaurant located on the waterfront. They normally had a cover band playing every Wednesday night on the patio so we opted to sit outside by the water. A south wind blew gently warding off the mosquitoes that are generally a nuisance of Texas gulf coast summers.

Sharing some appetizers and drinking a couple of beers, we sat and talked until the band started playing. The group was actually pretty good and they played songs from the eighties and nineties that Angie and I had grown up with. Before long we were dancing and drinking stronger drinks.

We were approached several times by guys who wanted to dance with one or the other of us. One younger man squeezed his way between us, apparently wanting to be sandwiched by our bodies. Angie simply took my hand over his head, and in a graceful turn brought me around in front of her, leaving the wannabe *sandwich meat* behind.

Our continued dancing like lesbian lovers seemed only to fuel the guy's persistence. Maybe he liked the idea of a threesome, or maybe it was just Angie's legs. She did have an awesome pair.

Wannabe left us for a moment then returned with drinks for Angie and me. I guess we both felt sorry for him then and allowed him to dance with us for a while.

Even though it was outdoors the music was still too loud to talk over. I had to stop dancing often to yell a question at Angie or lean in close to hear her answer. Eventually wannabe gave up on us and moved on to a new girl that showed up on the dance floor.

We took a break, gulping some water before starting on our next drink. As the night wore on the dancers became bolder, influenced by the alcohol that was ingested so liberally. It was amazing the amount of confidence a person could acquire from a few drinks, making even the worst dancers think they were sexy.

After watching and laughing for a while we returned to the dance floor to show them how it's really done. We drew the immediate attention of two incredibly attractive men that joined us on the floor. They were *hot.* Too hot to walk away from, so we danced with them through a couple of songs.

My partner introduced himself as Jason and when the dance was over he asked for my number. I tried not to look too excited but inside I was jumping for joy. Just the fact that he'd asked gave my self-esteem a boost that it desperately needed. It felt great to know that a nice looking man found me attractive enough to ask for my number.

I realized just how badly Dan's rejection had affected me. Somehow I had lost sight of what I had to offer. I didn't give Jason my number but if I'd been single I would have.

Someone requested a slow song and when the group started singing Angie lay her head on my shoulder. "This was mine and David's song," she said as tears welled up in her eyes. It was time to go. We left her car after informing the bartender that we'd be back to pick it up the next day and I drove Angie home.

As soon as we were in the car Angie's quiet tears turned to sobs. Her body shuddered violently as anguish ripped through her.

"I just can't do this anymore Kat." She cried as tears poured from her eyes. "It hurts so bad."

I was caught off guard by her sudden show of emotion. She had always seemed so strong, maybe too strong. I'd never seen her cry like this before. I thought maybe it was the alcohol but I'd been out with her many times and seen her totally sloshed. It was more than just the alcohol. I was at a loss for words not knowing what I could say to comfort her. I pulled over to the side of the road and held her hand until she eventually cried herself out.

"Come stay with me tonight." I said "You can sleep in the guest room and I'll take you home in the morning."

She shook her head at my suggestion. "No, I'm okay now. I want to go home. I need to be there. That's where it all is."

I wasn't sure what she meant but I assumed she was speaking of her clothes and toiletries. "That's okay," I said. "I have stuff you can use for tonight."

She shook her head adamantly again. "No," she refused, "I need to go home."

Reluctantly I acquiesced and headed once again to her house. By the time we arrived I had to help her inside. She was so drunk she could barely walk. I managed to get her into her night clothes then tucked her into bed. Taking her spare set of house keys I locked the door behind me on my way out.

The next morning I was up at seven. Though still tired my internal clock would not allow me to sleep longer. Determined to go to the gym I got up and pulled on my gym suit.

"Ugg"! I exclaimed in disgust when I looked in the mirror. The suit had fit perfectly just a few months ago, now I boasted what I absolutely hated the most, the dreaded muffin top! The sight made me want to lose weight before I wore the suit out in public again. I opted to wear a baggy shirt over it.

Fixing myself a quick cup of coffee, I grabbed my bag and headed out the door. Angie wouldn't be up for a while so I'd pick her up after my workout.

Stepping up onto the elliptical I tried to remember the last time I had been here. It had to have been at least six months but it may as well have been a lifetime. After only three minutes I was winded and had to back off the resistance.

My plan had been to do forty-five minutes of cardio then weights but after only twenty minutes on the machine I was drenched in sweat and on the verge of overheating. I was definitely out of shape. *Starting over from the beginning!*

Stopping for a moment I took a long drink then headed for the weight machines. An hour later I left the gym soaked with sweat and every muscle in my body shaking with fatigue. No doubt tomorrow I would regret pushing myself so hard today.

Angie had left a voice message so I headed to her house as soon as I left the gym; from there I took her to get her car. She looked sorely hung-over but there was a sadness about her that was so out of place on her normally happy face. She didn't seem to want to talk so I didn't push her. She probably just needed more sleep.

Stopping together on the way back we ate brunch then went our separate ways. I had a few errands to run and wanted to call Dan. My call went straight to voicemail so I sent a text message. Back at the house I managed to do a few chores then headed to the bedroom. I was going to need a nap before working tonight.

THREE

I met Angie in the locker room at six-thirty as she was pulling out a can of coffee she'd brought from home.

"I decided we should have something good if we were going to be here all night. I've had this since my last trip to South America with David. " she told me. Her expression told me what she didn't say. That she had been saving it for something special and no longer wanted to keep it hanging around in her pantry.

She was looking somewhat better and I decided it must have just been the hang-over that influenced her appearance from earlier in the day. She did however seem a bit more preoccupied than normal and I noticed her several times just staring into space.

The E.R. was dead. With only one patient in holding and none in the waiting room it promised to be an easy night but I knew better than to hold my breath.

Including myself there were five nurses and two techs working the E.R.

The patients trickled in slowly, a young man with a scalp laceration, a woman with a dislocated shoulder, and another man with a broken nose. The night was highlighted by the John Doe who arrived with a foreign object lodged in his rectum. Seriously! The things people do for fun. Luckily for him, the docs were able to remove it without having to take him into surgery. I wasn't sure how he was going to explain the hospital visit to his wife, but then again maybe she had been in on it. We managed to triage all of the patients, treat them and send them home by midnight.

At one a.m. more people began showing up. I don't know why they waited so long to come, but they all seemed to show up at the same time. Were they holding out till the last possible moment? Or did they only come for a doctor's excuse so they don't have to go to work?

Peeking out into the waiting area there must have been twenty people including the patients' extended families and children. One woman must have had five kids with her, waiting for her husband to be seen. *Really why can't they get someone to watch the kids?*

Even though the waiting room was starting to fill up none of them were emergent situations so we pulled them back as they had arrived. The first man was a frequent flyer and I'd seen him around many times. He had pyoderma – festering ulcers of the skin that oozed of pus and smelled putrid.

From the looks of it he had let it go for a while now and I wondered if he didn't have money for the meds. I gave him an IV of steroids then sent him to the shower, after which I applied a generous amount of antibacterial ointment to his ulcers and sent him home with a steroid pack and a large tube of ointment.

Angie came and got me to help her with an arrival via ambulance. Three people involved in a shooting. One of them was apparently dead on arrival. One was going immediately to surgery. We were left with a very large, young woman. She had taken a bullet to her back but it was lodged near her shoulder blade. It was not life threatening and one of the residents was able to remove it with a pair of forceps.

She was not very forthcoming with information about the shooting but what she did tell us did not add up. We knew she had to be lying, although we didn't know why.

After removing the bullet the doctor wanted her to remain in observation for a while. She complained of extreme pain and was unable to move herself so six of us gathered around and moved her from the stretcher onto a hospital bed, all four hundred pounds plus.

She had orders for a foley catheter and I truly wanted to leave that task for the floor nurses, but coming from the floor myself I knew how busy it could get and how much I'd hated it when the E.R. nurses had pushed stuff like this off on me.

I grabbed a foley kit, two nurses and a tech. A resident was in the room still making a few notes and observing. There was a nurse on either side of her, each holding a leg and the tech was holding back her pannus. I was left with the task of crawling in and inserting said catheter. And I do mean crawl in.

As soon as her legs were pulled apart the room was filled with the distinct odor of what we refer to as "twat rot." I thought the resident was going to puke; it was that bad. I steeled myself and moments later I was up to my elbows in Va-jay-jay! Not the best place in the world to be, but hey – this was all just part of the job. At least it wasn't a digital dis-impaction.

As soon as I got urine return I filled the balloon and strapped the tubing to her leg. I had done my good deed for the night. She was now ready to go to the floor.

A few hours later the waiting room had once again emptied out. Thankfully family members had left to take kids and others home.

Dean came down from the lab to see if anything needed to go up.

"What shift are you working now?" I asked surprised at seeing him again.

"Three to eleven but it normally turns into a twelve hour shift" he replied, "tonight I'm pulling a double for coverage". The phone at the nurses' station rang and Sandra, one of the nurses answered. After a brief conversation she hung up and announced, "Ambulance is on the way, apparently there was a bar-fight. He's going to have cops with him."

"Guess I'll hang around then" Dean said "They'll probably want labs."

It was almost an hour before the ambulance arrived with a man strapped down to the Gurney. The EMS team, Adam and Andrew frequented our E.R. so I knew them quite well.

Adam was tall and slender but in good shape and a nice looking young man of about twenty five. Andrew was massive. In his late twenties he was at least six feet tall and built like a tank. Flat facial features gave him the appearance of a Mongolian. He was always smiling but he was definitely one to be reckoned with.

"We had to subdue him" Adam said speaking of the man on the gurney, "and it took six of us!" he said matter of fact. "We guess he's probably hyped up on something. He's settled down some but you may want to get your labs before we unstrap him."

"Good idea," I said grabbing an assortment of colored tubes heading his direction. Already a group of residents had gathered around the man who seemed to be semi sedated. "Was he given a sedative?" I asked Andrew. "We gave him nothing," he replied, "we had no idea what was already in his system."

Adam stepped up and began filling me in.

"Patient is a John Doe, male, approximate age mid to late thirties. He was involved in an altercation in the parking lot of Madrid's bar. The other guy was hurt pretty severely and was flown out to one of the larger hospitals in Houston.

There were four cops on the scene when we arrived including the one that will be standing guard. This guy seemed to be on drugs or having some kind of mental problem so they wanted him to go to the hospital to get checked out before he goes to jail."

Angie was next to me now listening to Adam. "Nice looking guy." She said studying him. I looked at him again. He was a nice looking man, but even laying there seemingly relaxed, there was something off about him. As I approached the group of residents I announced

"I'm drawing labs and I'm going to need orders for them." The doctors headed for the computer.

"We're putting in orders right now!"

As I moved closer his eyes flittered open and he tried to jerk away from me. In my career I had seen many drug induced behaviors but never anything quite like this. The look in his eyes was wild and bewildered. He snarled at me sounding almost animal.

"It's alright," I told him "I'm just going to get some blood." He seemed to relax again but I worked as quickly as possible.

He was hot to the touch so I drew blood cultures also. Labs drawn I gave them to Dean who headed upstairs to run them.

"Let me know about the tox screen ASAP," I said.

Angie was a bit shaken. "He reminds me of something I've seen before in South America. We need to be very careful with him."

The patient needed to be thoroughly examined but neither I nor the doctors were comfortable letting him out of the restraints. It was finally decided that we would draw some Ativan and if he got too aggressive we'd administer the shot of sedative. Angie and I would do the assessment while the residents and the policeman assigned to him watched.

Talking to him as we moved and worked around him we began our assessment. I noticed that when I got near him his eyes would shift and his head would turn as if he were trying to identify a scent. We started the basics of trying to obtain vital signs but Angie needed one of his arms free to do so.

The patient seemed okay until the cuff started tightening around his arm. He began thrashing and fighting, trying to break free. I grabbed the syringe with the sedative and prepared to give the shot intra muscularly.

The patient was still thrashing and three residents came to hold him down while I gave the shot. I managed to get the needle in but when I drew back there was blood return. "Damn it," I said attempting to relocate the needle.

The series of events that followed happened so fast no one could have been prepared. The patient swung his head to face me, speaking through clenched teeth. "I'll have you." He said. Before I could react he raised up on the table throwing the residents across the room as the straps that bound him snapped in to.

He grabbed the syringe, now containing the mixture of medication with his blood and stabbed it into my chest, just above my right breast. I stumbled backward as liquid fire spread out from the injection site through my entire chest and down my arms. I screwed my eyes shut against the pain as the muscles in my chest constricted making it difficult to breath.

Without thinking I reached up and pulled the syringe out of my chest then struggled to get back on my feet. Angie was coming to my aide as the man jumped up from the table. He grabbed her and bit into her throat like a wild beast, tearing away the flesh, barely missing her carotid artery.

The residents rushed in again but the man moved lightning fast. They had no chance of subduing him. Dropping Angie to the floor he raced from the room tossing those who came too close around like rag dolls.

Someone pushed the button that would alert security but by then the man had busted through the plate glass window that led to the parking lot, escaping into the darkness.

I dropped to my knees by Angie. She was pale and bleeding but a quick assessment told me her wounds were only superficial. She was in shock. With a blank look on her face she looked up into my eyes, "They're here too!" she said. "I can't believe they're here too."

The rest of the night was spent giving police reports, filing incident reports, and cleaning and stitching each other's wounds. Dr. Robinson, a resident on the plastics team worked on Angie's neck.

The bite was on the left side of her neck just below her ear. A circular cut indicated where his teeth had penetrated the flesh, this part was surprisingly clean. However he had jerked down with his mouth tearing the flesh further leaving jagged edges to work with. The entire left side of her neck was a deep purple color that ran down onto her shoulder.

Dr. Robinson assured her that he knew what he was doing and one hundred and ten tiny stitches later the tear was completely repaired. We were all thoroughly impressed with his stitches.

One of the residents had a fractured arm from being thrown across the room and ortho was busy splinting it. Another resident, Dr. Ruiz pulled me aside to examine where the needle had penetrated.

As painful as it had been there was only a relatively small bruise, about three inches across. Compared to what Angie had suffered I was embarrassed at the attention. "The area looks clean enough," Dr. Ruiz was saying "but who knows what kind of pathogens you've been exposed to with his blood. That was a considerable amount he injected into you."

Dean came down and drew labs on both Angie and me for screening purposes. There was more paperwork to be filled out as well as employee health forms. We both had a bag of IV antibiotics and decided it best to start prophylaxis against HIV. Thankfully we did have samples of the patient's blood. "I'll let y'all know the results as soon as they come in." Dean assured us.

The E.R. was a wreck. A million pieces of glass covered the floor and papers were everywhere. I hadn't noticed before but a desk with a computer on it had been knocked over in the skirmish.

Housekeeping had been called but still had not shown up. I picked up a piece of the glass. It was thick, tempered glass, similar to what they use in automobiles. If I remembered correctly all of our windows were hurricane rated to withstand flying objects. It had to have taken a lot of force to break through that window.

I felt I should stay to help clean up the mess but the night supervisor insisted I go home. Dr. Robinson and I tried to convince Angie to stay in the hospital in observation, but she politely refused. I asked if she would at least come home with me so I could check on her but again she refused. "I'm a nurse Kat," she said "I will come back if there is a problem."

Physically exhausted and mentally drained we left for home. My adrenaline had kept me awake despite the dose of the sedative I had received but now it was spent. Pulling into the driveway I could barely keep my eyes open. My last memory was pulling the drapes to and crawling into the comfort of my bed.

I awoke suddenly startled by a scraping sound, uncertain if it was real or only in my dreams. I lie quietly trying to determine the source. Hearing nothing more I moved to get up.

I gasped with sudden pain. Once again fire seemed to burn through my tissue, shooting out in all directions of my chest and into my shoulders and neck. I sat hunched over on the side of the bed for long moments then slowly got up.

Walking over to the mirror I pulled my scrub top off. I had not even changed before getting in the bed. It was painful to raise my arms over my head but I managed to free myself of the smock then pulled off my pants. The bruise had gotten bigger but other than that there were no visible signs of redness or swelling. My fingers were tingling with every movement.

I was glad that I didn't have to go back to work for a few days. Jackie had called before Angie and I had left the hospital and told us both to take a few days leave and call her if we needed more time.

It was only one o'clock but I was wide awake now. Going to the kitchen I made myself a cup of coffee then dug around for some Tylenol. Taking a couple I headed for the bathroom and jumped in the shower. I dressed quickly and left to get some fresh air and something to eat at the local sandwich shop.

The aromas that hit my nose as I opened the door to the sandwich shop were almost overpowering. Bacon was frying in the kitchen and the smell was so strong I could taste the salt in it. But it wasn't just the bacon frying now that I smelled. I could also smell the cold grease spatter from previous days that hung stale in the air. Breads, herbs and cheeses all came together in a somewhat nauseating combination. Somehow I wasn't as hungry as I had thought and I definitely no longer wanted a BLT. I ordered a turkey sandwich and opted to eat outside on the patio. My nose had not been this sensitive since I was pregnant.

I was un-wrapping my sandwich when my phone rang so loudly I almost jumped out of my seat. With each ring vibrations shot through my nerves causing my head to throb. Turning the ringer down as low as it would go I answered the call. It was Dean and he seemed to be shouting on his end.

"Hang on a sec." I said adjusting the volume again. He was calling to give me the results of my tests.

"First of all," he said "the patient had no drugs in his system. Also he was negative for HIV, Hepatitis B and C." I breathed a sigh of relief. "Your blood work also came back negative for those but it looks like you need to be immunized for Hepatitis B." he continued.

"No," I replied "I've had it four times now and have been told I'm a non-responder and should not have it again." "What about the cultures?" I asked already knowing it was too soon for growth.

"Nothing in the culture bottles yet, "he said then hesitating "I am looking at something else, I'll let you know if anything comes of it. For now you can stop the HIV prophylaxis but I would keep taking the antibiotics at least until the cultures have time to grow." Hanging up the phone I leaned back in my chair, took a couple of deep breaths, and then ate my sandwich.

Pulling up to the house I saw a familiar blue sports car in the driveway. I smiled. Dan was finally home! Inside I heard the shower and could smell his body wash, I could smell Dan. The closer I got to the bathroom the stronger the scent.

I was excited. I had not seen my husband in over a week. My pulses quickened. I have always been a very sexual person and the fact that he was less than willing lately was driving me mad. The smell of him in the shower was so very arousing, there was no way I was going to take no for an answer this time.

I was peeling off my clothes before I ever reached the bathroom. Once there I headed straight for the shower, opened the door and stepped in behind him. Our eyes met as Dan turned to face me.

Water dripped from his hair down onto his striking face. Neither of us said a word, we just stood looking at each other taking each other in. Dan was a handsome man with strong features, deep blue eyes set perfectly below black hair.

My eyes swept over his face then to his chest and shoulders as desire bloomed deep in my belly. I moved first, touching, caressing his muscular shoulders, down his arms, then over to his waist.

The fire that had started was growing hotter with each touch of his flesh beneath my fingertips. My shoulder was still aching but I didn't notice the pain. I wanted him desperately – every part of him. For too long I had gone without him buried inside me. I needed him, needed his touch, his approval.

Still looking into his eyes I sank to my knees there in the shower, water streaming over my head and down my back. I kissed his thighs and felt his immediate response. My mouth moved over and opened allowing his hardness to slip inside the warmth. He gasped as my lips slid over his plush crown, my tongue caressing the velvety skin.

I didn't take my eyes off of his as I began sucking him, swirling my tongue around his crown. With one hand I grabbed him at the root and began stroking up and down as I continued sucking and licking. His hands were on my head now, fingers in my hair, his hips moving in gentle rhythm.

I reached between his legs and grasp his backside then slid my hands down the backs of his legs. He reached for me, pulling me to him, kissing me deeply. There was hunger in his kiss that I had not felt from him in years. He grabbed the back of my thighs and lifted me up, pressing me against the shower wall. My legs wrapped around his waist as he slid me down onto him. I gasped feeling the penetration.

Pulling away from the wall he carried me into the bedroom, laying me back on the bed. His strong arms lifted my pelvis to meet his as he began moving inside me. My body arched wanting more. His arms shifted higher under my back moving me further onto the bed.

Backing out he flipped me onto my stomach and pulled me up to my knees. He was behind me now and I spread my legs for him to enter as he cupped my heavy breasts in his hands. His lips were hot against my neck and ears. With each stroke I moaned, and pushed back against him feeling his fullness inside me.

Slowly, deliberately he moved, in and out, harder and grinding. Repositioning again he pulled me up into his lap, guiding me down onto his erection, pushing up deeper into me. I was reeling, my head flung back, moaning in ecstasy. My hips were rocking and pressing into his as he pulled my head down to meet his kiss.

He turned and was once more on top of me, his body covering mine, his hands by my head. Our rhythm grew faster until I could no longer stand the intensity. I cried out as my release came, my body tightening and convulsing with his continued movement. Then he too released, moaning as he came, spilling out inside me, and leaving him spent.

We collapsed next to each other, sweaty and tired. Long moments I lay there, trying to catch my breath. When at last my breathing slowed I turned on my side to face him. Gently I stroked my fingers along his jaw, as I studied his face. "I love you Dan," I whispered.

Dan had suggested that we get out and spend some time together and I was more than happy to oblige. We had a quiet dinner then a leisurely walk along the waterfront stopping frequently in front of the establishments to dance to the music the bands were playing, or window shop.

My sense of smell still seemed to be in overdrive and I went out of my way to avoid the open air florist as well as the cigar vender. The sweet smells of flowers and tobacco were just too much. However, I found myself leaning close to Dan and breathing deeply, enjoying his scent. My hearing was affected as well and I discovered I could listen in on conversations across the patio. I wondered if it had to do with the meds I had taken....

On the way home I got a text from Angie. She was having some problems and decided to go to the hospital. She was already in a room and just wanted to let me know. As much as I was looking forward to a glass of wine with Dan I wanted to make sure Angie was okay. Dan said he'd wait up for me, so I left for the hospital without ever going back into the house.

Angie was in room 213 A in the medical wing. When I arrived I was surprised at how bad she looked. Her neck was swollen and there were angry red streaks running out from the wound in every direction. Another bag of IV antibiotics was infusing. Angie looked frightened.

"I'm glad you came." She said when I entered the room. "I really need to talk to you." I sat down next to her, the nurse in me trying to get a better look at her neck. She noticed my look and told me "if the antibiotics don't bring the swelling down by tomorrow morning they are going to re-open and drain it."

"Are you hurting?" I asked already knowing the answer.

"Yes, quite a bit," she said smiling, "but the docs have prescribed the good stuff to help me sleep."

Her expression turned serious again. "I'm worried Kat," she said. "I feel different and..." her words trailed off. After a moment of silence she started up again. "Do you remember me telling you about my trip into the jungles of Peru?"

"Yes," I said "a little." Again she hesitated.

"Something happened there, I saw something that I had hoped never to see again, but I'm almost positive what I…..we saw…..last night was the same thing I witnessed in Peru."

She swallowed. "Please promise you'll listen to me no matter how crazy I sound." I nodded. Then Angie broke into a story about Peru. One I'd never heard her tell before. She told me of how she had been traveling with a medical group deep in the forest to bring supplies to a Peruvian tribe.

There had been a rash of what everyone thought were animal attacks and one of the young men lay in fevered fits having suffered a bite in the throat, much like the one she now had. The team did everything they could for the young man but nothing seemed to help. The fever got so high they thought it would cook his brain. The villagers were hauling in water from the river to help cool his body but it barely helped. There was no ice to use.

The village people kept him restrained because of his incessant thrashing. He screamed out in thirst but refused water and foamed at the mouth like a rabid dog.

Then one night, when his fever finally started to break, he broke free from his bindings and ran out into the forest. The villagers and medical team assumed he had died in the forest because they had been unable to find him.

Two days later, however as Angie was following a trail to the river she heard a whimper. Not too far off the trail she saw him. He was kneeling over the body of one of the village women. His face was at her throat and he was drinking the blood that flowed from a gash at her jugular. The woman was still alive but Angie was afraid to move. She stood there and watched until the woman had gasped her last breath and the blood stopped flowing.

"When he finally stopped drinking he turned and looked at me with those same wild eyes our patient had. I thought he would attack me too but he just ran off into the trees. I ran back to the village and told them what I'd seen.

They brought the woman's body back and cut off her head then burned her. When I asked why they told me to put her soul to rest. They believed that the man was now a "pishtaco" or vampire. Afraid that the woman might also become one they took no chances." Angie looked at me. "I know it sounds crazy but it's true and now I think they're here."

I sat quietly for a moment trying to process what she was saying to me.

"So you think our patient was a vampire?" She nodded. "And now you've been bitten by a vampire. Oh Angie," I said "You know we'll do everything we can for you. We're not going to let you die, vampire or not." Angie threw her head back and laughed almost hysterically.

"I'm not afraid of dying Kat," she said "It's you I'm worried about. Don't you realize that in every vampire story you've ever heard you have to receive their blood to become one of them? Kat you got his blood. He said he would have you and I'm afraid he'll come looking for you." I looked at her in astonishment.

"But he bit you. IF he's a vampire and IF his bite doesn't turn you then what if it kills you?" She was in tears now as she answered her voice escalating.

"I have lost everyone and everything I have ever truly loved. My Husband is dead, my son is dead and so are both of my parents. I have spent the last three years just biding my time trying to fill the void until I could go and be with David and Justin again. I would welcome death. It's the fear of living forever that I cannot handle."

I pulled her close to me and let her cry. "Kat, "she said pulling her sheet up to wipe her nose. "If I'm right about the blood you are going to need help. Promise me that you will find someone to help you. Promise me that you won't try to figure it out on your own."

She was very upset and not wanting to upset her further I promised, although I had no idea what I was promising to do. "And Kat," she said once again, "promise me when the time comes you'll let me go."

Stepping outside of her room I asked her nurse to give her the pain meds. Angie needed to sleep. I was hopeful that she would be thinking rationally in the morning.

FOUR

Crossing the parking lot my mind was reeling with Angie's tale and the events of the night before. It was no small wonder that I nearly jumped out of my skin when someone grabbed me by the arm.

I wheeled around to see an older man dressed in an overcoat and fedora which I thought odd considering how warm it was. My hand flew to my chest at being startled, and I blushed to see that he appeared to be no threat.

The man removed his hat doing an informal bow then replaced it on his head as he started to speak. He was taller than I and looked to be about sixty years old although his age had not impaired his mobility.

"Sorry to startle you ma'am, I was just wondering if you knew anything about the attack that happened here last night?"

Assuming he was a reporter I told him I was unable to make a statement for the hospital.

"I'm not a reporter," he said "more of an investigator. I hear someone was bitten." He piqued my curiosity.

"What organization are you with?" I asked wondering why anyone would be investigating what had happened.

"I'm not formally with an organization." he said, then cocking his head in a knowing sort of way "I also hear there was a needle stick with a transfer of blood from the attacker."

My back stiffened. I wasn't ready to share personal information with a complete stranger. Moving closer he extended his hand and I took it thinking he meant to shake hands. Instead he merely used it to hold me in place. His eyes met mine and began searching my face.

"The blood," he said looking straight into my eyes "isn't infected with bacteria or viruses. It can't be cultured in a lab, but it WILL bring a fever and it WILL bring the blood thirst and YOU WILL need someone who understands and can help you."

I tried to pull away. *Who was this man?*

"I know it was you," he said "I can smell the blood in you.

He was scaring me now. "Please let me help you. You're going need help…soon." I jerked my hand away from him and turned to run but what he said next stopped me in my tracks.

"Don't you find it odd that you can smell and hear things from so far away? Your vision will change too." He moved closer again. "Your body is preparing to give birth to a new life."

I turned angrily "What are you telling me? That I'm going to have some demon child?"

He shook his head, "Not a child, a new LIFE; a new you." I turned again but he grabbed my arm before I could leave swinging me around to face him once more. He placed a piece of paper in my hand and closed my fist around it. "Remember," he said looking again into my eyes "I'm here to help." Then he released me and I was running. I didn't stop until I reached my car, and then drove like a mad man out of the parking lot and all the way home.

The man watched as Kat ran across the parking lot. Then getting into her car she sped away. He wondered if she realized just how fast she had coved the distance to her car. Silently he took out his phone and dialed a number. Someone on the other end answered. A smile lit the man's face.

"Nicolas," he said "so good to hear your voice."

The voice on the other end of the line replied, "Yours as well Stephan, tell me, to what do I owe this call?"

Stephan smiled again. "I have someone that needs to be followed and I can't think of a better man to do it." Nicolas said something to which Stephan responded. "Ah, yes." Then reaching into his overcoat pocket he pulled out a driver's license. Holding it up, he began reading. "Her name is Katherine Armand and you will find her at 3015 Pineloch lane. Once you find her she won't be hard to follow. She smells rather lovely."

I sat in the driveway for a long while, trying to gain my composure. Somehow I had to push my fears and thoughts down so they didn't show on the surface. I didn't want to waste any of my time with Dan. I wanted to give him my undivided attention, but I was still deeply rattled from the conversations I'd had with both Angie and the strange man.

Angie had been so sincere and I didn't doubt her story but the whole vampire idea was a bit much. I thought again about the burning sensation I'd experienced when the blood entered my body and the lasting tingling effects.

My sense of smell and hearing were heightened as the strange man had suggested, but was this just a coincidence? I closed my eyes and tried to shake off the feeling of impending doom.

Dan was home, and for the first time in ages things seemed to be on the right track to repair our marriage. I wanted this more than anything right now. The rest would have to wait. Taking a deep breath I steeled myself and went inside.

Dan was asleep in the recliner with a bottle of wine and two glasses on the coffee table. I went to the bedroom and put on my pajamas then climbed up into the chair, snuggling under his arm. He woke up and kissed me on the forehead looking at his watch.

"Have you been home long?" he asked.

"I just got back." I confessed. Dan lifted my chin and kissed me gently on the lips. Then smiling pulled the cork and poured two glasses of wine. I drank my wine while enjoying the warmth of Dan's arms and their strength as he lifted and carried me off to bed.

In the darkness of the new moon a tall figure crept along the edge of the forest that lined the property. Moving swiftly and keeping to the shadows it darted across the yard till it reached the southernmost wall of the house at 3015 Pineloch lane. The figure stopped, listening for a moment then moved around the house to the back door.

There was no one around to see when it darted through a narrow stream of light coming from the kitchen window. Had someone been watching, the figure moved so fast it would have never been noticed.

Nicolas Cristo stopped when he reached the back door. A quick sniff assured him that there would be no dogs to contend with. Already he knew the occupants of the house had long been asleep.

The vampire looked at the flimsy lock on the door and grimaced. A quick twist of the doorknob with his powerful hand and the lock mechanism broke inside allowing him entrance.

Trying to keep a vampire in would be as futile as trying to keep one out. When the woman went into her blood thirst she would have to be moved to a safer location. The vampire moved further into the house, familiarizing himself with the surroundings then made his way to the master bedroom.

The smell of sex clung heavily in the air as Nicolas stepped into the room. He paused near the door for a moment, the couple never stirring. *The man will pose a problem when the fever comes.* She would have to be separated from him until her thirst was under control. That could take weeks, maybe even months, but there was nothing that could be done about it.

Nicolas studied the woman as she lie sleeping, taking in her small nose and full lower lip. Perfectly arched, dark brown eyebrows outlined her brow bone. She was very attractive, and from the way the sheet draped over her hips and legs, it appeared she had a nice figure too.

The woman turned in her sleep grasping a pillow pulling it closer against her body. Nick moved closer, watching the rise and fall of her gentle breathing. Something about the way her hair fell across her face stirred old memories in the vampire. He closed his eyes against them trying to dispel them but the scent of the woman and sex drew them closer to the surface.

His eyes were filled with pain when he opened them again. He ran his fingers through his hair. *Don't do this to yourself Nick; you can't undo what's been done.* The vampire shook his head resolutely, bringing him back to the task at hand. The woman needed to be protected and he suddenly felt the weight of that responsibility. Yes, he decided, he would make sure that she wasn't alone when the time came. He would be there.

There was absolutely nothing that could prepare the human for the transformation that would soon take place. He felt empathy for her and was glad that Stephan had followed his instincts and found her. Had she been left alone, it was unlikely she would survive the fever. But on the slight chance that she did, it was quite possible her neighbors would not survive what followed.

Having seen all he needed the vampire turned. He needed to get out of the house and away from her scent. He could return again once his head cleared. He left then, leaving no trace that he'd ever been there.

Somewhere in Kat's unconscious mind she detected a new smell. Unlike the harsh, obnoxious sound of her clock that raked against her nerves causing alarm and forcing her awake, the scent wafted in gentle and reassuring.

Dreaming, Kat turned in her sleep, clutching her body pillow, pulling it ever close. The new scent wound its way into her subconscious until it became part of the dream. Now permanently imprinted in her brain it began changing, taking the form of a man. Not just any man, this one was tall, strong and incredibly handsome; a force to be reckoned with, and when he walked into the middle of her dream, she couldn't help but take notice.

FIVE

When I awoke the next morning I sensed something was not quite right. The bed next to me lay empty and an acrid smell hung in the air. I wondered if Dan had burned breakfast and decided I should give him a hand.

Pulling on a robe I went into the kitchen to find Dan pouring a cup of coffee. The smell still hung heavily in the air but there was no evidence that he'd tried to cook anything.

He wasn't wearing a shirt and I gently kissed him between the shoulder blades. His back stiffened and he withdrew from my touch, moving to the breakfast table.

My heart sank. The carefree and loving husband I'd had for the last twenty-four hours had retreated back into his hole where I could no longer access him. He was once again cold and indifferent and I wondered if I'd done something to cause this. His phone buzzed with a text message and he hurriedly turned his phone off.

"Something wrong," I asked looking at him over my mug.

He shrugged, "I have to go in to the office for a little while, I have some business to take care of but it shouldn't take long." I sighed. I wanted to spend more time together today. Hopefully Dan would finish up soon. Forcing a smile at him I simply said

"Okay." What I really wanted to say was please stay home and let the job wait but I held my tongue. The last thing I wanted now was to get in to an argument with him. The fact that he'd spent any time at all with me was an improvement.

Dan went to dress while I finished my first and started on my second cup of coffee. Not wanting to sit around and wait I decided to go workout for a while and headed to the bathroom to change.

Pulling out my gym suit I laid it on the counter. Dan had just finished shaving and was dabbing a spot where he'd nicked his lip. The bleeding had mostly stopped so he went to the closet for his shirt.

I hated letting him go like this, feeling that he was pulling away from me again. After fighting for my marriage for months we had finally connected for a few brief hours and I wanted more. I wanted to make him want to come home to me after work, wanted him to want me.

As he came out of the closet I pulled him close. He was hesitant I could tell but he didn't pull away. My hands went to his hair as my mouth found his, claiming the softness of his lips.

With my tongue I traced the edge of his lower lip igniting my desire for him. In a rush of passion I licked around and into his mouth, tasting his blood in the process. There was something powerful in the taste filling me with ecstasy for just a moment. Then the onslaught of his memories came and knocked me off my feet – literally.

The sudden impact of what I was seeing caused me to fall on my ass on the bathroom floor, hitting the cabinet as I fell. Images from Dan's memory swam through my mind as if they were playing on a movie screen. I saw Dan making love to another woman. She was tall and thin and beautiful and he was telling her he's he'd always love her.

When he was away on business she had been with him. When he was too tired for sex with me he made love to her for hours. In horror I closed my eyes to shut out the images but they kept flowing like a river through my head. He was going to be with her today. There would be no time with him later today; he wasn't coming back.

Dan is leaving me. The realization hit me like a ton of bricks. I looked up at him in desperation, tears now burning in my eyes. *No, no, no – this just can't be happening. Not when things were just starting to get better!* I wanted so badly to hold him and make him change his mind. I wanted to beg, whatever it took to stop him, but I knew it would do no good, he didn't love me.

He was kneeling in front of me, trying to figure out what made me fall.

"Are you okay Kat?"

His question provoked me to anger. I wanted to scream what the hell do you care. Why did he even bother to ask me such a question when I was sure the answer would not affect him?

"How long have you been seeing her?" I asked.

An expression of shock washed over his face but was quickly replaced by one of relief. He sat down next to me on the floor. For a long time we just sat there not looking at each other, and then he spoke.

"I am sorry Katherine for what I've done to you. I hope that someday you will be able to forgive me."

When he finally stood he squeezed my hand. The acrid smell was gone replaced by something bitter and sweet mixed. Leaning over he kissed me on the forehead. I looked up into his eyes and told him "goodbye." His eyes met mine. "Goodbye." He said. Then he was gone.

I was so numb. I wanted to cry but tears would not come. Instead there was just the emptiness in the pit of my stomach that couldn't be filled and wouldn't go away. There wasn't a question that I didn't already have the answer to.

How cruel, how brutally honest his blood had been. My emotions swung from one end of the spectrum to the other as the day progressed. I was hurt, I was insanely jealous, but I was angry too. I was angry at Dan for hurting me, angry at myself for not seeing it coming, angry at the blood for telling me, and angry at life because now I knew for certain that Angie was right. I had tasted Dan's blood and it had revealed his darkest secrets. But even worse than that, I had liked the way it tasted and found myself wanting more. I was changing.

Washing my face, trying to reduce the swelling around my eyes, I pulled on some jeans and a shirt. I needed to go to the hospital to see Angie. I needed to ask her some questions and I hoped she had the answers for me.

When I arrived at Angie's room things were not looking good. The swelling was not down and she had become septic overnight. She was on a new, stronger antibiotic and fluids, but she was losing blood somehow.

To make matters worse, when they had attempted to give her some blood she'd had a reaction. I could tell she was not feeling well. Not wanting to burden her with my troubles I left her to sleep and headed for the lab. If Dean was around I wanted to talk to him.

Dean was there and he greeted me with a flourish telling me to come and look at something. Inside his office he shut the door. The look on his face told me there was trouble.

"I just can't figure it out." He said. "There is nothing growing in the culture bottles, nothing on the petri dishes but something is changing the makeup of her blood and it is happening fast."

"Stay here a second." He said walking out of the room. He was back in a minute with a single petri dish. "This is one I made up on a whim with a blood agar," he said showing me the dish. The dark red agar had clear spots spreading through it, similar to the way acid loving bacteria clear a phenol red agar. "I can see the changes here but nothing grows from it." He told me.

"What happened with the blood reaction?" I asked. Dean scratched his head.

"Her blood is acquiring antigens somehow. She had received blood once before here and I checked her records. When I did the type and screen it was much different than the last time. It had changed again by the time the blood was hung. I've typed and screened her three times since last night using the same sample and it comes out different each time. Something is mutating her blood so fast that we'll never find a match and have time to give it. Whatever is causing the change is also "eating away" at her blood cells."

I interrupted, "you mean her cells are being lysed?" I asked. Dean shook his head.

"I'm not finding any signs of cell destruction, her bilirubin levels are normal. They are just disappearing like they're being consumed. I suspect this is happening with the blood agar as well. I can only assume that it might be happening to her tissue cells also. From what I can see we are running out of time for her. When I look at these changes all I can see is certain death."

I rolled up my sleeve and looked at Dean. "I want you to run the same tests on my blood and tell me what you find out." He didn't have to be asked twice. In a blink he had a tourniquet on my arm and filled ten different tubes with my blood. "Call me and let me know what you find out." I said on my way out the door.

It was incredibly hot outside when I left the hospital. I had not remembered it being this hot when I left the house but now heat was radiating off of my body like a brick oven. I moved quickly to the covered walkway and stayed beneath it as far I could. The shade provided little relief from the intense heat that seemed to be surrounding me, suffocating me.

Back in the car I turned the A/C all the way down and put the blowers on high. According to the display in my car the outside temperature was only eighty-five but that couldn't be right. It was just too damn hot right now.

Mary looked up from the nurse's station to see Kat walk into Angie's room. She also noticed the man who followed closely behind. He was six foot tall with wavy dark brown hair and brown eyes. His nose and chin were strong and accentuated by a mustache and goatee.

He appeared to be in his late thirties, but the chiseled definition that showed through his shirt spoke of youth and vigor. He stood listening at the door and when Kat walked out he followed promptly behind her.

Sue came walking up behind Mary. "Who was that?" she asked.

"I don't know," she replied as she watched him disappear down the hallway, "but whoever he is, he is definitely eye candy!"

Back at the house I paced restlessly. I was feeling nauseated and I attributed it to my nerves. My muscles were aching now, stiff and tender causing pain with each movement, and my anxiety was building. My head was starting to hurt as the muscles in my neck tightened. Like a speed freak, I was racing inside, crawling out of my skin. Hot flashes swept over me in waves.

Inside my head was filled with clutter and turmoil as my thoughts jumped from one idea to another. I wanted a cold shower to cool off but once I removed my clothes I couldn't bring myself to get into the shower. I ran my hands through my hair as I paced restlessly around my room. I couldn't stay here any longer. I was about to explode.

Thinking a workout might eliminate my excess energy and help get my mind off of things, I decided to go to the gym. Going to the bathroom I grabbed the suit I'd left on the counter that morning and pulled it on. It felt loose; in fact it was downright baggy on me. Just two days ago it had been so tight I didn't want to be seen in public in it. Now it hung like it was two sizes too big.

Running over to the full length mirror I stood with my eyes wide and mouth agape, staring at the muscle definition I had suddenly acquired. The ten pounds I had complained about for the last five years had vanished into thin air. My abdomen now boasted a six pack. The muscles in my arms, legs and back were cleanly cut and well defined.

Angie's words came back to me. *Promise me you won't try to figure this out on your own. If I'm right – you will need help.* Running to my car I dug around in the front seat until I found a small piece of wadded up paper that had fallen between the seats. My hands were shaking as I opened the paper and smoothed it out. It contained only the name Stephan and a phone number was listed below. It was time to call.

Looking for my phone I went back inside. Returning to my room I found my phone on the bed. My insides started racing again as I grabbed it, attempting to dial the number. My hands were trembling and didn't want to work.

Anxiety washed over me in waves and I felt as though I would be swept away with it. Too much had happened to me today. It was more than I could cope with.

I was sweating now and great drops of perspiration were flowing down my face stinging my eyes. My hair was soaked and I could feel drops of sweat running down my back and legs.

My hands were wet with sweat making it even more difficult to dial the number. I grabbed a shirt that was lying nearby and attempted to dry my hands and face. Focusing on the final number I managed to push it, and then send.

My chest exploded with one enormous heartbeat and I was falling. I hit the floor with a thud; my phone landing just inches away. I lifted my head and could hear someone answer "hello," a pause "hello." But I could not talk.

My head hit the floor again. I couldn't move to reach the phone. I tried once more to raise my head and speak, but nothing.....and then darkness fell over my eyes as the voice on the other end of the line faded into the distance.

Dean looked up at the clock and realized it was time to go. He chaffed that he would have to wait to talk to Kat. He had been calling her phone for hours now and not getting an answer.

As soon as Kat had left the lab Dean had gone to work testing and culturing the samples of blood she had given him. Of course it had not been long enough to grow anything from cultures but he had been able to type and screen her blood. He had also stabbed a petri dish containing blood agar.

What he saw already was incredible. The sample of blood from Angie had made large clear spots in the agar where the blood was being "eaten" up by an unseen force, leaving nothing in its wake. However the sample he'd take from Kat was forming clear rings.

On closer inspection he realized that the blood in the agar was being eaten up just as in Angie's sample. The difference was that it was being replaced with new blood. Kat's blood appeared to be reproducing itself as it "ate up" the blood contained in the agar.

Wanting to confirm his theory he took a unit of blood already typed and cross matched. The label identified it as B negative blood. He injected a sample of Kat's A positive blood into the bag. What should normally happen would be destruction of the blood cells as the two types were not compatible.

Amazingly when he checked two hours later the entire unit had been converted to Kat's A positive blood. Where Angie's body was rejecting all blood Kat's would accept all. This put a whole new spin on the term universal recipient. His head was reeling with the possibilities.

Just seven hours ago he had told Kat that Angie's blood looked like certain death. Now looking at the sample of Kat's blood the term "immortality" came to mind.

SIX

Time seemed to come to a standstill as I lie on the floor in my bedroom. Waves of fear and heat washed over me again and again. Everything went black. I was hurting everywhere and deep in the pit of my stomach I could feel the blade of a knife as it twisted in my gut. I was thirsty, dying, begging for something to quench the thirst and put me out of my misery.

Then someone was there lifting me up and carrying me. Voices were fading in and out. Faces moved in front of my eyes but they were all strange to me. I screamed and thrashed in agony in response to the pain of being ripped apart, put back together then ripped apart again.

The fever moved through my body and burned through my brain with the fury of a forest fire licking up memories like chaff. It was a purging fire and the intensity of the heat forged new connections in my brain while closing or destroying others. In the aftermath all that remained was charred and forever changed. But in the hot ash were seeds that had been previously dormant, now awakened and taking hold.

From the thirst there was no escaping or any relief from the pain. Finally after what must have been days, someone came with a cool cloth and held a cool drink to my lips and I drank.

Nicolas had remained nearby after his visit to the couple's room. He had smelled the change coming, and not wanting to be too far away when it happened, had set up camp just beyond the tree line.

His need to monitor Katherine closely meant that he would have to travel unnoticed back and forth to the house. This position allowed him to remain unseen as he moved about and he had already taken advantage of it. He had been present, listening to the drama unfold this morning when her husband's secret had been revealed to her.

Knowing how stress could push the change to occur even faster he had not let her out of his sight, following her everywhere she went. Katherine had never even noticed that he was following her, even though at times he had been just steps away. That she had picked up his scent once he knew, but she had been unaware of what it was.

A light breeze coming from the house told him what he's been waiting to find out. It was time to move. In a moment he was inside the house again. Another second and he was in the bedroom where he found Katherine on the floor, her hand reaching for her phone.

Recognizing the voice on the end of the line he picked up her phone. "I'm here with her," he said "I'll bring her over." Then he hung up. Picking her up off the floor he placed her on the bed. The fever was on her full force so he packed her feet, head and hands in ice. Still she thrashed around and cried out as if she were living in a nightmare.

Not wanting to be seen by her neighbors he waited until dark to move her. As soon as it was safe he picked her up and carried her across the yard and into the woods where his jeep was waiting.

He had packed her a small bag of clothing that her scent was strongest on. These were things she had worn recently and likely things she liked. It would suffice until she was better and could choose for herself. Reclining the passenger seat he buckled her in and headed to Stephan's. At Stephan's she would be safe.

It was nearly one a.m. when Nick pulled up to the gate of a massive house that sprawled over two acres of property. "We're here." He said into an intercom system. With that the gate rolled back and allowed him to pass inside.

He was met at the front of the house by Stephan who held the door for him while he carried Katherine in. Stephan pointed to a room at the top of the stairs. "She will be comfortable there."

Even carrying the extra weight Nicolas easily navigated the stairs. Turning into the room Stephan had pointed out, Nick placed Katherine in the bed. She was still burning with the fever.

Stephan called to his maid. "Sara, can you please see that the young lady is changed into one of the cool cotton gowns. After that I will attend to her."

"Yes sir," Sara said and skittered off to tend to it. The two men finally having a moment turned to greet each other with a warm handshake and pat on the back. Sara returned with the gown and the two stepped out of the room for a moment.

"It seems my friend that we just may have avoided a catastrophe," said Stephan "let us hope at least." Nicolas nodded in agreement.

"What of Orlando, do you think he will come for her?" he asked. Stephan looked thoughtful.

"It is my hope that he forgets about her. He was in a blood rage when it happened, now that it's over we can but hope that the women he's already seduced will keep him happy. But should he not forget, that is why I've asked for your help, at least until Katherine can think with a sound mind and choose for herself. Until then the pull of his blood will be too strong. She won't be able to resist."

"I'm not sure how I'm going to help?" Nicolas stated.

"Just stand in the way. Be strong for her. "Stephan replied.

Sara came out of the room and nodded and the two men stepped back inside. Stephan brought cool rags to wipe her face. The room itself was much cooler than the rest of the house. Nicolas looked around and noticed there were no windows. Stephan caught his glance and raised his eyebrows. "Her only way out is through the door. She will have to go through us to escape."

Nicolas knew it was in her best interest. In here she would be safe. If she got out she could hurt herself and others. "I'll stay with her tonight."

When Stephan left the room Nicolas went over and sat on the bed next to Katherine. Again he touched her forehead with his cool hand. She was cooler now and not thrashing about anymore but he knew that the fever could last for days peaking and receding.

Once again his mind drifted to a time long passed, evoked by the feel of her skin beneath his fingertips. For a moment longer he allowed his hand to linger on her face, his brow furrowing at the memory. With forced effort he removed his hand. *Stop torturing yourself.*

Standing up he moved to a shelf in the room containing a selection of books. Gathering a couple, he placed them in the recliner then slid the recliner against the door. Satisfied that Katherine could not get out without moving him and the chair he settled down to read.

Four hours later he awoke to the sound of cries. Katherine lay in the bed alternately kicking and rolling into a fetal position. He laid his hand to her brow. The fever was back stronger than before. Heat radiated off her body like a furnace. She began crying out for something to drink. Behind him the recliner slid across the floor as Stephan pushed his way into the room.

"She's very hot this time," said Nicolas, "should we put her in the tub?"

"That might be best." Stephan replied calling for Sara to bring ice.

Nicolas stepped into the bathroom and began filling the tub with cold water. Sara soon appeared with buckets of ice that she poured into the water. Going back to the bed Nicolas carefully lifted Katherine and carried her to the bathroom.

Gently he lowered her into the icy water. Steam rose up from the surface of the tub as ice and heat collided. Grabbing a rag Nicolas soaked it in the water and placed it at her mouth. At first she accepted the water but after only a moment she turned her head and cried out again.

"How long must we wait before we let her drink?' Nicolas asked

"It is better to wait until the fever has run its' course," Stephan replied "it would only feed her deliria and make her more dangerous. We will wait a bit more. Trust me." He said looking at his friend.

They left her in the tub until the ice melted and again she was starting to cool down. Nicolas lifted her out of the tub and placed her atop a bed of towels Sara had made. Once again the men stepped out while Sara dried and changed her.

Three days longer the fever raged and each time Nicolas and Stephan were there to cool her fevered body. On the fourth day the fever broke and Stephan said "It is time, she can drink now."

He produced a unit of cold human blood from a refrigerator in his study. Taking it into Katherine's room he tore back one of the corners. Katherine began reaching for it immediately asking for drink.

Nicolas lifted her head and put the open corner to her lips. She began drinking greedily, sucking the cold fluid down her parched throat, stopping only long enough to breathe, similar to the way an infant pulls back from its mother's breast then returns again.

The bag was soon empty of its contents but already the glassiness of Katherine's eyes was clearing. She looked up into the eyes of Nicolas Cristo with the wonder and mystery of a new born baby.

For so long I had been in the grip of the fever that when it finally left my body it left me cold and shaking. I was thirsty and I craved the blood I was first given. My fever gone, I was now in restraints.

Sara brought blankets to warm me and Nicolas, as I came to know him, released my bindings, checking my skin several times a day. I was afraid. Not of Nicolas or Stephan, they kept me well fed and I trusted both completely. I was afraid of what I'd become.

My mind was still hazy and fragments of memories swam through my brain like the remnants of a dream, surreal and disconnected. My head hurt and I strained against the pain to put it all back together, sorting through the real and the imagined. Slowly the pieces came together.

I slept, but my dreams were filled with terrors. My desire to hunt and kill for blood overpowered my human will. Had it not been for the shackles keeping me from escaping, my dreams might have become reality.

Often Nicolas would wake me from them and offer me the cool blood. It quenched my thirst but I still desired warm blood. I wanted to drink right from the throat, to feel the pulse beneath my lips. I wanted to hunt.

Eight days longer I was confined to the windowless room, but I was free to move about within. Nicolas was with me often, offering drink or reading a book to pass the time. With each passing day I grew stronger, my mind clearer, and the desire to kill for blood passed.

I remembered my life as it was before but the fever had forever changed me. I was no longer that woman. Only a small part of her remained inside of me. Stephan had been right. I truly had been reborn.

On the ninth day I was brought out of the room and showed around the house and enormous grounds. It felt so good to be out, unfettered, free. Though I was much stronger now Nicholas walked slowly, taking his time. Offering his arm for support he led me out to the veranda.

I'd been gone for two week and knew nothing of friends or family. I needed to check on Angie. Nicolas brought me my phone that had been turned off to save the battery. When I powered it back on I was bombarded with missed calls and voicemail.

"Mom," Callie's voice said, "dad and I are really worried. Dan says he doesn't know where you are. Please call me." I called her first.

Callie was my only child and I had poured myself into her life. We had gotten along wonderfully until she turned thirteen. After that it was pure hell. Callie became moody and irritable, rebelling against me every chance she got, fighting for her independence. We couldn't talk without an argument and somehow our conversations always came around to the rules of the house.

At first Dan had been supportive but over time even that stopped. No matter what I did to appease her it was never enough. I was always too demanding; I just wouldn't let her grow up. She was grown after all and knew everything. I was just some old fashioned fuddy-duddy who wanted to make her life miserable.

When she finally graduated high school I'd had enough. So when she mentioned moving in with her dad I was more than happy to let her. All of my friends at work had told me it was normal and she'd come around once she realized she didn't know it all. That had not happened yet but at least she'd call and say hi now and again.

Callie was so relieved to hear my voice. I told her that I'd been really sick and staying with a friend but was much better now. She asked why Dan didn't know. I told her Dan and I were separated. Oddly enough the memory did not cause the pain I expected. For that I was grateful.

The next eight calls were from Dean each one sounding more excited than the last. I stepped outside to make that call. It was early and I had forgotten that he might still be asleep until he answered the phone. He had been asleep and his voice sounded groggy, but the instant he realized who I was he snapped out of it.

"Where the hell are you and why did you just drop off the face of the earth? I've been calling you for days now. Do you have any idea how worried I've been about you?" He was clearly upset and I knew I had a lot of explaining to do.

"I'm sorry Dean. I didn't mean to worry anyone but I've been really sick."

"Where are you? Were you in the hospital?"

"No, I – Some friends brought me to their home and have been taking care of me."

There was silence for a moment and his voice was lower, softer when he asked. "Where is Dan? Why isn't he taking care of you?"

I saw no reason to hide the truth so I told him. "Dan left. He won't be coming back." I heard a sharp intake of air over the line and another moment of silence.

"Are you okay Kat?"

"Yes, I'm ok."

"Okay. Good. I have some stuff I need to talk to you about."

He started buzzing about all that he had discovered and wanted to meet me in private so we could discuss his findings. I told him I was out of town and unsure when I'd be back.

At his persistent pleading I asked Nicolas where we might meet him locally. We decided on a bistro not too far from Stephan's house. Nicolas would go with me. I was not comfortable venturing out alone yet.

Three hours later Dean, Nicolas and I were seated around a small wooden table under an umbrella. Dean eyed Nicolas suspiciously when I introduced him as one of my friends whom I'd been staying with. I knew he was trying to place him and coming up short. He had known me long enough to know my circle of friends and Nicolas was not one of them.

Dean raised his eyebrows with recollection. "Oh yes, I remember," he said, "I saw you waiting for Kat outside the lab last time she was there. You've shaved since then." I looked at Nicolas in surprise. He simply shrugged his shoulders.

For the next forty-five minutes Nicolas and I sat and listened to Dean explain what he'd learned in the lab and his theories of how it could possibly be the biggest breakthrough in medicine the world has ever seen, possibly a link to immortality.

When he finished I just sat silently for a moment. Not sure how much I could or should tell him. After a long moment I decided to try to connect with the scientist in him. I started slowly. "Even being immortal would not be without sacrifice," I said, "How many immortals would the earth contain before extinction?"

I could tell he was processing what I'd said so I continued. "I have been experiencing some changes since I received that blood," I wanted him to understand without just blurting it out. Nicolas shifted uneasily in his chair. "Some of these changes have been quite painful." I continued "At the very least they are life altering."

"Is that why you went away?" he asked, his eyes searching my face.

"Yes," I replied.

"But your blood," he stated defending his position, "it could heal Angie." He must have seen the look of horror that crossed my face because he sat back in his chair suddenly.

"Angie is never to get my blood." I stated with a vehemence that startled even me. "She made me promise I'd allow her to die." Dean's face went white. I'd said enough. I had accidently confirmed his theory about my blood.

Dean shook his head. "Ok," he agreed. Reaching across the table I squeezed his hand. It was unbelievably warm and I thought I felt him shudder when I touched him. I looked into his face, my eyes pleading. "Destroy that blood," I said "it can't fall into the wrong hands." Dean's hands returned my squeeze and he nodded to assure me it would be done.

"There's one other thing," Dean said, "Some people came to the hospital looking for you. They said you had been reported missing but they were asking all the wrong questions and too many of them. They came up to the lab snooping around to, wanting to know about your labs."

"You didn't give them anything did you?" I asked, wondering why anyone would be interested in me.

"Of course not, I played absolutely dumb. I didn't trust them and besides, that would be a major HIPPA violation."

I laughed the mood suddenly lighter, "Yes, and we both know you're concerned about HIPPA."

"I am when it serves my purpose." Dean stated." "Regardless, your paper records show nothing without the actual blood, and that is put away in a safe place along with the petri dishes I made. Just watch your back."

"I will," I stated "Thank you."

103

"Do you think he'll destroy it?" Nicolas asked when Dean had left.

"Dean is a good person," I replied. "He'll do the right thing.

SEVEN

Dean went over his conversation with Kat a dozen times on his way home. What exactly had she been trying to tell him? That she had alluded to the possibility of immortality he had felt certain. And she had stated not to give her blood to Angie because Angie didn't want to be kept alive. But did she mean indefinitely? Had Kat already discovered something that he was only beginning to look at? It was possible, Kat was pretty good in the lab too, but – no it had more to do with her illness and her time away.

Kat had definitely changed, at least physically, since the last time he'd seen her just a few weeks ago. She was pale, very pale, and there was something about her eyes. He couldn't put a finger on it but she seemed to look at him as if she could now see through him. And then there were her hands.

He shuddered again when he thought about how incredibly cold her hands were. "Maybe," he thought laughing to himself "the guy in the E.R. was a vampire and now Kat is too." Dean's smile faded instantly. Pulling to the side of the road he did a U-turn and headed to the hospital.

Back in the lab Dean took out the unit of blood he'd carefully hidden in the back of his refrigerator. Applying gloves he took a syringe and removed a sample. Then with utmost care he placed the sample into six heparinized blood tubes, labeling them each with a simple KAB.

The rest of the blood and the syringe he had used he carefully placed in the incinerator, locked the door and turned it on. In five minutes the entire contents of the incinerator were reduced to nothing more than ash. Satisfied he left the lab.

Once home he went into his closet, moved back his clothing and opened a hidden door revealing a small refrigerator. Removing the tubes from his pocket he placed them on the top shelf. This was where he kept his most secret experiments.

Only he knew the KAB on the tubes labels stood for Katherine Armand's Blood. Closing and locking the door of the refrigerator he replaced the outer door and moved his clothes back to cover it.

He had no immediate plans for the blood. He was simply saving it for a rainy day. It was late when he climbed into bed with his laptop. Opening his search engine he placed the cursor in the box and typed in "VAMPIRE" than hit enter.

One by one I went through my calls. Some I returned, some I deleted, others I just left for a later date.

Jackie was one I did call. I still needed my job but I also needed more time off so I spoke to her about extending my leave. She understood and said to take my time. I had plenty of both sick and vacation time accrued.

Then I asked about Angie. The report was grave. She had gotten much worse and was in and out of consciousness. I needed to go see her. She needed me now. I just wasn't sure I could do it.

Coming down the stairs Stephan called to me to join him in the parlor. Entering the room I saw him and

Nicolas admiring some swords on the wall. Stephan
turned to me.

"Katherine, do you know how to fight?"

"Not really." I replied.

"Add vampire tactics to the course description
Nicolas," He laughed. I had jokingly told him I needed a
Vampire 101 course and he had risen to the challenge.
"Katherine must learn to fight like a vampire."

Stephen still called me Katherine but Nicolas had
begun referring to me as Kat, the two of them sharing bits
of information with me as it seemed necessary. The
information most important to me: (1). I could still go
outside in the sun. (2). I could still drink a bloody-Mary. I
was about to do both!

I took my drink outside to walk about the grounds.
The house was nestled on the top of a hill in Texas hill
country. From my vantage point you could see for miles to
Austin, the nearest town.

Stephan owned several hundred acres that spread
out around the house in all directions. Except for the
property immediately surrounding the house it was un-

improved land filled with scrub oak, cactus, and rock. There were also some caves in the area that Stephan had mentioned. You could easily get lost if you didn't know where you were going and wandered too far.

Nicolas followed me out to the veranda that was located in the courtyard at the back of the house. He had become a constant in my new world of variables and I was comfortable spending time with him.

As he approached my heart flipped in my chest. That I was attracted to him was an understatement. I just about melted every time he came near me and when he smiled it pushed me to the boiling point.

The times when we had touched sent sparks flying and I wondered if he felt them as well. If ever there was a god sent among men he must have been one of them. I'd had the privilege of seeing him without a shirt on several occasions and had not been the same since. Already I was an avid worshipper of his gloriously chiseled chest and shoulders that tapered into a perfectly trim waist, revealing a gorgeous loin of Apollo.

He was more than good looking, and I took every opportunity revel in his beautiful, sexy features. The set of his shoulders and his confident stride spoke of a man that was perfectly at ease in his body. I couldn't help but believe he would be just as confident in bed and secretly hoped I'd get the chance to find out first hand.

His thick head of wavy, dark brown hair sat beautifully above dark brown eyes and strong nose. His wide mouth and square jaw were accentuated by a day's growth of facial hair.

He was wearing a pair of worn blue jeans and a cream colored linen shirt un-tucked with the long sleeved rolled up to his elbows. The top buttons on the shirt were undone revealing the hair on his chest and I mentally followed it down behind the shirt to his happy trail. He was absolutely, breathtakingly gorgeous. I couldn't help but smile as he walked up.

The weather was beautiful and mild. Fall would be arriving soon; I could smell it in the air. Our conversation was mostly small talk about life and the way it could change without notice, then turned more serious as I broached the subject of returning to the life I'd left behind.

Nick, as I had started calling him, shifted uneasily in his seat. His expression revealing that he needed to say something but didn't know quite how. I waited. Slowly and deliberately he began.

"You know Orlando may come back looking for you." He said studying my face as he spoke, looking for a spark of recognition at the name. I frowned, the name was completely unfamiliar and I was unsure of what he was talking about. He repeated himself "Orlando, the vampire that gave you his blood."

With startling realization I understood who he was talking about. Chills ran up and down my spine at the memory of the vampire's crazy eyes and what he had said to me. At that time in the hospital I had not known his name.

"He told me he would have me." I whispered.

"He what," Nick nearly shouted. Fear and uncertainty crept over me as I recounted the night in the E.R. Nick listened intently. "We didn't know about that." Nick said referring to himself and Stephan. "We had hoped that he would never come looking for you, but it sounds like a high possibility."

"But," I protested, "I still have the right to choose whether or not I'm with him don't I? This is America for Christ sake." Nick threw his head back and roared with laughter. It lightened the moment.

Reaching over he gave my hands a squeeze. There was such depth in his eyes as he held them captive, his thumbs lightly stroking my knuckles before reaching up to brush a stray strand of hair behind my ear; the backs of his fingers caressing my cheek.

"Of course you can choose," he said. Then back to a more serious tone he added, "And the longer you're kept away from him the better your chances of resisting."

Not understanding I looked at him imploringly. Seeing my expression he tried to explain. "The blood," he said "that now flows through your veins will call to Orlando. If he wants to find you he will – there is nothing we can do about that. The same thing that draws him to you will pull you to him once he is in your presence. It is a very powerful force, but the longer the separation the weaker it becomes. What it comes down to is – how strong is your will?"

"This all seems so unfair," I said "to be pulled against you own will."

Nick smiled, "It's not so different from going and having a few drinks and next thing you know you wake up with a stranger. Only being a vampire the urges are far stronger and usually last much longer. The longer you stay together the more bound you become to each other."

"So it's mating in a way?" I asked.

"I guess you could look at it like that," Nick said. "Only Orlando already has at least three other *mates,* "he said putting emphasis on the word, "hell he nearly has a harem".

Then slowly he added while watching my face. "Judging from what I've seen about you, you're not likely to want to share a mate." *Nick was there when Dan left?* I thought about Dan and my discovery of his other lover.

"No," I said, "that is not something I'm willing to do at all." Nick stood up.

"Then there is only one thing to do. Keep you as far away from Orlando for as long as possible and pray when he does show up." Reaching for Nick's hand he helped me to my feet. He squeezed my hand and added.

"I'll be there for you when the time comes."

"Can I ask you something?"

"Of course you can."

"Dean said you were with me at the hospital?"

"Yes, I had followed you there. I had been watching you and wanted to be close when you needed me."

"So you were there when Dan left me?"

"Yes, I was in the next room."

"I smelled your scent." *He was the sweetness that mingled with the bitterness from Dan!*

"I thought you might. Look I wasn't trying to pry – I was only trying to keep you safe."

"No, no – I don't mind, really. I'm just glad someone was looking out for me. Thank you."

Nick sighed in relief, "You're very welcome Kat."

When Nick had agreed to keep an eye on Katherine for Stephan he'd had no clue how deeply involved he'd become. At first it had been her vulnerability that had kept him around. She had needed help and there was no one else who could give her the kind of help she needed.

He had truly been concerned about her when the fever had taken her, feeling responsible for getting her through the ordeal. He'd told himself once the fever broke he'd be on his way. But that was not the case. The more time he spent with her the more he wanted to be around her.

Common sense told him he should walk away. Getting too involved with her would probably end him up with a broken heart. But after these last few weeks he wasn't sure he could. He had made the mistake of touching her, feeling her skin beneath his fingertips and now he couldn't stop.

She had depended on him yet somehow he was now dependent on her. The firmness of her body pressed into his chest as he lifted her, the gently touch of her hand on his arm, and the way her eyes lit up when he came near her. All of these things had somehow started filling the void in his soul and giving them up now just wasn't an option.

I spent two more months at Stephan's house, leaving only twice to visit Angie. The last time was to tell her goodbye. The illness had ravaged her so she was barely more than a skeleton, her eyes sunken deep into her head.

She had hung on for so long fighting her inevitable death that I had started to think maybe she had changed her mind and really didn't want to die. I was torn inside. I knew I had the power to restore her health. It would only take a small amount of my blood and she would be well again.

I struggled with the pain of losing Angie if I gave her what she wanted and the pain of the guilt I would carry if I did not. In the end she won. I held her hand and told her I was okay and that she could end her suffering her on this earth and go be with David and Justin and her parents.

I told her she would always be my dearest friend and would never be forgotten. Then Angie let go. It was just that simple and that hard at the same time. One minute she was breathing and the next her heart stopped altogether.

She had wanted me to allow natural death and so I did. When her heart stopped the nurses just turned the monitors off. It was as if she had waited to tell me goodbye before allowing herself to die. She had made it. And I had kept both of my promises….

I had a memorial set for her next to David's and Justin's grave stones. There were no funeral arrangements to be made as I had decided to have her remains cremated. There was a reason for her telling me about the woman in Peru and I took it as her last wish to ensure there would be no coming back once she was departed. I carried her ashes to the grave site of her husband and son and scattered them there. "Be at peace Angie." I said as the wind carried her away.

I was in a strange mood afterward and had wandered again out to the veranda. Nick came out looking for me after a while.

"Are you okay?" he asked.

"I'm not sure." I replied. I wanted to cry but no tears would come. Somehow I couldn't shake the feeling of guilt for not helping her. My insides were in turmoil over whether or not I should have used my blood and also knowing it was too late anyway.

I was angry too at Orlando for killing her. I tried to explain my feelings to Nick and he listened to me vent. When I finished he began to speak, slowly the way he did when he was choosing his words carefully.

"I think I understand how you feel about losing your best friend. You shouldn't be angry with yourself though. You gave her what she really wanted. She told you she didn't want to live as a vampire. Please don't punish yourself for not being selfish."

I tried to listen to him. I wanted to believe what he was saying was right. It just didn't feel that way. "As far as Orlando," Nick continued, "I don't think his bite was sufficient to kill anyone. Vampires bite people all the time, take small amounts of their blood and leave without any harm coming to the person. He didn't even take her blood. Our saliva prevents blood from coagulating right away, but I've never see it cause a serious reaction."

"Then what did kill her?" I asked angrily. Nick shook his head.

"I'm not sure Kat, maybe she just lost her will to live. The only thing you really need to know is that you didn't do it. Angie didn't die because of you." I knew Nick was right. I just wished I didn't feel so empty right now.

The rest of my time at Stephan's was spent in Vampire 101. I had gained significant strength and speed as well as improved hearing, vision and a sense of smell a dog would envy. However, my newfound abilities lacked the discipline and training that would keep me alive. For an older man Stephan was surprisingly strong and fast but he preferred to leave that end of the teaching to Nick.

One morning early Stephan came to my room.

"Put on something you can move in that won't get in your way, and then come down stairs. There is something I want to show you."

I quickly pulled on a pair of jogging pants and a tee shirt. Meeting Stephan at the foot of the stairs I followed him into the parlor. There on a table up against the wall were a couple of swords. Stephan gestured toward the swords with his hand.

"Choose your weapon," he said "today I will show you basic stance and moves in sword fighting."

I could not for the life of me figure out why I'd need to learn to fight with a sword and said as much as I walked to the table. There were only two swords there and both looked identical to me. Stephan saw the query on my face and explained.

"They are both the same, but it is customary to allow your opponent first choice."

"Ok," I said picking up the one nearest my reach." Stephan smiled at my choice.

"In time," he said "I will teach you how to examine a sword for signs of damage and weakness. For now the closest one will do."

"So why do I need to learn this?" I asked skeptically. Again Stephan laughed.

"You will find Miss Katherine that, as a vampire, it is always good to learn what you can, if for no other reason than to fill the time. Acquiring knowledge can keep you from being bored. As you will no longer be bound by the time constraints of a mere human, you will be able to learn a great many things, possibly things that you've always wanted to learn but never had the time. My Dear Miss Katherine, you now will have the time."

I thought about his words for a second as he turned to a chair to remove his shirt. In my mind's eye I saw myself playing the electric guitar in a rock and roll band and laughed to myself. Somehow I could not grasp the concept of "living forever" I had been pre-programed for thirty-six years with finite mentality.

Bringing my thoughts back to the present I received a shock. Stephan had removed his shirt placing it on a nearby chair. Up to now I had not seen him except fully dressed. Now as he turned to face me I couldn't help but react.

"WOW! The words were out of my mouth before I could stop myself. Stephan laughed as he turned to flex for me.

"Not bad for an old man huh" he said making light of the situation. Not bad was an understatement. The man, though somewhat shorter than Nicolas, was in terrific shape. His muscles long and lean wrapped around his arms like snakes. The same lean muscles showed at his waist and back. There was not an ounce of fat anywhere on the vampire. When he raised his sword his pectoral muscles tightened, showing off his chest even more.

Curious I asked "Just how old are you Stephan?"

"I was turned when I was sixty-two." He replied. Then he added "But I was born in 1705. I was considered ancient at the time. Back then most men didn't make it past forty." My jaw dropped and I lowered my sword. Stephan continued.

"I learned to use a sword as a boy and have always preferred it over any other method of combat, though I have lived through many different eras, each more advanced. There is something fluid and graceful about wielding a sword. That is why I choose to pass down the art. And who knows; if man continues on his current path and annihilates himself we may someday fall back on the simplicity of the sword."

My mind was reeling with questions now. The shock of discovering how old Stephan really was had thrown me into a tailspin. After all, how long did I really want to live I wondered. After raising your kids and a few good years of retirement what else was there to live for? Work forever? Do nothing forever? I suddenly understood what Stephan had meant about learning what you could, but what about when you knew it all? Did you ever learn it all?

"Can – Do vampires have kids?" I blurted out. Stephan looked thoughtfully for a moment.

"I have heard that it can happen," he said "if you mean through conception, but that would be *extremely* rare, I've never known anyone personally that became pregnant." I wasn't sure if this was good news or bad news. At the moment I didn't want to have any more kids, but I might if I got bored a hundred years from now.

"So if we usually only make children or offspring – whatever it is called by transfer of blood to an already existing human, then who was the first vampire and why does the blood work on humans?" Stephan studied me for a minute.

"That is a question most new vampires don't ask for many years, if ever." He stated. And one regretfully I don't know the answer to. I do have my own theory though, if you're interested." I nodded. "Well then," he started, "Are you familiar with the term "Nephilim"? He asked.

I nodded. "Actually I am. The idea that at one time Angels interbred with human women."

"Yes exactly." He stated. "I believe that they really did exist, and I believe that we are the descendants of the Nephilim, via proxy. You see when you cross breed two totally different species you are able to have offspring. Such as it is when you cross a horse and a donkey. You get a mule that carries the traits of both species; however the mule is always sterile and cannot reproduce after its kind. But now through cloning, it can.

124

The same with the Nephilim; Two totally different species come together to have offspring, as I recall – mighty men!" Stephan was referring to the scripture in Genesis. "But the offspring themselves cannot reproduce through copulation, they had to find another way and the answer came through the blood. Isn't it true that the child always carried the father's blood?"

"But what about the few that do have children," I asked "How is that possible?"

"My guess would be time," he said "over time the bloodline is not as strong and the offspring are able to reproduce."

"Now," said Stephan "We have a lifetime or more to finish this conversation. Let us begin our lesson with swords. Today we will begin with the grip, pommel, and the forte."

Watching Stephan with the sword I realized just how graceful he was. His movements were fluid and flowed like a precise choreographed dance. It made me feel even more awkward when he had me mimic his movements.

The parts of the sword I had learned easily enough, but wielding it was an entirely different matter. "The rhythm will come in time with practice." He assured me seeing the frustration on my face. "Just continue to focus on the movement."

I learned a lot during the time I spent with Stephan, including some basic history of the vampires that existed in and around my area. There were no set rules on how to live once you became a vampire and many integrated their human philosophies into their new existence.

Some vampires gathered others around them in large "family" groups, while others chose to live alone. Orlando, as it turned out was a "prodigal son" so to speak, having left a large family in Cuba coming to the states to enjoy his fortune. He was a pimp of sorts, the kind of young, attractive, well-dressed man that surrounded himself with beautiful women and wore a lot of gold.

He had a weakness for illegal drugs and being a vampire could only enjoy them through the blood of humans. So he kept a few "feeders" around him, supplying them with all the drugs they wanted. In return he got to

126

feed off of them, enjoying the drugs as well. I mentioned that when Orlando was in the hospital he had no drugs in his system.

"That is because he was on a blood thirst." Stephan said. "A blood thirst is what happens to vampires that don't take care of themselves." He explained. "Even we need to eat sometime, when you continue pushing yourself past your limits your innate survival instincts take control. One tends to become a little crazy and out of control when that happens."

"So," I asked "he went too long without eating and his body's preservation instinct took over?"

"Exactly," said Stephan "My guess would be he was enjoying himself a bit too much on the drugs and forsook his nourishment. It's not the first time it's happened with Orlando and I'm sure it won't be the last."

"How did you find out about me?" I asked.

"Five o'clock news" he replied." I just had to check it out. The artist's sketch looked too much like Orlando to dismiss it. After that it wasn't hard to find the nurse that was stabbed and determine if there had been a transfer of blood"

"I'm glad you did Stephan," I said "Thank you."

Everything I learned I associated to what I knew from my human life. This survival instinct was apparently the human equivalent to the fight or flight phenomenon often experienced when a human didn't eat causing their blood glucose levels to drop leading to a chain reaction ultimately ending with too much adrenaline.

Even humans could get pretty wild from that so I could understand how much worse it could be for a vampire. I made a mental note to self – Eat right or you might kill someone you don't mean to.

By day I worked with Stephan and nights I spent with Nicolas. This was easy to accomplish since I now required very little sleep. I still got hungry and was able to eat pretty much whatever I wanted. However my taste had changed and I no longer wanted much of what I used to eat. I had taken a liking to sushi and it had become a staple for my diet. An occasional rare steak was also appetizing.

Night became my favorite training time. One reason was that I immensely enjoyed the time I got to spend with Nicolas. With each passing day our friendship grew. Once the sun set he and I would roam the city where I learned to jump fences, scale buildings, and disappear down darkened alleyways.

I also learned how to hunt and how to defend myself. I became aware of my fangs; how they felt when they descended through my gums and I learned how to control them. This was easier said than done when the desire to feed was on me. It was more a lesson in self-control than anything. Nick wanted me to be a fully functional person. I couldn't be that if I allowed my feral nature to overrun my will. I had to fight to maintain control over my appetites. He assured me it would get easier with time. Until then, he'd be there to help me.

Spending so much time together allowed us to get to know each other. We often found ourselves sitting on the top of one of the skyscrapers, looking out over the city talking. Not only was Nick beautiful to look at, he was a good person, not that he was without his share of demons.

Behind his smile there was a sadness that I got an occasional glimpse of. Surely after so many years on this earth it would be impossible not to have been broken a time or two but I wondered what had caused the pain that he was still carrying.

Nick shared with me how he had become a vampire. Not near as old as Stephan, Nick's family had come from Romania in the early eighteen-hundreds. They traveled in groups still known today as gypsies, preferring to stay away from the towns.

His family raised goats and it was his job to take them out to pasture. One night while he was sleeping in the field a bear came out of the woods and attacked the flock. He awoke disoriented with the animals going crazy, not seeing the bear until it was too late. The bear turned its attention to him slashing through his chest and neck then went back to the goats.

Someone lifted him from the ground and carried him away from the bear. Nick had thought he would die, his life's blood flowing freely from the gash at his throat. Then the man did something strange. He sliced open his wrist and placed it to Nick's mouth forcing the warm liquid down his throat.

Nick awoke days later deep in the woods in the cabin of an Old gypsy named Esmerelda. He was bound hand and foot and thirsty for more blood. The old woman cut the throat of a goat and brought the blood for him to drink. She fed him like that for days until the blood thirst had passed then let him go.

Nick never knew who the man was that had turned him, although he was sure Esmerelda did. He didn't know if he should be thankful for his act or not. He had saved Nick's life but his humanity had been lost in the process.

While Nick was with Esmerelda she had taught him all she could about his new life. He stayed with her until he was strong enough to travel then went back to live with his family.

At the time of Nick's conversion he was thirty-eight and I asked Nick if he'd ever married or had any children. "No," he replied bluntly, there was anguish in his face when he answered.

I wondered why he'd never married. He was such a handsome man; surely he could have had his pick from the women of the time. I decided not to ask any further since it apparently pained him.

Nick sat quietly for a while staring blankly out into the darkness. After a few moments he spoke hesitantly.

"There was someone….a long time ago … that I thought I could have made a life with." He paused breathing deeply. "Things didn't work out for us and since that time I've not had a long term relationship. Being a vampire complicates things."

He didn't have to tell me the story for me to hear the pain in his words. My heart ached for him. I knew firsthand what it was like to lose someone you loved. That night something changed between us. An unspoken pact that glued us together – we both understood loss.

We discovered that we had many things in common. The types of music we liked the books we read, and our love for everything outdoors. Nick was very intelligent and well read.

It was nice to be around a man again, especially one as good looking as Nick, and to be able to talk about pretty much anything. It was especially nice to look up and catch him staring at me in a way my husband rarely had.

Nick's profession for quite some time now had been private investigator. He was ~ quite literally ~ good at sniffing things out. He and a friend worked in the same line of business so they helped each other out when needed.

Stephan had called asking Nick for help when he knew I needed looking after. For that I was very thankful.

The other reason I loved the night was how good I could see in the dark. My vision had changed so much that I could now see just as clearly as if it were midday.

This night vision came in handy while out hunting, but when it came to hunting humans, whom we rarely did, not just any would do. If we were going to kill, it at least should be for the greater good, not just to satisfy the hunger of a vampire.

It was necessary to make sure we had the right person. This is what Nick referred to as the art of selection. An accidental bump to the nose, or a scratch on the skin would normally bring about a drop of blood. As I had already learned, just a drop is all it takes to find out a whole lot about a person. Needless to say, it was easier for me to hunt a child molester or rapist than a hard working father of four.

Children were off limits and I shied away from family pets. Truthfully, there would never be a reason to touch a child with the unlimited supply of thugs. But hunting was for survival mode with all the other avenues available. Butcher shops would collect blood when requested, and there was always the rejected units from would be blood donors. Not to mention I really didn't require feeding that often.

EIGHT

Tasting blood told me more that the persons thoughts and experience though. Over time I could detect certain nuances in the blood that I associated with illness and disease. This could prove to be a valuable tool when I went back to being a nurse, if I ever went back to being a nurse.

It became apparent that the local law officials were aware of our existence. It was also apparent that they were more than happy to allow us to go our merry way and not interfere in our business.

At one point we were littering the area with bodies and very few of them wound up in the news. The ones that did make it to the news were always connected to some local gang the cops were trying to bring down.

Like killing two birds with one stone, they could allow us to get rid of one unwanted while framing another unwanted for the crime. It did start me wondering though who the vampire was that had his fingers in the local law enforcement.

My time at the big house had gone by quickly and soon I would be going back to my own house. One afternoon as I strolled about on the grounds I had stopped to watch the Koi feeding along the lilies in one of the small ponds. Lost in my thoughts of returning to my old life I didn't see the flash of movement behind me.

Suddenly someone grabbed my arms from behind, knocking my feet out from under me. I was on my back on the ground in an instant, my attacker pinning my shoulders. Without thinking I swung my legs up wrapping them around my assailant's neck then flung them back toward the ground flipping him over my body and into the grass in front of me.

My legs still tight around his neck, his arm shot into the air. "Uncle!" he called out. I swore as I released my grip. It was Nick. Standing up I glared down at him, my hands fisted at my hips. He smiled up at me.

"Guess you can take care of yourself after all." I couldn't stay mad at him.

"You scared me," I said plopping down on the ground next to him. "I didn't hear or smell you sneaking up." I said jokingly.

"I stayed down wind," he retorted with a laugh "and found you with my eyes closed." I gasped.

"What exactly does that mean?" I asked indignantly.

Nick pushed up onto one elbow looking at me, the humor gone from his eyes. Now they were dark and filled with desire. The air around us charged and heated. A delicious shiver ran up my spine. I was drawn to him, pulled by an unseen force causing muscles to clench from deep within.

"Just what Stephan said," His voice was low, sexy and filled with longing.

"What did Stephan say?" I asked leaning closer, surrendering completely to the pull. Nick reached his free arm around my waist and lowered me down on the ground next to him. I didn't resist as his lips met mine, his greedy tongue licking and tasting inside my mouth.

Hungrily his mouth moved across my cheek whispering in my ear.

"That you smell lovely" he answered.

We spirited away to a small cave we had discovered on one of our outings. There hidden from the rest of the world Nick spread out the blanket we'd brought. Turning to me he offered his hand and I accepted, kneeling with him.

His hands were on my face, bringing my lips to his, wandering to my neck and up to the back of my head; His fingers tangling in my hair as he pulled me closer. A fire ignited in my lips and traveled to my groin as muscles deep in my belly clenched. His lips were soft, enticing my own lips to part allowing his tongue to invade my mouth then move down my neck, slowly, tantalizing.

"I want you Kat," he whispered in my mouth. I moaned feeling the pull in my groin and the growing wetness between my legs.

My body arched hungrily into him, aching with desire and the need to be touched. His eyes moved deliberately down my throat stopping at my breast as he began to unbutton my shirt.

My chest heaved as he pushed the shirt from my shoulders, allowing it to fall to the ground. He kissed me again, a low moan escaping his lips, his hands stroking my breasts.

Gently his fingers traced the delicate lace of my bra, his eyes burning into my breasts. Inserting his fingers into the cups he pushed them down so that my breasts were now exposed. Gently he stroked my nipples with his thumbs, first one then the other, teasing them between his thumb and forefinger.

The feeling was divine and another moan escaped as it radiated to my groin. Pushing the straps off my shoulders he kissed where they had been as he unhooked my bra, and tossed it aside.

Trailing my fingers to his belt line I found the hem of his shirt and pulled it off over his head taking in his chiseled chest and shoulder muscles. I ran my fingers through the hair on his chest, feeling the power in the muscles below.

His head dipped, his mouth moving across my breast, stopping at my nipples sucking and flicking them with his tongue, causing them to bead up and harden under his touch.

His mouth returned to mine, one hand holding my head to him, the other cupping and kneading my breast. My hands were in his hair again, fisting and pulling him closer to me.

My breathing was ragged and my pulse quickened. Pushing his hips into me I felt his erection hard against my belly, straining against his zipper. He pulled me tighter into him, rocking his hips against me.

I moaned into his mouth as my hands traveled to his waistband unbuttoning his pants. Slipping a hand inside I found him hard and thick, and muscles clenched achingly in my groin. I pushed his pants down, allowing his erection to spring free.

He lowered me onto my back and hovered over me, kissing my neck. Moving a knee between my legs he pushed them apart and positioned himself comfortably between them. I raised my pelvis up to meet his, grinding against him.

His mouth made its way down my neck past my breast then on to my stomach. I felt the pop of a snap, heard the tear of the zipper and with one quick jerk my pants were off.

His hand moved between my legs and I spread them wide to his touch, pushing against his hand, feeling the friction. He slipped two fingers inside me, moving them around, pushing against my clitoris with his palm.

"Oh, baby you're so ready for me. Do you know how hard that makes me?" I wanted him inside me. I wanted him now.

"Nick please, now" I begged, stroking the hard thickness of his cock.

"Not yet baby." He said moving back, leaving me bereft. I knew what was coming as he lowered his head to the apex of my thighs. My head pushed back against the ground as his mouth found my sex and his tongue parted the moist folds, his fingers still moving inside me.

My body convulsed as his velvet tongue sucked and licked at my clit, pushing me toward orgasm. I fisted my fingers in his hair, moaning as waves of pleasure swept from my groin out to the rest of my body.

His fingers had found that sweet spot and he moved them expertly massaging inside while his tongue excited my sensitive clit. I could feel the flutter of my labia as muscles inside squeezed around his fingers, holding them inside.

I was building with intensity, ready to explode around him, wanting to release. "That's right. Come for me baby," he urged, "Come in my mouth. The desire in his sexy voice pushed me over the edge as I convulsed with the orgasm.

"Oh god, Nick – fuck," I cried out as the waves moved through me. He moaned against my sex as his tongue lapped into the entrance of my body. His thumb now on my clit massaged me, prolonging the effects that continued to echo throughout my core.

He moved, pulling my hips up to meet his. "I'm going to take you now," he said as he slowly pushed into me, penetrating into my wet depth. "Ahhh," I gasped as I expanded to accept his thick length. I closed my eye as my head pushed back, overwhelmed by the delicious feeling of him filling me, stretching me as he pushed in to the root.

A cry of sheer pleasure escaped my lips as he began to move. I tightened around him and the pleasure showed on his face. His balls slapped heavily against my backside as he moved in and out. With each stroke he grazed my already oversensitive clit, exciting it even more. My hips moved with his, pushing harder and tightening more with each stroke.

Then I was calling out with each thrust and he was moving faster and faster. My body shook as waves of pleasure exploded from my groin spreading out in another orgasm. Then Nick was exploding, pulsing, emptying out deep inside me; calling out my name as the intensity tore through his body leaving him shaking.

He collapsed down on me, into my arms. I lay there in his arms for long moments, my entire body trembling as if chilled to the core. He pulled me closer, wrapping himself around me.

And it was just us, Hidden from the rest of the world; Two vampires clinging to each other.

NINE

The day regretfully arrived that I had to return to my own home and attempt to return to my old life. Stephan had extended an offer for me to continue living at the big house with him, stating the house was far too large for just him and Sara. The offer was very generous, and I might have taken him up on it, had it not been for the business I had left unattended for the past two months.

Coming out the front door, he made his way down the front steps to where Nick and I were putting my few belongings into Nick's jeep. "Katherine," he said as he hugged me and kissed me on the cheek, "You are always welcome in my home."

I returned his kiss. "I know, I replied. You haven't seen the last of me." I had become quite fond of Stephan and felt I owed him a great deal. He had, after all, saved my life.

Everything loaded; we said our final goodbyes and climbed into the car. Stopping at the gate I turned to look at the big house again, the house where I had been re-born.

As Nick pulled out onto the main highway my thoughts turned to what lie ahead. My paycheck had continued while I was out on leave and was deposited automatically into my checking account. Also, my mortgage payment was automatic from my account.

Other bills though, such as water, gas, and electric had not been paid in my absence. Secretly I hoped that maybe Dan had paid them, but that was highly unlikely. He had left to make his new life with his lover – of that I was sure.

Nick reached over and squeezed my hand. Looking up from my reverie I gave him a forced smile. I was concerned about what surprises might be waiting for me at the house. Nick's hand moved to my cheek then down to my chin, tipping it up towards him he smiled, his unspoken meaning understood. I was glad for Nick's company and equally glad that he would be staying with me for a couple of days until I was well settled. With that reassurance I settled back into my seat for the drive home.

It was nearly two o'clock when we pulled up into the driveway. My car, still sitting in the garage where Nick had put it before we left, had two flat tires from non-use. I wondered if it would even crank after all this time.

The house was hot inside and no lights were on, a musty, closed up smell permeated the air. A quick flip of a switch told me the power was off. *Apparently Dan didn't want to pay the bills!*

I went to the guest bath and turned on a faucet. A low groaning gurgle escaped through the pipes. *Water is turned off too.* I shook my head; well at least I was prepared for that. What I wasn't prepared for was the site that awaited me in the living room. A pile of mail lay near the front door mail slot, and a pile of trash stood where my sofa once was.

The dining table and chairs also were missing as well as were the bar stools from the breakfast bar. Shock went through my spine and spread throughout my body. I was instantly angry.

Dropping my bags in the middle of the floor I ran to the bedroom, Nick right behind me. My bed was still there, but the large dresser was missing. Then I saw the note on my pillow. I grabbed it up and read it growing angrier by the minute. It was from Dan.

Katherine,

I've decided to let you keep the house but since I am letting so much go I am taking the furniture and appliances. Tash didn't want the bed so you can have that as well. Expect to receive divorce papers from me as soon as I can have them drawn up. I would like you to sign ASAP so that I can get on with the rest of my life.

Dan

So this was how it would be then. His regret for what he'd done to me - gone - disappeared the instant he was in her arms.

"Who the hell does he think he is?" I said, my voice getting louder and higher. "Of course *she* didn't want my bed! I wonder did he tell her he fucked me in it the night before he left. And the house was mine before we married so it's not his anyway."

Nick was behind me now, holding my shoulders, attempting to calm me. I was shaking with uncontrollable rage, tears streaming down my face unbidden. "He had no right." I screamed again. In that instant I wanted to kill him. Blinded by the onslaught of new and repressed feelings of hurt I moved to take action. Nick grabbed me by the arm and pulled me into his chest. "Let me go I screamed."

"Where are you planning to go?" he asked calmly.

"I'm going to kick his ass…. I'm going to tear out his throat!" I replied angrily.

"No," Nick said, still holding me tight, "that won't do any good and it's just not worth it." Again I tried to pull away, but Nick's arms were much stronger than I. "Please stop," he begged. "Let me help you with this. There are much better ways to deal with this. If you go over there now, in this state of mind, you will kill him and people

149

will see you. I won't let you take that kind of risk. It's just furniture, it can be replaced. It's hard enough being a vampire without being hunted and always running."

As Nick continued to talk to me I started to relax. Something about his voice was so comforting to me. Maybe because he had been with me during the change, helping me through.

He was right. I would kill Dan now if I didn't get control of my anger. It wouldn't just be a domestic dispute called in. I was strong enough to snap his neck with one blow, and I'd probably break *Tasha's* neck too just because I could.

"Ok," I finally said, lowering my voice. "I'm ok now, you can let me go." He released his grip slowly and turned me around to face him. Lifting my chin he smiled down at me.

"There's more than one way to skin a cat, and we will skin this one legally!"

Dan's note had said appliances too. As we looked around the house once more we realized the refrigerator, washer and dryer were gone. I couldn't believe I had walked right by and not noticed them missing before.

Opening cabinets I found much the same. Dan and his harpy, as I had decided to call her, had left nothing but miss-matched items. There was no way to cook or eat even if I'd had power. I just stared in disbelief.

I would have never done something like this to him. Would have never believed Dan would do this to me, yet here I stood in an empty house.

Nick gently pulled at my arm. "Come on, let's go," he said. "We can't stay here until we have power and water at least. We'll go stay at my place while we take care of that stuff."

I looked up surprised. "Your house," I asked.

"Yes," he smiled. "I have a house near here." I hadn't realized that before, but I'd never really asked him either. "I have several houses," he said "the one I'm currently living in is not far from here."

I needed some more clothes from my closet. After getting those packed I grabbed a plastic bag and stuffed my mail into it, then flinging it over my shoulder; I gathered my other bags and followed Nick out the door.

Today was Saturday. I wouldn't be able to do anything until Monday when the utility companies were open. Locking the door behind me I looked again at my poor car. I would need to come back and take care of that. Luckily, I noticed my tool box still stood in the corner of the garage. At least Dan hadn't taken that.

Thirty minutes later we were pulling into a very long, pavestone driveway that led to a sprawling house on the bay. Great pecan trees littered the property, providing shade. The house itself was an older, single story dwelling that had been updated over the years. There was a separate garage, connected to the house by a large covered patio.

Nick got out and came around to open my door. Taking my bags, he led me inside. The interior was very rich looking with stained wood paneling, stone flooring, and granite countertops.

"This is very nice Nick," I commented looking around. "How long have you lived here?"

"I bought this house in the seventies." Nick said. "I own several homes and don't stay in any of them too long. I just kind of circulate." He said smiling.

"How often do you move?" I wondered frowning.

"No set time, just whenever necessary," he said. "Most people have forgotten me or moved away by the time I come back. I just pick up and start again." I shook my head. I still had not been able to wrap my head around this *methuselah* life span.

My life for now was still pretty much the same and I really had not given it a lot of thought. Now hearing Nick talk about moving around made me depressed. Nick must have read my mind because he leaned over and gave me a quick kiss.

"Come," he said "I'll show you your room, and then we can get something to drink." Great! I thought. Even though the alcohol really did nothing for me I still savored the thought of a bloody Mary.

Since our little escapade at the big house our relationship had changed. Still I was not sure exactly what it had become, friends with benefits possibly? That we enjoyed each other's company was evident, we spent hours together every day. When it came to sex Nick was even better than what I had imagined and I took advantage of him as often as possible. He did not disappoint.

Whatever our relationship had become I was immensely enjoying it and in no hurry to jump into another serious relationship. Neither had I gotten any vibes from Nick that he wanted to take it further. As long as he was happy with what we had, I was happy too.

The room where I would be staying was large, boasting its own bath and walk in closet. Pale green in color, it had a queen bed covered with a green and maroon quilt. I put my bags down on the foot of the bed.

"Let me give you a quick tour," Nick said. His room was at the other end of the hall. It was larger and very masculine looking. Sitting on a dark wood floor was a king bed also of dark wood. A leather covered bench sat at the foot of the bed and deep burnt orange and brown accent rug lay in front of that.

Nick turned to me with a wicked grin. "Just because you have your own room doesn't mean you have to stay there." I smiled back.

"I'll keep that in mind."

On our way back to the kitchen Nick pointed out his study, a large game room with a pool table, and a sun room. The living room and kitchen were large open area's that, more or less flowed into each other.

A large stone fireplace with a bearskin rug stretched out before it was the centerpiece of the living area. I had never seen a real bearskin before and stooped to touch it. It was much thicker than I had imagined, and quite soft. A thought crossed my mind.

"Is that....?" I asked pointing to the bearskin rug.

"One and the same," He said smiling. "I've had to pamper it along though or it would have not lasted."

Stopping in the kitchen to fix some drinks we moved outside to see the back yard. It was huge. A strong south wind, not evident in the front yard, was constant here in the back.

We walked for a hundred yards before the yard dropped off steeply into the bay. A metal staircase driven into the embankment led down to a long pier and boat house. Nick started down the stairs motioning for me to follow.

Once on the pier he took my hand and led me to the boathouse. We were protected from the wind in here and I stopped to tuck a wayward strand of hair behind my ear. Securely tied up in the slot, bobbing gently with the rise and fall of the waves was a sleek twenty-four foot boat.

"Go ahead and hop in if you like." Nick said.

Carefully I stepped down into the boat, grabbing a bar on the console to steady myself. I knew very little about boats but this one seemed to be equipped for fishing I noted seeing rod holders. There were padded bench seats in the front and back and two large ice chests with cushioned tops.

"It's very nice." I said, sitting down on one of the benches. "Do you fish often?" A broad smile spread across his face.

"As often as possible," he replied. "I also use it for water sports occasionally." He pointed to some chrome tubing coming off the top of the console. "This allows you to pull a wake board or you can drag a skier from the back." "How about you, do you fish?"

"My dad used to take me fishing off a pier, but I've never been on a boat before." I frowned remembering the time my best friend had invited me out on her boat and my mother, afraid I'd drown, had not allowed me to go.

"Well, we'll have to fix that," Nick said smiling.

Back in the house we were both starting to get hungry and decided on going out for sushi. The sushi bar was one I'd seen many times before but had never eaten there. Due to my recent introduction to the delicate cuts of fish, I was sure this wouldn't be my last visit.

Once seated, Nick fired off a quick text message. The waiter appeared a moment later and we ordered. I opted for the seared blue fin tuna and a glass of Saki. Nick ordered some smoked salmon and a beer.

As we waited for our food to arrive, Nick reached across the table and squeezed my hand.

"I don't want you to feel like I'm in your business," he said, "but I'm checking up on something that may help you with your divorce situation. That is, if you want my help."

The scene from earlier in the day leapt into my mind and I tried to suppress my anger. Dan might as well have kicked me in the gut. I had, as gracefully as possible let him go without a fight knowing that I had lost his affection. I had fully accepted the responsibility for my part in our failed marriage. I was not, however going to allow him to use me as his door mat.

"I can use all the help I can get," I said with resignation.

"Well then after lunch," he said smiling, "There is someone I want you to meet."

As it turned out Nick had a friend who had been practicing law for over four-hundred years. According to Nick, he'd practically written half of them and knew the in's and out's and every loophole there was. His name was Dorian Finch, a nice looking young man of about thirty with a pleasant demeanor and a firm handshake. He shook his head and smiled when he heard the story.

"I tell you," Dorian said, "I've seen it all a hundred times over in my day. The trick is to get the jump on him and file first. It gives us a bit of an upper hand in the situation. I'll get my girls working on it and have if filed by Monday morning. I have friends in the system. We'll get him served so fast it will make his head spin."

"All I have is his work address," I said, "I don't know where he's staying."

"Even better," said Dorian, an impish gleam in his eye. "Nothing like getting him served at work to rattle his cage."

As we stood to leave, Dorian shook my hand once again, smiling warmly.

"Katherine, "he said, dipping his head slightly, "It's been a pleasure. You don't need to do anything but wait to hear from me." Then turning to Nick "I'll need you to turn over a few stones – see what you can find out to help us."

Nick nodded, "Will get right on it." he said.

I exhaled long and slow as we left Dorian's office. The events of the last two and a half months were mind boggling to say the least. Throw on my issue with Dan and there seemed to be a mountain standing in my horizon, threatening to block the sun for a while. This problem at least had effectively been handed over for someone else to deal with. Immediately my mountain had shrunk in size.

Mentally I pulled down my to-do list and checked it off- at least for now. Tomorrow I would check off a few more. Nick wrapped a knowing arm around my shoulders as we walked back to the car. I liked the feel of his arm around me and I leaned into it, relishing the closeness.

On the drive back to Nick's we passed a small church with a graveyard that I hadn't noticed before. My mind wandered to thoughts of Angie. I missed her, missed her and grieved more for her than I had Dan. Soon I would have to go back to work and she wouldn't be there. I wondered if I would be able to work in the same area – or same hospital for that matter. We had so much history.

I had never known how much she was really hurting inside and the realization of that pained me. She had never let on at all, just threw herself into helping other people. Now I ached inside wondering if I had made the right decision.

Should I have let her die the way she did. She had so much life left to live. I wondered if she would have hated me if I'd saved her. Then I wondered if it would have really been saving her at all.

My life was changed. I could go back to work but it would never be truly what it was before. Life for me was filled with the makings of horror films and Frankenstein monsters. I had accepted it, embraced it even, but would Angie have been able to? I would never know. For now I just kept telling myself that I gave her what she wanted.

Back at Nick's I showered, washing away the sticky coating of sea-salt I was plastered with. The water was warm and felt wonderful running over my head, warming up my core.

Outside the sea air was cold and damp, chilling me to the bone. It was only September but already the sun was setting earlier and it was getting cooler. Drying off I wrapped my hair, turbine style in a towel and put on my night shirt and yoga pants.

A fire was burning in the fireplace and Nick was in the kitchen opening a bottle of wine. He smiled when I entered.

"Glass of wine?" he offered.

"Absolutely," I accepted.

I felt nervous for some reason, and although I knew the wine would have no alcoholic effect on me I hoped for placebo effect. Nick noticed my restlessness.

"What's wrong?" he asked looking a bit concerned.

"Just a lot on my mind," I said forcing a smile, "A lot to do before I go back to work this week."

Nick put down his wine glass and walked over to me. Reaching up he stroked my cheeks with the backs of his hands, dropping them to my shoulders caressing my arms. Stopping at my elbows he held me there for a moment, closed his eyes and breathed deeply.

Opening his eyes he muttered, "You've been stressed. You will need to feed soon. Tonight we will rest. You should try to sleep and conserve your energy."

Something about the way he touched my cheek set off sparks deep inside. He was so close and I loved the way he smelled, it was tantalizing. I caught myself mimicking his actions as I closed my eyes, breathing deeply.

Maybe it was just the attentiveness and care he displayed, or possibly his nearness. Whatever it was I was suddenly incredibly aroused in his presence, the effect much different than before.

Desire bloomed deep down and spread through me. Warmth spread within my belly, clenching muscles deliciously and setting nerve endings on fire. My breathing increased and waves of energy swept up and down my spine.

Opening my eyes I found myself staring directly into his. His pupils were dilated; his chest rapidly rising and falling, with bated breath. Then he had me, his arms wrapped around me, as his mouth claimed mine.

My lips parted as his tongue pushed its way in, his hands in my hair as the towel fell away. My fingers dug into his shoulder blades attempting to pull him closer. His mouth moved to my neck, kissing me down the front of my throat, a day's growth of beard teasing my senses, fanning the flame that had started.

I could taste his arousal with every kiss. Pushing me against the cabinet I felt his erection against my hip, fueling the raw lust I was now engulfed in. Wet and wanting I pulled his head to mine our foreheads resting together. I was panting, being driven by unseen forces.

"I want you," he said breathing heavily, his eyes glowing almost red. "I know you want me too." I answered by taking his lower lip in my teeth. In an instant he lifted me into his arms carried me into the living room and deposited me onto the bearskin rug.

My hair now freed from the towel hung in damp, curling strands down my back. Nick pulled off my tee shirt exposing my breast and beaded nipples, his mouth going to them without hesitation.

"Oh Nick please," I begged, "I want you to fuck me now; I need to feel you inside."

164

Nick moaned against my breast. Pulling back he placed his thumbs in the waistband of my pants, pulling them down my legs. As he did he slowed, and a deep, guttural sound came from his throat. I responded with my own moan, lying back on the rug, bringing Nick with me.

His hands moved up my legs to my thighs and higher finally finding me with his fingers, and exciting my clitoris. My body arched under his touch.

Tilting my pelvis I pushed against his hand, wanting more. His hand moved spreading my legs wider, his mouth now on me, claiming me with his tongue.

Hungry and raging with desire I grabbed his hair, running it through my fingers. "Ohhh," I cried out as Nick moved once again. Now he was on his knees straddling me. Sitting up I grabbed the hem of his shirt and pulled it off over his head tossing it to the side. My hands went to his pants releasing the button and zipper then pulled his pants down.

Loosed from the confines of the fabric his erection sprung free. Nick stood, removing his pants the rest of the way. He was a beautiful, splendid example of manhood and I wanted him, every part of him. I wanted him inside me….I wanted him in my mouth.

Before he could kneel again I was on my knees, taking him greedily into my mouth with both hands at the root.

I was eager to taste him and pleased that he swelled even larger in my mouth. I licked over the small slit in his crown tasting the sweetness of his pre-cum.

"Ahh – Kat," he said sucking air through his teeth, "Suck on me hard baby."

Hollowing my cheeks I sucked deeply, rolling my tongue along the thick heavy veins as I withdrew, then took him deeper into the recesses of my mouth. I continued to jack the base of his cock with my hands as I bobbed my head slowly along his length, taking him almost completely before returning to his crown.

Swirling my tongue around and around the head of his cock I grabbed his balls that shrank up tight with my touch. His hands were in my hair guiding me back and forth as he rocked his pelvis into me, fucking my mouth with his exquisite cock.

Sensing his pleasure made me want to give him more. I began moving faster, sucking harder with each thrust. I could feel my own dampness spreading down to my legs. I moaned against him and felt him swell again as I allowed my teeth to scrape gently down his exquisite length.

He shuddered violently calling my name as he came thickly into the back of my throat. "Kat baby," he said through clenched teeth. "Oh fuck what you do to me." I swallowed only to accept more of his cum as his cock pulsed repeatedly into my mouth. I continued to lick down his length until he stopped quivering. Long moments later he withdrew, still partially erect.

I let my head fall back. I wanted him now. My groins ached to have him inside me and he was there, crouching in front of me, talking through gritted teeth.

"Is this what you want," he asked holding his cock in one hand, and his eyes lit up like hot, glowing embers as he fingered me with the other. "You're so wet baby, so ready for me!" Still holding his cock in one hand he began to jack it up and down his length. It was so hot to see him holding himself, pleasuring. "I'm ready for you too." He said as he pushed me gently onto my back, moving between my legs.

My pelvis tilted to feel him against me. Then he was inside me, lifting and pulling my hips to meet his thrust as he stretched and filled me to my limit.

"Yes," I screamed as he pounded against me again and again. Then he shifted forward with my legs over his shoulders, coming straight down hard and fast, filling me up with each stroke. He rolled his hips into me exploring every surface, seeking out my pleasure spot and I gasp as my core constricted, tightening around him.

"Come on baby," he growled, his mouth at my ear. "Let me hear you. Come for me now." I was breaking apart, shattering into a million pieces, moaning in ecstasy as I came on and on with every stroke. Then Nick found his release and collapsed on top of me, breathing rapidly into my hair as he pulsed repeatedly inside of me.

I was sated and I didn't want him to move. Raising his head he kissed me deeply before rolling to his side, taking me with him, never breaking our precious contact. We held each other as our breathing slowed, arms and legs entwined. There on the bearskin rug, in front of the blazing fire, we fell asleep in each other's arms.

I awoke suddenly some hours later. I was still lying on the bearskin rug with Nick cuddled against my back, his arm wrapped around me. We were naked but Nick had pulled a small blanket off the couch and covered us with it. I was shaking and there was a sense of hollowness in the pit of my stomach.

The anxiety had returned. I needed to feed – Now! Nick stirred as I attempted to unwind from his arms. "What's wrong?" He asked me as he sat up. I tried to speak but words failed me.

The light from the fire illuminated my body. Nick touched my arm and felt as a shudder passed through me. "Shit!" he exclaimed jumping to his feet and pulling on his jeans and tee shirt. My voice back I started to talk.

"I need…"

"Yes," Nick snapped, I know."

I was scrambling to my feet now, pulling my clothes back on. The anxiety had passed for the moment. Nick switched the light on and assessed my face, pulling my lower eyelid down to look more closely at my eye. "Fuck!" he exclaimed again. "Get some shoes on, we need to move now." Running to the room I grabbed some socks and a pair of tennis, hopping back into the living room as I put them on. "I'm sorry," I managed, "sitting on the couch to tie the shoes.

Nick came over and sat by me, already in his shoes I noted.

"I'm not mad at you Kat," he said, "I' m angry at myself for letting you go this long. And I probably pushed you over the edge tonight. You need to feed before you go into an all – out blood thirst." I was shocked and scared when he said the words.

"But, I've been eating." I said feebly, feeling a little anxious again.

"You've been eating human food," Nick said, "and that is ok for a while, but your body needs blood for your health and strength. You haven't fed in over a week, and since we left Stephan's you've had a lot of stress dumped

170

on you." He stood up and held out his hand to me. "Ready?" he asked.

We left the house on foot in the cover of night. My senses heightened even more as adrenaline coursed through my bloodstream. Running helped reduce the effects of the adrenaline but I was still in full hunting mode. My fear of going into blood thirst made it even worse.

We had just gotten into town and had not been able to *mark* any selections. Tonight would have to be a necessity kill and choices would be limited. I hoped that someone up to no-good would be out and about for us to find.

My thought's turned to Dan. *I should be ripping his throat out!* "Nick smelled the surge in adrenaline just in time to grab my arm and stop me from going after Dan. "No," he said, we'll find someone here soon. I promise."

We were in the city now, moving along the bayou that meandered through town, and ducking into alleyways avoiding the light. I stopped and rested my hands on my knees, fighting the sudden strong desire to break into a house and feed on the family.

171

I was getting more tense and irritable by the minute. Nick pointed to a two story building along some dark streets. "Up there." He said, and we moved around the corner and climbed to the top.

A few streets over a man walked alone on an unlit corridor. He would have to do. Stealthily we moved from rooftop to rooftop until he was just below us. In his arms was a bag with a gallon of milk. I felt ill. *Was he bringing this home to his children?* I closed my eyes against the thought. *If not this man then who; and how many more would die? I needed to feed quickly.*

As if in answer to an unspoken prayer a Cadillac swung into the alley, and three men jumped out surrounding the man with the milk. All of them had knives and were swishing them around threating the man, demanding his money. I breathed a sigh of relief and jumped off the roof into the darkness.

Nick was on the ground just an instant before me. Alarmed and confused by our sudden appearance, the attackers turned their attention to us. "Run," I yelled to the man with the milk. He did, leaving us alone with the three.

The fight was short. They had no chance against us. In just moments the first one to move was impaled on his own knife by Nick, the second and third had their necks broken instantly.

We moved them off further into the dark and feasted. As I drank in the blood I saw the horrible things they had done and felt justified in my killing. I was glad they had come along when they did. Glad the man with the milk was still alive. Sated, we put their bodies into the car and, leaving the windows halfway down, drove it off into the water.

Nick and I returned to the house just as the first rays of the sun were glowing over the horizon, highlighting the tops of trees and painting the sky the most fabulous hues of vermillion, orange, and purple.

Together we sat out on the pier and watched the sun make her glorious appearance. I had never seen anything more lovely than this sunrise over the water.

I never went back to sleep. Having fed, I was full of energy and glad of it for all I had to do. Nick had busied himself ferreting out information on Dan. Taking out a note pad Nick had asked me a series of questions about him. "What were his favorite colors, foods, restaurants, movies, books, etc., what was his full name, what were the names of his parents, did he have siblings/children/pets. I answered the questions to the best of my ability, realizing that my answers may be wrong. I really didn't know Dan like I had thought I had.

I left Nick working on his computer and took his jeep to go pay some bills and get my tires taken care of. With any luck I could also procure some beef blood from a local meat packer. I didn't ever want a repeat of last night.

The utilities were not a problem. When I told the girl at the water company I had been sick for two months she took pity on me and waived the re-connect fee. Besides I had never been late before.

Back at my house I opened the garage door and found my tire tool. Removing the two flat tires I took them down to a tire shop to have them checked and aired up.

After replacing the tires I checked the battery. Surprisingly, my car cranked right up so I drove it around the block. It was low on fuel so I stopped and filled the tank before returning it to the garage.

Nick met me at the door at his house. He had successfully hacked into Dan's work computer as well as his personal laptop.

"I have some stuff I think you should see before I hand this over to Dorian." He said with a touch of concern in his voice. Leading me into his study he pointed to a stack of papers. "I came across a file in his email server. He has saved all of these since 2004. I made a digital copy as well but I printed these for you to read. Those are in order starting with the earliest date."

I took the stack of paper from him. It was as thick as a ream of paper and I wondered what Dan would have been saving since 2004. That was the year we were married.

Nick pulled a chair out for me. "Sit." He said. I did, and sank back into the chair as I started reading. These were all emails back and forth between Dan and the harpy. Some filled with endearment while others were downright raunchy. I couldn't believe what I was seeing. I didn't want to read them.

Anger washed over me anew as I flipped through the pages. *All those years wasted; Wasted on this sorry son-of-a-bitch. How could he? Why? Why didn't he leave me back then?*

I thought of the opportunities I'd passed up, duty bound to stay faithful to a husband who was no longer interested in me. And Now, to find out he'd been seeing that home wrecker harpy all this time.

Page after page I turned. I didn't want to read it all. I couldn't read it, my mind reeling from the shock. In a daze I skimmed for information, my eyes seeing but my mind not comprehending. I was overwhelmed to the point of drowning.

Nick sat quietly as I looked. One fourth of the way through I stopped. I couldn't look anymore. The hurt and anger was rolling over me in waves. My eyes burned with unshed tears.

Defeated I turned to Nick. "Is there anything more I really need to see in these?" I asked waving the papers at him. Nick took them from me and placed them on his desk, and then pulled his chair so that we were sitting toe to toe. Leaning forward he kissed me.

"I know this is hard for you Kat," he said softly but there is one more thing you must see." He took the stack and flipped it over revealing a sheet he had tagged with a sticky note.

Careful not to get them out of order, he opened up the stack and removed the one page. Then he pulled his chair around so he was next to me. This email was dated April 2012, this year. I read only the highlighted area.

Baby please, please be patient with me. I know you're anxious and I know how you feel about me still living with Katherine, but please…

I am almost ready to take my leave. Just a few more months- ☺ I have been saving now for a while and have $250,000 in an account that Katherine knows nothing about. I want this for us, to start our lives together. I won't be able to keep saving once I leave Katherine, as she is paying the brunt of the bills. Please give me just a little more time. I'm doing this for you and you know my heart belongs only to you. We will be together soon – I promise.

Dan

"Oh, Fuck – This is enlightening! And I get screwed again! So he really was making much more than what he told me." I was beside myself with anger. "How many times can he just slap me in the face? I felt sick to my stomach.

How long had he been saving money while I paid the bills? That's a hell of a lot to save in eight years." I started to rise up out of my chair, but Nick pushed me back down, a look of satisfaction on his face.

"Kat, Baby," Nick said excitement in his voice, "this is our smoking gun. You are entitled to half of this and I've found the bank account to prove the money exists. We have copies of his statements.

He's been saving since before you married but a very large portion of that was accumulated after your marriage. Anyway, its money he brought into the marriage. You had no pre–nup so it's not protected from you. Any judge will give you half, but if we can get this into Reichert's court you may get more."

"Who is Reichert?" I asked starting to feel redeemed.

"Another good friend," Nick said, "of Dorian's and me." Then grinning he added, "He's also a vampire!"

Nick and I met once more with Dorian to give him the information Nick had dug up thus far. He had assured us that the suit had been filed Monday morning and we could expect Dan to be served sometime this week.

Things were looking very good for my case and I was very pleased with Dorian's and Nick's work. Nick was still doing some digging and, as much as I didn't want to know more, I was anxious to see what he might find.

By Thursday the power and water were back on at my house so I decided to go over and clean up. I still had no appliances or furniture but since Nick was in no hurry to get rid of me I saw no reason to rush out and buy any. Still I wanted to make sure the place was taken care of, and to make my presence known to any would-be vandals.

The day had turned out to be quite warm so I pulled on some old shorts and a cropped tank top and gathered some cleaning supplies. Nick offered to tag along and mow the grass for me while I cleaned up inside so we rode together in the jeep. I would drive my car back to Nick's when we left.

I was just finishing up, putting some stuff away in the garage, when Dan pulled into the drive. After all I had recently learned about him I didn't want a confrontation, but I wasn't sure how to avoid one either.

To my horror I realized he had brought *HER* with him. How dare he bring *HER* onto my property? I knew he was only doing this to get at me. *He must really hate me bad to go to such lengths to hurt me!* Unwilling to let him know how bad it chaffed me, I put on the politest face I could muster.

Dan climbed out of his sports car, nicely dressed and swaggered up the drive, looking as good as ever. Judging from the expression on his face, he was mad. I hated the fact that I was dirty and sweaty, but glancing down at myself I realized I had never looked better. My body was as nice as the ones on the cover of any fitness magazine and today I was wearing the perfect clothes to show it off. I decided to step out into the light and give my audience a show.

As I walked out of the garage, Dan suddenly didn't appear as confident. I was gloating inside as his gait noticeably slowed; his eyes wide with surprise. Patiently I waited in the full light of the sun for him to regain his composure. It took him two seconds, but he did summon it from somewhere. Scowling at me as he approached, he handed me an envelope. "You have officially been served." He said.

Nick rounded the corner from the back yard carrying the trimmer. He had taken his shirt off and the muscles in his back, chest and shoulders glistened in the sunlight from the sweat that ran liberally off his body.

In that moment I loved him – loved him for showing up so hot and undeniably sexy. He looked absolutely glorious and his timing could not have been better. He walked up to me, his pants hanging just right on his narrow hips revealing that beautiful touch of a god on his abdominal muscles.

"Is everything alright Kat?" he asked planting a kiss firmly on my lips, an impish grin on his face.

"Yes babe," I replied. "Dan is just leaving."

He smelled a divine mix of sweat and Nick and I imagined sliding my naked body against his sweaty, slick one. My thoughts weren't lost in my expression because Nick made one of his low growling noises. "You keep looking at me like that and I'm gonna have to fuck you." He said not caring that Dan could hear.

Dan had turned ashen as the blood drained out of his face. I'm not sure what had the biggest effect on him, the sight of Nick, or the fact that I was moving on. Either way the look on his face was a sight I would cherish for the rest of my long life. I couldn't see the harpy's expression, but she was growing fidgety in the car. I could smell her discomfort.

As Dan drove off I did a little dance. Round 1 was a K.O. in less than ten seconds!

TEN

Friday morning started off in a flurry with my alarm clock going off at four-thirty. It was my first day back to work and I was a bit apprehensive about it. I had taken all the time off that I could afford to, but I still was not ready to return to work. *Maybe I never would be,* I thought grimly. However, it had to be done.

I was scurrying around getting my things together when there was a knock on the bedroom door. I hoped I hadn't wakened Nick making too much noise.

I opened the door to find Nick standing there with two cups of coffee and a sleepy smile on his face. He was wearing nothing but a pair of pajama bottoms and again I admired his chiseled upper body.

"Morning," he said as he handed me one of the cups. "Oh – Thank you, good morning!" I said taking the cup from him. I took a sip, instantly beginning to relax as the hot liquid slid down my throat.

"You're up early; I hope I wasn't disturbing you."

"I wanted to get up and see you off, maybe have a cup of coffee before you left."

"A person could get use to this," I grinned. We walked together out into his back yard and sat at a small table under the stars. It was another incredibly clear sky and the wind had died down to a gentle breeze. We sat quietly for a while listening to the sound of the sea. Nick broke into the silence.

"I was thinking of taking the boat out this weekend and hoped you would go with me. Maybe catch a few fish. The weather is supposed to be great all week."

"I'd love to," I said, feeling a little excited, "I have to work tomorrow though."

"We can plan for Sunday then. I have gear that you can use. You may want to get a license."

"I'll do that," I said getting up. My cup was empty and I needed to get moving. Nick followed me into the kitchen where I poured us both a second cup of coffee.

Thirty minutes later I was dressed and ready to leave. Nick stopped me at the door and surprised me with a hug and a kiss. He lingered for a moment like he wanted to say something, then dismissing his thought; he kissed me on the forehead.

"Have a good day at work," he said as I got into my car.

"You too," I called back.

As I drove in to work I thought about the events of the morning. My relationship with Nick was evolving, moving in a direction that both allured and scared me at the same time. Nick was such a caring and giving person. For years I had lived with a man who did nothing but take. More than I had ever realized before.

Being around Nick allowed me to see what I'd missed out on. Simple actions, like making me a cup of coffee, were such a huge deal. No-one had ever done that for me before, except maybe Callie, certainly not Dan. Of course having only Dan to compare Nick to, sure made it easy for Nick to look good.

Then there was the off the charts, mind blowing, toe curling, body shaking, multi orgasm, totally amazing sex to think about too. It wasn't like I'd slept with hundreds of guys or anything but I'd had my fair share.

Without a doubt Nick was the best hands down. Nick was truly gifted in the love making department and he already knew my body better than I did. He knew just how and where to touch me, just the right angle, the right amount of pressure, the perfect flick of his tongue. OMG – just thinking about it was making me wet and wanting.

But in my heart I know it's not just the sex – although the sex is truly awesome. It's the fact that he's a good man. It's because I feel so safe when I'm with him and comforted in his arms. It's because when I was going through the absolute worst experience of my life, Nick was there for me.

I wondered how Nick really felt about me. Did he want more with me? What did he want to say to me this morning? Did he already consider me his lover? Should I ask him? No, I thought not. I didn't want to mess anything up.

Nick stood at the door watching as Kat drove off to work. He worried about her. She was strong, and for the most part, could take care of herself yet she was so new to this life.

Something about her made him want to take care of her. He had wanted to make coffee for her this morning and he had wanted to sit outside and enjoy life with her. She was so easy to be around, so easy to like.

Kat wasn't the typical, high maintenance, dramatic, over-reacting female. She had taken the worst that life could dish out and handled it with grace, never complaining. She was tough, and accepted life as it came.

The fact that she seemed happy just to be with him blew his mind. Her genuine appreciation for what most people took for granted spoke volumes.

He recalled the excitement in her eyes this morning when he'd brought her the cup of coffee. You would have thought he had just given her a diamond ring.

That smile for a simple cup of coffee! How would she have looked if it had been a diamond ring?

He had wanted to tell her, or at least hint to her how he felt, but decide not to at the last minute. Was she still in love with Dan? He didn't think so - she appeared to be over him, but that didn't mean she was ready for a serious relationship.

Was he ready for that kind of commitment? He had been a bachelor for so long now, but it was so refreshing having her here in his home. His life was no longer empty.

Maybe he could convince her to stay for a while. Nick sighed. Kat was pretty independent and may not want to stay much longer. Then there is the problem of Orlando.....

I looked up at the time. It was six-fifteen Saturday evening and the night shift would be arriving soon. I had survived my first two days back to work.

It hadn't taken me long to get back into the flow of things. I was in my element. These last two days had been busy and I was thankful. I needed my mind to stay occupied, less time to spend thinking about Angie.

A few things had changed since the last time I had worked. In my absence Jackie had hired a new nurse named Teresa. She was pretty and funny and fit right in with the rest of the staff. There was also a new group of doctors with the start of the fall semester.

The most important changes though, were the ones that had occurred within me. My heighten sense of smell had come in very handy, along with my ability to read a person using their blood. This was incredibly useful when trying to identify a medical problem.

As I had discovered on my outings with Nick, not only do people have their own unique smell, disease process do too. One of the easiest for me to identify was the scent of diabetes. There were so many diabetics around me it was easy to confirm. Their blood was much sweeter than other blood and a bit thicker.

Other scents were not so easily identifiable, as I had nothing to compare them with. I was making notes as

I went along. It would take time for me to sort it all out and connect scents with specific nuances in the blood, but it could be done. This was a new approach to the head to toe assessment – via vampire.

I started another small notebook as well. This one contained a last name, address, and a small smear of blood on the page. So far I only had one name. When I thought about it I cringed.

When tasting this patient's blood I saw him violently beating and kicking a woman repeatedly, then turning and doing the same to a small child. I had been so furious I couldn't go back to tend to him for a while.

As a result he had won a *special* place in my heart and had inspired me to make what I now referred to my expendables list. If anyone else ever saw it they would simply think it was an address book. To me it was the name and location of my next blood meal!

The sound of a pen tapping on the counter brought me back to the present. I looked up to see Shay, one of the night shift nurses, smiling at me. "Ready for report when you are."

I gave report as quickly as I could then left, stopping to buy a fishing license on my way home. I was excited about the boat trip in the morning. On the way out the door I spied a rack of bikinis. A pink and orange floral one caught my eye and I decided to buy it. I hadn't bought one in years and wasn't sure if my old one fit anymore.

Most of my clothes were pretty loose fitting these days, but a new wardrobe hadn't been a priority. Maybe I would go buy a couple of new things when I was off later this week. Bikini in hand I headed home.

Nick was just taking some steaks off the grill when I arrived. He had made some au gratin potatoes and a salad as well and I was thoroughly impressed. Opening a bottle of red wine he poured a glass using a small aerator. The wine made a slurping noise as it passed through.

"Does that really work?" I asked. Nick grinned,

"I don't really know but I like the noise it makes."

"Me to," I laughed as he poured a second glass.

The wine, the steaks, everything was just perfect and afterward we sat around, like two kids in a toy shop, pouring glass after glass of wine through the aerator just to hear the slurping sound.

"It actually does open up the flavor," I said as I swirled my wine around in my glass. Wish I could still get a buzz on it though." Nick looked thoughtful and rose suddenly, holding up a finger.

"Don't go anywhere, I'll be right back," he said as he disappeared around the corner. A moment later he returned carrying a crystal decanter with clear liquid in it.

"Hold out your glass." He ordered, a smile playing on his lips. I did and he poured in a small amount of the liquid.

"Swirl it in with the wine. It tastes better that way."

"What is it?"

"Madam," he said taking a low bow, "your wish is my command!" He poured some into his own glass, swirling it around, and then held up his glass.

"Cheers!" We clinked glasses and took a sip even though I still didn't know what it was. It was good. In fact it was really good and went down smoothly warming me all the way down. Nick smiled. The effects of the beverage were immediate as a feeling of euphoria swept through me. I took another sip.

"Don't drink too much too fast," Nick warned, "This should last us a couple of hours."

He was right. This stuff was strong and I was feeling really good. It was better than any alcohol buzz I'd ever had. All of my cares vanished along with my inhibitions. The world was a wonderful place.

We moved into the living room and Nick started a fire in the fireplace again as the effects of the elixir began to wear off. Nick was sitting on the floor, leaned back against the couch and I was between his legs, leaning against his chest. His arms were around my shoulders making me feel so safe.

He sat silently for a long while and I thought maybe be he had fallen asleep. Reaching up I put my hand on the back of his head, running my fingers through his hair. His hand closed over mine as he brought it to his mouth and started kissing my fingers.

"What is that stuff you gave me?" I asked.

193

"Wolf bane extract." He said sounding distracted. I swiveled so that I could see his expression. He was gazing down at me with darkened eyes, looking a bit lost. "Come to bed with me," he said imploringly, and I melted under his gaze.

We were up before the sun was the next morning and I busied myself loading snacks and drinks into one of the coolers on the boat. The other cooler had only ice in it. Once our gear was loaded we headed out into the bay.

At first it was misty over the water but as the sun rose higher in the sky the mist burned off into a beautiful sunny day. I was glad I had bought the new bikini and Nick seemed to appreciate it as well.

We stopped for a while and Nick showed me how to cast with his bait caster reel. I had used one before when I was younger and I quickly got the hang of it. Once he was comfortable with my casting ability we took off again.

About ten minutes into our ride Nick slowed the boat and pointed. I followed his finger out and saw what appeared to be a large flock of gulls. Throttling the motor he headed straight for the birds. As we approached them Nick circled around wide, putting the wind to our backs. He killed the big motor and jumped to the front of the boat, putting in the trolling motor.

"When we get close," he said, "start casting underneath the birds. Something is chasing bait up to the top so we should be able to catch whatever it is." I was skeptical of the rubber lure he had put on my hook but figured I'd try anyway.

Suddenly I saw a shrimp jump out of the water and skip several times before diving below the surface again. I cast just to the spot where it had been and started reeling back in.

Almost immediately something took my line and started running. I let out a squeal of excitement and gave a quick jerk to the line to set the hook as my pole bent against the weight of my catch. I was ecstatic! I had a fish.

I looked over at Nick and saw that he had one too. Both motors were now off. We were just drifting through

195

the midst of this great flock of birds. Nick quickly reeled his fish in and netted it, then came to net mine. I was so proud. It was long and freckled and beautiful. Nick told me it was a speckled trout and measured it. "It's a keeper," he said throwing it into the cooler with his. "Now get your pole back in the water, the birds are still working."

We fished like that for probably thirty minutes catching fifteen more trout, but a few were too small to keep. The flock was starting to break up now as the fish moved on. I was glowing with a silly grin plastered on my face. Nick laughed and kissed me. "You did good," he said, "I might just have to make you my first mate!"

We had limited out on trout at our first stop so we spent the rest of the morning just riding around. Nick pointed out some of his favorite fishing spots and we watched as one man pulled in a huge drum. At eleven o'clock we headed back to the dock.

Nick had a cleaning station in the boathouse and he showed me how to fillet the fish. I wondered if they were any good for sushi. My nose told me probably not. As we walked back to the house together I put my arm through Nick's.

"Thank you for taking me fishing," I said, "I had the best time."

"It was my pleasure, Kat," he said.

At four o'clock Nick and I were sitting out on the patio when a gold sedan pulled up into the drive. Nick looked quizzically at me and I shrugged my shoulders, not knowing who it was.

A small balding man wearing dress pants and a short sleeve white shirt emerged from the car carrying a brief case. He approached casually and I assumed he was a door to door sales man.

"Can I help you?" Nick asked.

"That you might be able to do," the man said. "I am looking for a Mrs. Katherine Ann Armand."

Oh shit, I'm being served again! "I'm Katherine Armand," I said. The man extended his hand to me and introduced himself.

"My name is Andrew Dole and I am here on behalf of Mrs. Angelica Marie Hudson." *Is he talking about Angie? Yes, he must be – Hudson was her last name.*

"I'm sorry, I don't understand." I said.

"Yes, excuse me for barging in on you un-announced." The man continued. "I am the executor of Mrs. Hudson's will. Mrs. Armand, you have been named as her sole beneficiary and I have some paperwork for you to sign. Would you happen to have a place where we can get out of the wind?" I was stunned, looking at Nick with bewilderment. Nick intervened.

"Right this way sir," he said rising from his seat and helping me to my feet. With Nick holding me up I managed to stumble into the house and sit at the dinner table. Mr. Dole opened his brief case and removed a large stack of papers. Taking a pair of glasses out of his shirt pocket, he put them on and began going over the paperwork with me. He explained as he went along.

"Mrs. Hudson has no surviving children and has named you as her sole heir. I have spent the last three weeks taking care of any debt her estate owed and am here now to present you with the balance. She has bequeathed it all to you, to do with as you see fit.

I was in shock and at a loss for words. Mr. Dole began going through the stack of papers. "If you will, just sign at the bottom of each of these documents as I go over them."

"Okay." I muttered. He flipped the first sheet over.

"This states that you are entitled to the residence at 11051 Fairport Dr. South, Clear Lake Texas. All taxes have been paid and there is no lien against this property." I nodded and took the paper as he passed it to me, signing my name at the bottom. This was Angie's house, a very large home in an upscale neighborhood. He turned the next page.

"This states that you are entitled to one 2011 Acura Integra..." My mind began wandering as he read the VIN number, lost in my own thoughts. I just could not believe this was actually happening. Angie had never said anything about a will before. I snapped back to the present as he pushed the paper toward me saying something about the Audi. *What? Another car?* I signed the paper.

One page after another he pushed across for me to sign. A boat, her furniture, her clothing, her bank accounts, her retirement account, her jewelry - *I never saw Angie wear jewelry!* The list went on. Mr. Dole turned the final page and peered at me over the tops of his glasses.

"Mrs. Hudson has some frozen assets as well."

"Frozen?" I asked.

"Yes, she and her husband, you see, they had sperm and ova saved. This document gives that to you as well.

What am I going to do with those? Can I leave them where they are? I signed the document and lay the pen down hoping there was nothing more to sign. This had been mentally exhausting.

"There is one last thing." Dole said as he handed me a large zip-lock bag with an assortment of keys inside. Also inside the bag was an envelope with "Kat" written across the front in Angie's handwriting.

"You may take possession of the house immediately. Once the paperwork is completed I will send you a copy of the deed. There is nothing more you need to do for that. The cars are both parked in the garage at the house. The boat is in a rented slot on the bay as is stated on the paper work. Do you have any questions for me?"

I shook my head numbly. I had questions but didn't know where to start. "Good then," he said, "I'll be on my way, and let you get back to your afternoon." He stood then, muttering about information on bank accounts and paperwork for transferring retirement funds. Nick got up to show him to the door. I was overwhelmed.

"Oh, Mr. Dole," I called after him. He turned to face me.

"Yes?"

"How did you know where to find me?" I asked. "One of your neighbors saw me at your house. They told me you were staying here."

"Oh." I had forgotten about telling Jim. He had said he would keep an eye on the place for me.

"Good day Mrs. Armand."

"Good day, Mr. Dole."

When Nick returned I was still sitting at the table staring at the stack of papers.

"Are you Okay?" Nick asked.

"Yes, I suppose so, that was all just a bit mind boggling." Nick pulled me to my feet and into his arms.

"You don't have to do anything about this right now. If you want I can look at it with you later or have Dorian go over things with you a little slower."

"Okay," I agreed. "I'm just not ready to deal with it all right now." Even the letter from Angie would have to wait. I couldn't read it – not right now.

That evening after dinner I tried to read a book in an effort to take my mind off of other things. Stretching out on the couch, I saw Nick walk out the back door. He had been pretty quiet all evening and I assumed he had a lot on his mind too. I had become too comfortable here and needed to get back to my house. Even though he didn't seem to mind me staying with him, I didn't want to overstay my welcome.

Unable to focus on the book, I decided to go talk to Nick. I didn't see him in the back yard so I walked down to the pier. He was sitting down at the end, his legs dangling above the water. Climbing down the metal steps, I walked out and sat down next to him.

"You've been quiet tonight," I started, "everything alright?" He reached over and took my hand.

"Yes," then hesitating, "I've wanted to talk to you about something, but I don't want to put any more pressure on you."

Oh no, here it is. He needs his space back. "Look," I started, "I know you're probably ready to get your life back to….."

"No Kat," he said gently cutting me off, "it's not that." His voice was low. "I was hoping that maybe you would consider staying here." He paused, looking at my face trying to gauge my reaction. I was surprised, this was unexpected. He continued. "I don't want to pressure you. I know you're still married and …" His voice trailed off.

"I just – I want to be with you Kat – and I want you to stay. Will you stay?" My heart must have skipped a beat and for the second time that day I was at a loss for words. Was he asking me to move in with him? As a roommate," I wondered? I just needed to be sure so I didn't embarrass myself. He was looking at me with trepidation, waiting for a reply.

"Do you mean stay in the guest room?" I asked. He let out his breath and ran his fingers through his hair.

"Well you can if you're more comfortable there, I just was hoping…" His eyes were wide now and I could hear the panic in his voice, smell the adrenaline from his fear.

I had never seen Nick this vulnerable – ever. He was always so in control. Now the sight of him like this melted my heart and I wanted him. I knew I wanted to be with him.

"Kiss me." I said. He looked at me; his eyes still wide, then he leaned over and kissed me, not understanding. "Again," I said, "kiss me again." This time he smiled, his body relaxing as he let out the breath he had been holding.

He kissed me deeply and my body responded to the touch of his lips, pulling deep down inside as our tongues tasted one another. I pulled away from his grasp just long enough to say, "Yes, I'll stay." Then his mouth found mine once again.

Sometime during the night a thundershower passed through, waking me with a roll of thunder. Nick was breathing gently into my hair, his arms cradling me against his chest, and one of his legs between mine.

I felt so safe here in his arms, protected from the rest of the world. His tender embrace, like the rain now falling gently on the roof that shut everything else out, surrounding me, gently cradling me. And with that thought I drifted off to sleep once again.

I woke the next morning as the first morning light filtered through the curtains. I was still draped with Nick and when I attempted to dislodge myself he pulled me back against him. Pushing his hips against mine I could feel his erection and laughed.

"What are you doing?" I asked amused.

"Just wondering if we should try this out and see if it works in the morning." he replied, a smile in his voice.

"Oh, I'm sure it will work, just not sure how long it will hold up." I said giggling. With that he rolled me onto my back pinning me to the bed.

"And why would ya be thinkin' that?" he asked me, attempting an Irish brogue. "Is there somethin' I be needin' to prove to ya now lassie? I was really laughing now and he was wearing an enormous grin. I was squirming, trying to free myself from his grip but he retained his grip on me with one hand as his other hand found its way up to the apex of my thighs. "Oh, what have we here now," he said continuing with the mock Irish. "I think I've found me pot o' gold."

"Oh Nick, let me up, I've got to pee," I protested. His eyes widened with mirth.

"Is that so lassie? Ev'n better," he said. Pushing aside my panties he slipped a finger inside me, stirring me with desire immediately as he began moving it around.

"Oh, Nick-" I gasped, "you don't play fair." His body was now reacting to my response and a low growl escaped his throat, his eyes hooded with dilated pupils. His mouth was on my breast as he continued to stimulate me with his fingers. I spread my legs to accept his body as he moved between them, my hips pushing against his hand, wanting, needing.

He removed his fingers and pulled off my panties then lowered himself inside me, slowly, gently, stretching and filling me. I moaned in pleasure as he took me. Rising up on his knees he lifted my hips up to meet his. I wrapped my legs around his waist, holding onto him and pulling tighter as he thrust hard and deep into me.

"Oh Nick," I moaned, "You feel so wonderful inside me baby." The intensity accentuated by my full bladder.

"You like that?" Nick asked through gritted teeth. "Do you know how much I want to give you what you like?" His hands and elbows were now by my head, supporting the weight of his body.

My feet were on the bed pushing my pelvis up harder and faster to match his rhythm, the intensity building, my muscles squeezing tighter and tighter against him. In sweet release I exploded around him, crying out as I came, causing him to release deep inside me. He continued to push in and out as he moaned loudly.

When at last he stopped he rose up onto his knees again, then swinging one of my legs across in front of him, collapsed behind me so that we were spooning, never breaking our precious contact. Nick leaned up behind me and brushed a kiss against my ear.

"And top o' the morning' to ya," he said with a wicked grin. I was laughing again.

Later that morning Dorian called to let me know we had a court date set for mid-December. Since there were no children involved we were not required to have mediation. He had also managed to get it into Reichert's court.

When I asked about settling before court he informed me that he would be negotiating right up to the court date and I could settle if I wanted to. However, Dan now wanted part of my retirement. He was not likely to agree on anything less than fifty percent and was willing to go to court believing his money was unknown to us. It would be in my favor to go in front of the judge.

This was Dorian's area of expertise so I listened to his advice and tried not to worry about it. The court date was three months away. There was no reason to dwell on it for now. Hanging up the phone I mentally checked another item off my to-do list.

The paperwork from Mr. Dole sat on Nick's desk in his study. I wasn't ready to read over all of it now, but I did want to read the letter. At least I thought I did. Going into the study I retrieved the envelope from the zip-lock bag then carried it outside. I wanted to be alone when I read it, not sure of how it would affect me.

I decided to go down to the pier. It was a calm day and I could sit against the boat house. I opened the envelope and took out the contents. It was several pages thick and I knew it was because of Angie's large, loopy handwriting.

Unfolding the pages and flattening them against my lap I started reading. I noted the date. She had written this just before she died.

August 13, 2012

Dear Kat, If you are reading this letter it is because you gave me what I truly wanted and allowed me to die a natural death.

I cannot begin to tell you how difficult my life has been since David passed, and again when Justin left me at such a young age. Mom and Dad were older and I accepted their passing much easier but it still left me so alone.

But this letter is not to complain about my misfortune in this life. This letter is to thank you for being there when I needed you.

Thank you for being my friend when I was new to the hospital and afraid I wouldn't fit in. Thank you for being a shoulder to cry on when David was killed and for stepping in and taking his spot in the birthing class.

Thank you for holding my hand and telling me I could make it through the long hours of labor with Justin. Thank you for being there to hand him to me and tell me how beautiful he was. Thank you for going with me when I had to put him in the facility, and for helping me choose the casket and clothing he was buried in.

You were at every funeral, at my side, being strong for me when I could not be. You have been my closest and dearest friend and I cannot tell you enough how much it has meant to me. Please don't mourn for me or second guess yourself- you did the right thing.

This bite in my throat is not killing me, my heart is. I no longer have the desire to go on. Please don't feel bad that I want to leave you. It's not you I want to leave behind but my empty house.

Everything that I have is yours. I have had it set up that way for a while now. I don't mean to put extra burden on you. Please use this however you see fit.

Your friend always in life and in death,

Angie

I folded the letter back and the tears came unbidden, hot, burning my eyes, streaming down my cheeks into my lap. I sobbed, my body heaving as the grief poured out from some unseen well buried deep within my bosom. Again and again, shaking violently as waves of grief racked my shoulders pulling me down, down, down.

Then I felt his arms around me as he pulled me between his legs, his chest against my back, as he wrapped himself around me like a protective cocoon. My Nick; my sweet, precious Nick was enveloping me once again in the protection of his arms.

ELEVEN

I stood staring with my mouth gaped open at the document in my hands. I couldn't believe it. Angie had a DNP from Johns Hopkins? I had no idea she had gone to school there and certainly no idea that she held an advanced degree. Why had she wanted to be a floor nurse when she could have done pretty much anything she had wanted?

I was standing in the study of her elegant home going through a file cabinet. Apparently there was much about Angie that she had kept private. Just two days ago I had stood in the kitchen at Nick's with a similar stupefied look on my face when Dole had handed me the paperwork for Angie's (mine now) bank accounts. Yes – plural – accounts. Four checking and four savings accounts to be exact, with a sum total of one hundred and forty million dollars in them.

But that wasn't all. She had investments in all kinds of stuff making more money than I could dream up and a retirement fund to boot. I couldn't figure out why she even needed the retirement fund but maybe it just kept her from paying more in taxes.

Honestly, I was shocked but hurt as well. Angie had been my best friend and I knew so little about her. That she really didn't have to work I did know, but this – this was off the charts. *She really didn't have to work.*

I thought briefly about one of my last conversations with her. *Money isn't everything Kat – what would you change that you can actually change with money?* I was just now starting to get a glimpse into her soul. I was blown away. Why did she work? I wouldn't have. Then again, I haven't made any plans to quit yet either.

Putting the document back into its folder I pulled out another folder. Maybe she had gotten this when her parents died, I speculated, and didn't want to quit then. I just couldn't wrap my head around it.

Angie had always dressed nice, but not extravagantly. She had a nice car, but nothing over the top. Even her house, though nice, is very modest for the money she had. I would have never figured her to be a multi-millionaire.

Now it is my money and I'm not quite sure what to do with it all. I damn sure don't want Dan to find out about this while we're still married. My head is swimming. One of the file drawers is nothing but receipts from charity organizations. I should continue to give to the ones Angie felt strongly about.

As I look around the study I see a picture of Angie and David. They were so happy together. Again I feel a surge of regret at not giving her my blood and making her better. She had so much – life, so much everything and she could have found someone else that she would have been happy with. Wouldn't she?

I remember the words from her letter. *It's only the empty house I want to leave.* Yes, I remember plenty of times that she complained about the house being too big after Justin had died. I wondered why she didn't sell it and buy a smaller one.

I lost interest in the filing cabinet and started looking around the house. I had been here many times before but had never really looked around. There were many pictures of Angie with David and photos of her and Justin. It was so sad that they were never able to take one with the three of them together.

I walked up the stairs past Angie's room to the room that had been Justin's. I had never been in his room before. Opening the door I stepped inside. Everything was in its place. The bed sat in the corner next to a window, a toy box sat against a wall filled with toys, a chest of drawers still filled with clothing was on yet another wall and the closet still filled as well.

Then down low on the wall, close to the window I saw where a child had scribbled with crayon all along the baseboards. Angie had never had it repainted. I finally got it. This house held everything she had of Justin and David. That was why she couldn't sell it, why she couldn't leave. Even the bed showed evidence of that Angie had spent time on it, maybe crying, maybe just remembering.

I had come to the house to try and figure out what to do with it and was no closer to an answer now than I was before. The two cars sat in the garage and I decided to try and crank them. Amazingly they both fired after just a minute. Satisfied I shut them off and returned inside.

There was just too much to do here and it was going to take me a while.

I had to decide what to keep and what to get rid of. After that I would decide what to do with the actual house. Maybe I'd ask Nick for advice or Dorian. For now the task just seemed overwhelming. I was getting agitated to and would need to feed again soon. I'd stop by the meat packing house on my way home and pick up some of the blood they'd saved for me.

I lie sprawled across the bed fully sated from the beef blood I'd gotten earlier. Nick leaned up on his elbow and began sliding his fingertips gently up and down my legs in small circular motions. He was in an introspective mood and I watched as he continued the movement back and forth. It was very arousing, the feeling of his fingernail against my flesh, tickling and teasing, yet his expression remained pensive.

Reaching over I ran my fingers through his hair. He closed his eyes breathing long and deep. "Penny for your thoughts?" I asked wondering if something was wrong.

When he opened his eyes again they were filled with primal lust, his mouth set hard in a thin line, setting my groin on fire instantly. He moved quickly pulling my nightshirt off as I lay there; pushing his hands up my thighs to my belly then grasping my breasts, cupping and kneading them.

My breath became ragged and my heart began racing, fueled by his arousal. I was wet, my sex begging to be taken. His tongue was on my breast then he moved trailing his mouth down my stomach.

I lurched off the bed under his touch, burning with desire. I reached for his pants and found them undone. His eyes were on me like coals of fire as he sat up to remove his jeans, freeing his erection.

"I want you, now. I want you like I've never wanted anyone before." His voice husky, breath bated. I reached for him and found his cock, squeezing tightly. He moaned and a shudder ran through his body.

I had never seen him quite like this, so intense, so wanting, so carnal. He knelt before me lifting me up into his powerful arms. He pulled me tight into his chest and again whispered in my ear, kissing my face, fisting his hands in my hair.

"Katherine," he spoke again I want you, do you understand? I want you." My hands were on his neck and in his hair and I was pulling him to me.

"I want you too Nick," I said panting, begging. Grabbing me under my backside he lifted me up, fingers digging into my flesh as I wrapped my legs around his waist. He pulled back and looked into my eyes again, anguish on his face, in his voice as he slammed into me, filling me violently again and again.

"I want you Katherine. I want you to choose me…. Fuck, I need you to choose me!" I was lost in him. Hanging on for my life as he fucked me hard and fast, driven by what? Fear maybe. I cried out loudly in my orgasm,

"I choose you Nick. I want you too. I need you too." His orgasm shook him violently as he called out to me.

"Oh, Katherine, fuck – I need you….. Fuck, I don't want to lose you." Collapsing, he fell onto the bed, still holding me in his arms. He was spent, as was I, but I felt unsettled. I didn't understand his anguish or his fear. I wanted to assure him, to hold him a while longer. I ran my fingers through his hair and pulled his face to mine, kissing him tenderly.

I loved this man. The realization came as a shock, but I was in love with him. I wanted to tell him but I was suddenly afraid. I choked on my tears that were now burning in my eyes. I pulled him close again.

"I choose you Nick," I said kissing his forehead. His eyes were wide again with an unreadable expression as he pulled me tightly against his chest, and wrapping me in the security of his powerful arms we fell asleep.

TWELVE

I was still entangled in Nick's arms and legs when I woke the next morning. Turning on my back I felt a sudden gush of liquid. Scrambling out of the bed I ran to the bathroom.

"Shit, shit, shit." I cursed along the way. Nick had startled awake when I jumped out of bed and was now standing in the doorway.

"Are you alright?" he asked concerned. I let out a breath, shaking my head.

"I'm ok, I just started," I said. Nick was lost.

"Started what?"

"My period," I replied. Nick's mouth dropped open with a look of shock.

"You're still menstruating?" he asked.

"Yes, of course. I'm only thirty-six." I said indignantly. Nick shook his head.

"Kat, that's not what I meant. Vampire women don't menstruate. I've never met one that did." Now it was my turn to look stupefied.

"You mean to tell me that every other vampire woman gets to go without this pain in the ass, and I get stuck with it. That's just my luck!" Nick looked amused for a moment but didn't laugh.

"Are you sure you're really menstruating?" he asked me.

"Of course I'm sure." I said rolling my eyes.

"Then you need to see a doctor."

It's just my period. It's completely normal."

"No it isn't, not for you, not anymore. I want you to go see a doctor about this." I was getting irritated now, this was a little unreasonable.

"What am I going to say? Doctor I'm having a period. She'll laugh me out of the office."

"Not if you go to a vampire. They will know what to check for and if nothing is wrong fine. But I would feel better if you get checked out."

"I don't know any doctors that are vampires." I tried one last argument.

"I do." Nick said his voice soft and coaxing. "Please go. I'll go with you if you want." I rolled my eyes again. I didn't need him to go with me but I didn't want to argue. Maybe Nick was right. So many other things had changed. Why not this?

"Alright," I conceded, but you don't have to come with me."

Nick made a quick phone call to his doctor friend and she cleared a spot for me on her schedule to come in immediately. He quickly wrote out some directions to her office and handed them to me. I was feeling a little nervous now. Maybe I would like Nick to go with me.

It was a nice office in a suburban part of town with a comfortable waiting area. A sign above the reception window read "Dr. Julian Lee – OB/GYN – Specializing in fertility. The waiting room was spacious and only three other people were seated when I arrived with Nick in tow. They were all human and I wondered how many vampires this doctor saw. How many even existed for that matter.

I had only been seated for a moment when my name was called. Nick threatened to stay in the waiting area but I insisted he come with me. "You wanted this – you can come watch."

Doctor Lee was an attractive woman with Black hair and blue eyes. She was kind but seemed more excited than concerned. She had me come back as soon as I got to her office.

"Let's see what we have here." She said as I sat up on the table. Putting my feet into the stirrups I scooted my behind all the way down to the edge. She would do a vaginal exam then a trans-vaginal ultra sound.

Nick sat quietly next to the exam table. "Everything from here looks normal," she said as she finished the exam. "Let's look with the ultra sound." She inserted the probe into my vagina and started moving it around.

I could see the screen a little but it was her face I wanted to see the most. I couldn't read an ultra sound, but I was pretty good at reading faces. A smile came to her lips as she moved the probe taking pictures as she went. When she finished she put the probe up and turned to face Nick and I.

"I must say that this is a first for me. I've never seen a vampire woman that actually menstruated. Not in five hundred years of doing pelvic exams."

"Do you see a lot of vampires?"

"Honestly no, not many vampires are in need of healthcare. The ones I do see are generally new ones like you. Most of those are here to find out why their periods have stopped."

"So there's nothing wrong with me?" I asked.

"No," she replied. It's a perfectly healthy, viable uterus that has a lining sufficient to sustain life. Your ovaries also are intact and appear to have follicles on them.

This is extraordinary. When women turn to vampire they always lose both. They tend to "dry up" for lack of a better word and cannot support life. Ovaries stop producing follicles. It's as if those parts of the body age, but yours are like that of thirty-six year old human's."

"That means I could still get pregnant. Could I have a vampire child?"

"You could sustain life provided you have a viable fetus, human or vampire it should grow. I'm not sure where you will find a viable sperm from a vampire though. This was news.

"You mean male vampires still produce sperm?"

"Yes, their sexual organs remain intact and they still produce high amounts of testosterone, but due to the higher core temperatures the sperm are greatly weakened, many of them dead."

I was thoughtful for a moment. As a nurse I had heard every story in the book. Even men with vasectomies had been known to "miraculously" father children. Dead sperm or not, anything could happen so I needed to take precautions. For some reason the thought of having a child with Nick didn't scare me like it had with Dan. I smiled at the thought. I wonder if Nick would feel the same way.

Doctor Lee brought me out of my reverie.

"Would you mind if I put my findings in an article that goes out to the vampire community?" It seemed harmless enough but I didn't want to wind up being a guinea pig somewhere.

"As long as you don't use my name."

When we left the office Nick put his arm around me.

"Are you happy now?" I asked. He smiled and kissed me on the nose.

"Yes," he said. "Happy and turned on."

I raised an eyebrow, "Really?"

"I was just thinking how much fun it could be if I was the one holding that probe."

I smiled at him shaking my head. That sounded HOT!

The next two weeks went by in a blur. I had so much on my plate to deal with. I still had not gotten back to Angie's house. Every time I thought about it my brain cluttered. I just didn't know where to begin.

She had no relatives that would want any of her personal effects and selling it or throwing it away was out of the question. I didn't have room for most of it so just leaving it where it was seemed to be the best idea. I had decided to keep her Acura and sell my car and the Audi. The Acura was much newer and I could now afford the maintenance on it.

Work was much the same and I was getting along with Teresa well, which was good since we worked a lot of shifts together. I hadn't seen Dean in a while and wondered where he was but was too busy to stop and call most of the time.

Nick was busy on a job doing what he did best which lately had kept him out till the early morning hours. Dragging in he would shower then snuggle against me in bed waking me with his arousal. I didn't mind – in fact I loved knowing that he came home to me every night. I would never tire of that. This job was pushing him mentally and he needed a release. I was more than happy to provide that release for him, and I reaped the benefits as well.

Callie called and we talked for a while. I updated her on the divorce, and then told her about Nick. She sounded excited for me and couldn't wait to meet my tall, dark and handsome. She was planning to come into town for the Thanksgiving holidays which were coming up in a month. "Bye mom, I love you," she said as she hung up.

That was a first. I was glad to see that she was coming around and didn't still hate me. I wondered would I ever be able to tell her about the other changes in my life. The sudden fear that I might outlive my daughter gnawed in the pit of my stomach. I couldn't deal with that now. I had years before I would have to worry about that.

THIRTEEN

On Tuesday I received an unexpected call from Dean. He was off work and wanted to meet me for lunch. We decided to meet at Topper's where we could sit outside by the water. I gave him a hug when he approached and he shivered.

"Your hands are so cold. It's like wrapping an ice pack around my shoulders."

It was odd. My extremities were always icy, but I felt like a furnace on the inside. I hadn't realized how I felt to other people though.

"Cold hands-incredibly warm heart." I said jokingly. "I haven't seen you around the hospital in forever," I said as we pulled out a chair from an umbrella covered table.

"I'm fully staffed now and haven't been out on the floor in a while. Plus I'm working on my school and my other little side projects with every spare minute so I don't hang around and chat." He looked tired and I wondered if he was getting any sleep.

"You didn't bring Nick with you today?"

"Not today, he had some work to finish up." The waitress wearing a very mini skirt approached and sat a basket of bread and butter on the table, taking our drink orders and giving us each a menu. She left and returned promptly with our drinks.

"I wanted to tell you about something I found in Angie's blood," he said when mini skirt left again. "I thought you might want to know. I 've just been so busy with other things… and I wanted to give you some time too." I looked at him expectantly. He continued,

"I ran an ANA – antinuclear antibody test – on her blood. Her numbers were off the chart. I'm thinking she had a severe autoimmune response to something. I was looking for a foreign body that was causing the problem but maybe it was her immune system that did the damage.

I think it became so severe that it attacked her blood cells, effectively killing her." I remembered what

Nick had said about the bite. That and the fact Angie had lost her will to live. It all made sense.

"You may be right," Mini skirt came back for our orders.

"I've done some other research," Dean said when she'd gone. Grabbing my hand he looked me in the eye. "I know you're a vampire."

I eyed him warily. Dean was a friend and I had wanted him to know, but at the same time I was afraid of what he'd think. He gave my hand a squeeze, studying my expression. I made no move to affirm his suspicions but I didn't deny it either.

Dean considered Kat as she sat across from him. She had always been special to him. In fact he had secretly been in love with her for years. They had been so close before when she spent time in the lab, but for some reason he felt inadequate. After all, she was gorgeous and smart and he was, well – a lab nerd. What could she ever see in him?

He would do anything for her though and had kept quiet about his love for her when Dan came into the picture. He had known Dan was having an affair but refused to tell Kat, not wanting to destroy her. Now it was still the same. He would quietly love her in the background, watching her love some other man. *At least Nick is a good guy and will treat her right.*

Dean smiled tightly, "Relax Kat, you know I'm ok with it. I'll do anything I can to help you too." I let out my breath not realizing I'd been holding it, smiling to convey my thanks. That was more than enough for Dean.

"Can you tell me about it?" he asked excitement in his voice. "What was it like when you changed? You said before some of it was painful." His eyes showed genuine concern as he said it, like the thought of it hurt him on some deeper level. Looking around to make sure no one was listening I launched into my story.

I told him all the details I could remember including my conversations with Angie and Stephan at the hospital. I told him about the first changes I noticed and about the pain – days of writhing in pain – unconscious of what was happening around me. I told him of how Nick and Stephan had cared for me the whole time and the training they'd given me afterward.

"Stephan sounds like someone I'd like to meet," he said thoughtfully, and apologizing for the interruption asked me to continue.

I told him about my first experience with blood and how I could see what people had done when I drank it. His eyes widened with that information.

"Can you shape shift?" he asked me suddenly.

"I don't know," I replied hesitantly. "Nick and Stephan never mentioned anything about that."

"Oh," he said looking a little disappointed. "Just something I read on the internet. You know the internet is full of information and a lot of it is good info, no matter what people say."

The thought had not occurred to me and I decided maybe I could read up a bit and try to learn more about myself.

Another thought occurred to me. Dean should meet Stephan. They were the two smartest men I'd ever met and somehow I thought they would be good for each other. Together maybe they could answer some of the questions they both had.

Dean changed the subject to lighten the mood and started telling me about his school, what he was learning to work with in the lab and some of his private projects he was working on at home.

I was amazed by him. He was so intelligent. He had completed one degree and was now working on another, his main focus on DNA mapping but he was taking classes on anything microscopic. He became so animated with excitement when he started telling me about it.

He had lost me after just a few minutes but I was so happy for him I couldn't help but smile and listen. I wondered as I watched him if he would ever marry. I didn't know how he would have time in his life for anyone with all of his projects. *Too bad, he is a very attractive man. Smart and caring too. Can't ask for better than that. Maybe someday, some lucky girl will wind up with him.* I hoped she deserved him.

I left him at the restaurant after a quick kiss on the cheek and a tight hug.

"Remember," he said as I climbed into my car, "I'll do anything I can to help you, Nick too."

"I'll remember that." I told him before I drove off, "And I'll put you in touch with Stephan ASAP."

Dean stood staring after me in my rearview mirror. I knew he meant what he said and I was glad he was on my side.

Saturday morning I busied myself with the laundry and had just dumped a basket of towels onto the couch to be folded. The news was playing on the TV while I popped the towels, folding them to be put away.

A story came on about a jewelry store robbery in Houston. That sort of crime was so common I wondered why they bothered airing the story. They flashed a segment of an interview with the store owner showing his face for just a minute.

I couldn't believe my eyes. Grabbing the remote I turned the volume up to hear what was being said. The news moved on to another story so I re-wound and watched it again. The man's face flashed in front of me again.

It was Nick – or was it? It looked like him, almost exactly like him, but the voice was a little off, doppelganger maybe?

I didn't catch the name because of the questions running around in my head. I re-wound again, this time listening intently as they said the man's name. "The owner of the store, Elijah Keet, was …" the news announcer was still talking when I rewound again. Coming back to where they displayed the man's picture I hit pause and went to find Nick.

He was in his study and looked up surprised when I busted in the door. Seeing the alarm on my face he jumped to his feet.

"Are you alright?" he asked. I grabbed his hand and pulled him with me to the living room.

"You have to see this," I said pointing to the television. His face went even paler than it normally was when he registered what I was trying to show him.

Nervously he took the remote from my hand and pushed play. He repeated my actions – rewinding and re-playing the clip again and again. Then as if someone has socked him in the gut, he fell back into the couch. His fingers running through his hair, his face in anguish he folded over onto his knees, his shoulders shaking. It was then I realized he was crying.

It tore my heart out to see him like this. My powerful, sweet, wonderful man was hurting and I knelt in front of him, holding him, willing his pain away. Finally, he sat up, his eyes red rimmed and glossy.

"Do you want to talk to me about it?" I asked hoping he would share. Somehow I knew this was the source of the anguish I'd seen in his face before. Memories of our recent lovemaking came to mind. He took my hand and took a deep breath.

"Before I became a vampire I was betrothed to a woman named Adrianna – Adrianna Wheeler," he repeated he name with reverence. "I was so in love with her and her with me."

I fought against a twinge of jealousy at the thought of Nick with another woman, even if it was two hundred years ago. He continued,

"I worked so hard for years to put money away for our marriage. Then right before we were to be wed I was turned. We still wanted to be together but somehow her family found out. They refused to allow the marriage, tearing us apart, threatening to kill us both if we went against their wishes.

They left our group moving Adrianna away and forced her to marry another man immediately. Later I learned that she was with child. I always wondered if it might be mine but I never found out – until today. The man she was married to was named Keet."

I tried to digest what he'd just said. This couldn't be his son but a great, great grandson? The resemblance was too striking to not be his family. I was glad he had found out but afraid at the same time of what this meant for us.

"I'm sorry for your loss Nick," I said with apprehension in my voice. "Do…"my voice faltered. "Are you still in love with her, with Adrianna?" I forced myself to say the name, afraid of the answer I was about to get. I remembered too well the look of anguish I'd seen in his eyes.

His eyes widened then and he reached for me pulling me close. "Don't ever think that," he said kissing me softly. "That was many years ago and I am with you now. I don't want to lose you. I couldn't bear to lose you."

His words brought little comfort. He had loved her but was still did not say he loved me. I wanted so badly for him to love me the way I loved him. I wanted to tell him how I loved him but now I was afraid of being rejected. I wouldn't be able to handle that again. Not now. I would just have to be glad he wanted me around. I would take anything I could get from him.

I attempted a weak smile. "With your abilities to sniff things out you should be able to trace his family tree. Maybe find your son after all." He kissed me again and I returned it, giving everything I had to give wrapped up inside it. He had my heart for life, even if I didn't have his. I knew I could never be without him.

Nick now had a new project to work on – digging into the family history of Elijah Keet. He spent much of his free time online and searching through public records. I busied myself by calling Stephan and arranging for him and Dean to meet. This was the first time I'd spoken with him since I left his home and it was good talking to him. I thought of him as the dad I never had.

My real dad had moved away when I was a young child and I rarely saw him. As a result I had never been close to him, in fact I barely knew him. Stephan filled a need in my life that I never knew I had. Giving me words of wisdom and encouragement. He helped me to believe in myself. I felt incredibly fortunate to have met the man.

Stephan had been more than happy to meet with Dean and suggested we all get together for dinner one evening the following week. It was decided we would meet at Aruba's, a nice restaurant and bar located halfway between our house and Stephan's place. There was a Hotel nearby in case we chose not to drive home if it got too late.

I called Dean to give him the date and time then went to talk to Nick about it. I found him in his study pouring over some old ledgers containing names and dates. He had been hard at it all day and many of the documents were difficult to read. Fatigue lined his face and he was running his fingers through his hair.

"Nick I…." He cut me off immediately.

"Not now I'm trying to read something."

I was wounded. I knew he was tired but still I didn't deserve that. I considered saying something back but decided against it. Turning I left the room to go nurse my hurt feelings out on the pier.

It wasn't just that he'd been sharp with me. I could handle that. It was my knowledge of who he was searching for, and his recent revelation to me about his former love. I felt sick inside, my mind conjuring up my worst fears. *What if he still loves her? What if he never loves me? What if he no longer needs or wants me because he's found a connection back to her?*

I was so lost in thought that I nearly jumped out of my skin when I felt a hand on my shoulder. My heart in my throat, I turned to see Nick standing behind me. *What is it with these vampires always sneaking up on me?* I pulled my shoulder away from his grip. I was irritated that he'd startled me and still wounded from his outburst.

"Hey," he said softly, "I'm sorry. I shouldn't have snapped at you in there."

I wanted to cry as all of my insecurities bubbled up inside me spilling over. He reached for me again and this time I allowed him to pull me close. He kissed the top of my head then tilted my chin up kissing me on the lips. Gently caressing my cheek he tucked a stray hair behind my ear.

"I've been working too hard on this project when I have something more important to take care of. Let's get showered and go out for the evening. We both need to relax and enjoy ourselves for a change. Maybe I'll bring some wolf bane."

"Alright," I agreed. My mood brightened as we walked back to the house holding hands.

"Where are we going?" I asked stepping into the shower with him.

"I thought I'd take you out to Tommy's for dinner then we could go dancing afterward if you want."

I smiled, "That would be nice." The last time I'd gone dancing was with Angie.

I applied some body wash to a rag and began washing Nick's back and shoulders. His body was exquisite and I loved sliding my hands along his beautifully defined muscles. Veins ran like ropes up his arm and I traced them with my fingers.

Touching his body was so arousing. He turned in the shower allowing me to linger over his chest and svelte abdominals. He grinned and started soaping me up with his hands going first to my breast. Slick with body wash his hands glided across them. With a mischievous grin he moved his thumbs in circles over my nipples. I grinned back at him.

"Are my boobs the only things you're going to wash tonight?"

"No," he replied as he slipped his hand down to my sex and started palming it.

"I want my pussy to be clean too."

"Oh so it's your pussy now?" I asked, arching a brow at him.

"You're damn right it's mine," he said cupping it, and then gently slid a finger inside.

"Oh," I moaned my arousal mounting. I pulled his head down, kissing and licking down his neck as he continued to massage me, now using two fingers. I wanted him. I wanted him inside me. I wanted to give him every part of me. This man I loved so much; needed so much; wanted so much.

As I moved my tongue down his neck I sensed a small vein pulsing beneath my mouth near his shoulder and in that moment I wanted to feed on him. I wanted to take him into my body completely. I wanted this so badly I could almost taste his blood as it coursed through the tiny vein. My mouth sucking hard on it, my teeth ready to bite down.

"Ahhh," I cried out as I pushed away from him. *What am I doing? I can't feed on Nick.* Nick stopped when I pushed away from him, a hurt look on his face. "I'm sorry I…. "How could I tell him I wanted to feed on him? Was I still that out of control?

246

The atmosphere in the shower had suddenly become icy. Nick stalked out of the shower. "We'll never make it to dinner if we keep this up." I couldn't tell if he meant the petting or our emotional standoff.

Wrapping a towel around myself I went after him. "Please don't be angry with me. I'm so sorry. I….." Dropping my head I still didn't know what to say. Fortunately Nick softened a bit. He pulled me close again and kissed my forehead, "Find something pretty to wear and let's go have fun."

FOURTEEN

I chose a sleeveless, cream colored dress with deep pink flowers and matching peep toe stiletto pumps. The dress was made of a stretchy jersey fabric that draped perfectly showing off my figure and ended about four inches above my knees.

Twisting my hair up, I arranged it in a clamp allowing curling tendrils to hang on my neck and around my face. Makeup and jewelry on I went out to find Nick. He was waiting on the couch and looked up to see me when I walked out of the room.

His eyes lit up with a smile as he stood to his feet. "You look amazing!" he said planting a kiss firmly on my lips, "Absolutely beautiful."

"Thank you," I blushed, "You look terrific yourself, but then you always do. You smell good too." He was wearing a pair of jeans and a white button down shirt with an embroidered design down the left side. The shirt he left un-tucked with the top three buttons left open. I smiled as I took in the site. He was the embodiment of the

249

stuff dreams are made of. Taking my hand he led me out the door.

The food and wine at Tommy's were excellent and we lingered just a little while after dinner to finish a second glass of wine. From there we decided to go to Davenports, an upscale waterfront club.

We found a small table, thankful we arrived early enough and Nick went to get us some drinks. Moments later he arrived with a chocolate martini for me and a dirty martini for himself. Placing them on the table he removed a small vial from his shirt pocket and smiled. My eyes got big as he poured a drop into each drink. He had brought the wolf bane!

My chocolate martini was delicious and we were soon feeling the effects of the wolf bane. Nick led me out onto the dance floor and I learned he was quite a good dancer. A few more sips of my martini had me really moving, dirty dancing with Nick. The song ended and we returned to our table. I drank the last bit of my martini, enjoying the chocolate at the bottom of the glass.

I started feeling hot and a little strange and I thought it was the wolf bane. Little vibrations started in my skin, tingling and burning. I was getting uncomfortable and began fidgeting. I leaned over to Nick, "Do you feel that?" I shouted over the din. "Feel what?" Nick shouted back.

I was anxious and energy was moving through me pulling deep, deep from within. "Are you ok? Nick shouted again, "Do you need to leave?" I was hypersensitive, my skin crawling, nerve endings firing from an unseen source of stimulation. I didn't know what to do. "I think I……" I couldn't finish my sentence.

My body arched and I fell forward, grasping the opposite edge of the table, clinging to it as an orgasmic explosion rocked my body. I was instantly alive and aroused in a way I had never experienced before. Nick looked at me then his eyes caught sight of something behind me. His expression froze.

I was afraid, not knowing what was happening to me. I tried to see what Nick was looking at as another wave washed over me. I was panting in short, shallow breaths, my muscles tightening, clenching deliciously deep within pulling me to a climax. Sliding down from my stool I released the table and turned around, my back to Nick.

Momentarily I leaned against the table and grabbed the edge, my knuckles turning white as another wave racked my body. It was everything I could do to keep from screaming out from the pleasure caused by my own muscles clenching. As the intensity subsided I searched the crowd, looking for whatever it was Nick had seen.

I had a brief moment before the next wave started. It was like I was having contractions, only instead of intense pain it was intense pleasure, pleasure that had a source outside of my body, and it was calling to me, pulling me.

Releasing the table I straddled my barstool, leaning over the back like a feral beast as the next wave moved through me. Then I saw what I was searching for, my eyes making direct contact with his. It was Orlando and he was coming my way.

My body rocked with arousal as the vampire drew closer. I was burning, hot with desire and lust so carnal and primal it scared me. I was being pulled to him like a meteorite caught in the pull of gravity. There was no escaping.

The vampire was incredible handsome and he walked with the swagger of a man who was completely at ease in his body. His pants hung sexily at his hips and his deep purple shirt was open down almost to his navel, leaving nothing to be imagined.

The glint of a golden chain drew my eye to his perfectly chiseled chest. Unashamed I allowed my eyes to wander further taking in the whole man. His ripped abdomen and the bulge of his cock as it strained against his zipper. He was all male and nothing like what I remembered of him on the gurney.

He was tall with dark skin and darker hair and eyes. He flashed a smile showing brilliant white, even teeth. He was sexy and I was literally drooling as I looked at him. My brain was screaming no, but my body was in charge. I was squirming in my chair, my panties saturated from the wetness of my arousal.

I stood, sliding from the barstool again. Inside my brain a war was waging, part of me reaching for Nick; the other part was begging for Orlando to come fuck me where I stood. My blood was boiling and he was still twenty feet away.

My nipples were now hard, pushing against the fabric of my dress, visible to any who looked. I dropped my hand to my sex wanting to quell the throbbing. I was about to explode. Then he was there, taking my hand to his mouth and kissing my knuckles.

"Beautiful Katherine, I am here for you. Are you ready to be mine?"

I barely noticed the beautiful young woman that was with him, looking at me with a disdainful pout to her lips. She was wrapped in his other arm, hanging on his side but I didn't care, all I saw was Orlando.

I closed my eyes against him, trying to gain ground in my mental war. My brain was foggy, succumbing to the intoxication of my arousal. Reaching back with one hand I tried to find Nick's. I needed something to ground me, stabilize me.

Orlando threw back his beautiful head and laughed. "The vampire wants you but he has failed to make you his own." Somehow I pushed through the fog, fighting back against the will of my body. I fought with every ounce of sense I had available.

This was not what I wanted. I wanted Nick. Where was he? I turned back to where he had been sitting only to see an empty chair. "Come beautiful Katherine," Orlando was saying again, "Let me love you. I know how to love you." I groaned as another orgasmic wave pushed me closer to climax.

I was terrified of what was happening to me. I had no control, or did I? I wanted Nick, needed him and he'd left me. I was confused. I wanted to be away from Orlando, needed desperately to escape his pull. If I didn't get away soon in my intoxicated state I knew I'd wind up in his bed. I couldn't chance that. I had to leave. I did the only thing I knew how. I ran.

In desperation I bolted out the door of the club and down the steps, leaving my shoes behind. Somewhere in the distance I heard Orlando laugh again about me running away. I needed more distance between us. I needed to be able to run faster than my two legs could carry me.

Suddenly I was no longer on two legs but four running full out. Someone yelled "look at that wolf." But I didn't stop. I didn't know where I was going, just that I had to get far away from Orlando.

After what seemed like hours I slowed down. I was panting from heat and thirst. I wandered the streets and alleyways for hours not knowing where to go. Nick had left me with Orlando. He didn't want me, the realization tumbling down on me, suffocating me. My heart was breaking.

I didn't know where I could go. I couldn't go back to Nick's house. It was too far to Stephan's and I might freak Dean out if I showed up as a wolf. Finally exhausted I turned in the direction of my old house. At least I still had a bed there if I could get in.

I made it to my house around one-thirty a.m. and went around to the back. Pawing at the door mat to uncover the hidden key I realized I needed my hands. Just like that I was back in human form, buck naked on my back porch. Quickly I opened the door and went inside.

Once inside emotion flooded over me like the sea. My heart ached. Nick had abandoned me. He had promised he'd be there when I had to face Orlando and he'd left me alone. I was shaking from the adrenaline or maybe the coldness that had settled into my bones.

Mechanically I looked through my chest of drawers in the hope that something had been left behind. It was empty. Continuing my search I moved into the closet.

In the far corner on a shelf was a discarded tee shirt. Picking it up I shook it out, Dan's smell instantly filling my nostrils.

The thought of wearing his shirt now was almost unbearable but I needed something. I looked around the closet once again and finding nothing more pulled the shirt over my head, welcoming the soft warmth it provided.

Numbly I climbed into my bed, pulling the comforter up around my head. I was dying inside. The events of the evening burned in my memory, replaying again and again. *Let me love you Katherine, I know how to love you.* I shut my eyes tight – *Nick knows how to love me better than anyone.*

Dread gripped my stomach twisting it into knots as the cold emptiness spread further through my body consuming me. How could I let myself get so close to this man after what I'd gone through with Dan?

No longer able to withstand the force my mental dam collapsed and tears poured from my eyes, springing from a source deep in my chest. My body shuddered under the weight of my despair as I sobbed freely into my pillow, my breath coming in tiny gasps. I closed my eyes against the pain, but the tears still came, pushing past my eyelids.

I don't know how long I cried – minutes, an hour? Mentally and physically exhausted my body eventually ceased shaking and I began to drift. I imagined Nick being with me, how he would smell. I took a deep breath and I could smell him – faintly.

"Katherine," Nick's voice boomed into the house. I sat up in bed. *Was I dreaming?* Again he called out, "Katherine." *No it's him. He's really here!*

"Nick," I cried. Then he was there, scooping me up into his arms and again my tears began to flow.

"Oh god, Katherine, I've been looking for you everywhere. I was so worried, so afraid. My god baby, I'm so sorry." Nick pulled me close, his mouth covering mine, his tongue parting my lips, licking, tasting. I responded eagerly tasting the salt of my tears mingled with the taste of Nick. There was nothing I wanted more than to be right here in his arms. I pulled away, searching his face.

"You left me with him………..I thought……."

"I'm so sorry baby, I was an ass." His face reflected the shame in his voice. "The scent of your arousal for him was so strong. I couldn't stand it, I wasn't thinking straight. I should have gotten you out of there. As soon as I left I realized what a mistake I'd made. I went back to get you and you were gone. They said you had run away."

He kissed me again deeply, rocking me in his arms. Gently he stroked my face, wiping the tears from my cheeks, a pained look in his eyes. "Please come home with me, I want to take you home." I nodded in agreement. He kissed my hair then grabbed the hem of my tee shirt to pull it over my head. "Let's get you out of that shirt." He said scowling at the tee.

"I have nothing else to wear. I seem to have lost my clothes."

"Why? Did something happen to you?" he asked, concern showing on his face.

"I…… turned into a wolf……..I guess I lost them when I was running. I was naked when I got here." I was crying again.

"A wolf," surprise and relief registered on his face. He'd heard someone talking about a wolf looking dog running down the street. He pulled my hands up, studying them for a moment then began kissing my palms.

I hadn't even noticed the little scratches on them before. No doubt from running on the rough surface of the road. "We'll talk to Stephan when we go see him. Right now that's not important. Why did you come here? Why didn't you go back home?" he asked, his eyes were searching my face.

"I thought you didn't want me. I thought that was why you left me there. I didn't know where to go." Nick's face was filled with anguish and tears stung in his eyes.

"My god Katherine, I love you, of course I want you."

"You love me?" I asked. Little ripples of joy flowed from my heart out to every inch of my being. He looked at me warily.

"I know you don't feel the same way but…"

"Why would you think I don't feel the same?" I asked cutting him short.

"Because you pushed me away in the shower tonight, you didn't choose me and I was afraid maybe you wanted him."

I gasped. "Nick, I almost bit you, I wanted to feed from you. I was afraid I was going to hurt you."

Relief flooded his face. "Oh baby you couldn't hurt me like that. I've wanted to do nothing less to you now for weeks. I'm sorry, I just expected you to understand; when two vampires share and feed from each other…It's one of the most intimate acts we can do. I've wanted you – desperately to share with me. Knowing you want me too…"

"Of course I want you, I've told you that."

"But you haven't taken my blood. We haven't mingled our blood yet. That's how we're marked by each other." He frowned again at the tee shirt then without warning ripped it up the middle, taking it off my shoulders he tossed it in the floor.

"I'm sorry Kat," he said as he removed his own shirt and put it on me. "I just can't stand for you to be wrapped up in any other man's scent."

His possessiveness was more than welcome right then. I needed more than anything to feel that sense of belonging. He kissed me again deeply, his tongue invading my mouth and mine his, re-igniting the fire that had started earlier in the shower. I wanted him. Nick gently picked me up and carried me to his jeep.

"I'm taking you home now and we will take care of this tonight, in our bed." As bad as I wanted him at that moment I was glad he was taking me home first. He was right; my room was filled with too many scents and bad memories. They had no place in my life with Nick.

Back at Nick's he carried me in, not letting me walk. I didn't mind. My hands and feet were tender and I was relishing being so close to Nick's heart. *He loves me!* I couldn't contain the joy I felt at knowing this and wrapped my arms around his neck.

Gently he lowered me onto the bed. "Stay here, "he commanded then went into the bathroom. I heard water running and a few moments later Nick returned, lifting me into his arms again. "I can walk," I protested but Nick wouldn't hear me. "Have you seen your feet?" he asked me. I shook my head. "We'll have a bath then go to bed. I want your feet to soak just a little while."

The bathroom smelled of jasmine I noticed as Nick gently lowered me to the edge of the tub. The water was warm and foamy and I eased my feet in, noticing the small cuts on the bottoms. They stung as they entered the water for the first time.

Nick slipped his shirt off of me and I slowly lowered myself into the soothing heat of the water. Nick took off his clothes and grabbed one of my hair clips off the counter.

"Slide forward a little," he said as he stepped in behind me. Lowering himself into the water he pulled me back between his legs, my back against his chest.

My hair was hanging down around my shoulders and he gathered it from behind, twisting and securing it with my clamp. He pulled me closer then, my head resting against his shoulder.

The water was soothing and Nick gently stroked the muscles in my arms. They were incredibly sore I realized as his thumbs slid up and down along my bicep and triceps. Slowly he worked his way to my hands pulling them to his lips as he kissed each little cut on my palms and finger pads. With each kiss my arousal grew stronger.

Deliberately I pushed my butt back against him, pleased when I felt the firmness of his thick erection against my back. I moved in his arms, turning around to face him. His eyes were dark with carnal desire, appearing only half open over huge dilated pupils.

"Take me now," I whispered with overwhelming emotion, "mark me as yours. I want to belong to you."

He rose up from the water swiftly, powerfully, bringing me with him, his arms around my back and under my backside. I wrapped my legs around his waist, my hands resting on his powerful shoulders.

Water fell away from us in sheets back into the tub and onto the floor as he stepped easily over the side. Our bodies glistened in the bathroom mirrors as the yellow light reflected off our wet skin.

Nick's cock hung impressively, hard, thick and heavy, pulsing from the surge of blood in his massive veins. Still wet, he deposited me gently into the welcome warmth of his bed.

Desire raged inside me and muscles pulled and clenched deep within. The tender folds of my sex swelled and throbbed in anticipation of receiving Nick's thick cock. Joining me in the bed I urged Nick onto his back.

I wanted him inside me but first I wanted him in my mouth. I licked the tip of his thickness tasting the first drop of pre-cum, tasting Nick.

Giving my body fully over to my desire I took the head of his cock in my mouth. My tongue swirled around licking, sucking, moving him deeper into the recesses of my mouth.

Nick moaned deep and guttural, reflecting the depth of passion I was feeling for him. "Arrrg," he cried out, rising up and pulling me to his mouth. His cry was almost anguished but this time I understood. His cry was reflected in my emotions. I had never wanted someone so desperately in my life.

Tears sprung to my eyes and my body shuddered as an orgasmic wave moved across me. I moved to my back bringing Nick with me, spreading my legs wide to receive him. He moved down grasping my thighs, spreading them wider as his nose nuzzled into my cleft, his tongue parting the moist folds, stroking and flicking my clit.

I was on the verge of explosion. So many emotions spilling over in the form of tears as my orgasm pulsed through me intense and powerful, rocking my body.

Then Nick lowered himself into me. I screamed as already stimulated nerve receptors received the onslaught from his throbbing, pulsing cock inside me.

"Oh my god – Nick," I cried out.

"That's right baby, I want you to feel me in every nerve in your body." He pulled out slowly then pushed in with such force I shifted in the bed. He was buried to the root inside of me and the feeling of the stretch and fullness overwhelmed me. I fisted my hands into the sheets, bracing myself for his next wonderful slam inside me.

"Nick," I screamed as I came around him again.

"You. Are. Mine," he said between thrusts, punctuating each word, "and everyone will know that you belong to me." He shifted, lifting me as he swung up and around leaning against the headboard. He was still buried deep inside, my legs straddling his lap.

I kissed his neck and my tongue found the tiny throbbing vein once again. I felt as my fangs descended through my gums. This time I didn't hesitate but bit in, my mouth filling instantly with his exquisite blood.

Nick was exploding deep within me, filling me with his seed, hot inside my core as he came while I drank him in. My neck exposed to him was accepted as he bit down filling me with untold pleasure, driving me over the edge once again in orgasm.

We were one now, sharing the same blood, knowing every detail and secret about each other. Nothing was hidden. There was no shame. It was just two vampires bearing our souls to each other, promising undying love. Nick had been right. There was nothing more intimate than this. I would never forget it – not ever.

Before I fell asleep Nick turned on his side and pulled me close against him, my back to his chest. "Everything I have Kat is yours. This is our house and our bed. I never want you to feel like you don't belong here – not ever again."

I turned in his arms to look into his beautiful eyes, overwhelmed by the love I felt. I kissed him again pouring my soul into him. Willing him to feel just how much I loved him. I couldn't say anything for the flood of emotions running through me but he understood. He got me.

FIFTEEN

Orlando swung out of the sports car with a grace and ease that made his fluid movement appear effortless. He was perfectly in tune with his body and the way he carried himself reflected his self-confidence.

He was strikingly handsome and knew it, but not to the point of being vain or obnoxious. He simply used his knowledge to his advantage and he was not beyond flashing a gorgeous grin to swoon a pretty girl.

Over the years he had turned heads by the thousands and had strings of girls at his beck and call. A bit on the flamboyant side, he liked to impress people, thus the expensive sports car and gold chains. After all he had the money. Why not enjoy it with the people he surrounded himself with? By people he was referring to beautiful women with even more beautiful bodies. He was partial to the tall, leggy type with full pouty lips, but enjoyed beauty in many forms.

He was a worldly man, one who never turned down a party, or a good time. True, he was irresponsible, even reckless at times but there was no malice in his mischief and he would never intentionally hurt someone, unless of course they were trying to hurt him or one of his. Then he could become violent, he was a vampire after all, but generally he considered himself a lover, not a fighter.

Walking around to the passenger side door he opened it and helped his leggy brunette with ultra-pouty lips out of the car. Always the gentleman, he did know how to please the ladies. With his left arm he tucked her firmly against his side as they made their way up to the club for a night of drinking and dancing.

As the couple approached the club Orlando caught a scent on the wind. He stopped for a moment closing his eyes and breathing in deeply. Leggy brunette whined and pouted over having to stop but he paid her no mind. The image of someone that bore his blood came to him and he knew she was inside.

He smiled. He had completely forgotten about her, not that she wasn't attractive, but he had more than enough presently to keep him occupied. She was here though so he might as well have some fun. Maybe he could leave with two beautiful women in his arms.

The thought pleased him and he resumed his stride toward the club. He would find her quickly. He loved to watch a woman that was aroused by him and this one would be very, very aroused. A wicked gleam came to his eyes as he spotted her across the room.

She did not disappoint! Shorter than what he normally went for, she was still strikingly beautiful – and squirming with desire already. Only a few seconds away from her, he knew it would seem like an eternity for her.

What was her name again? He had to reach down through the fog of his last blood thirst to remember. *Oh yes, Katherine had been on her name tag.* He would have to remember that name. Part of pleasing a woman was remembering their name! He made a beeline for her- slowly, and bringing leggy brunette with him.

Katherine was with another vampire, but Orlando could tell from her scent the other vampire had not yet marked her. From the look on his face he was wishing he had. Leggy was pouting at him and at the girl now. *She better get used to sharing me, I have a lot of love to give – more than enough for just one girl.*

Just steps away now. *She would make love to me here on the floor if I wanted her to.* The other vampire left abruptly. *Ass, she deserves to be treated better than that! I would walk away if you just said to back off.*

Orlando was directly in front of her now, kissing her knuckles and speaking to her. There was definitely a fight going on inside. This was a first. Most women just caved. Katherine was resisting her primal urges and he respected that. *A woman who thinks for herself! She could be fun to have around.*

Orlando spoke to her again, encouraging her to give up the fight. Then suddenly she bolted, running right out of her shoes and leaving her purse behind. Orlando laughed loudly. He had never seen anything quite like this. This Katherine had just earned herself a special place in his heart. One day when he was ready to settle down, if that time ever came, he wanted to find a girl just like her, someone that would love him unconditionally.

He stood staring after her for several more minutes even though she was out of sight as soon as the door swung shut behind her. The other vampire walked back in through the doors searching the crowds. *He must have just missed her.* Orlando picked up the purse and shoes carrying them toward him.

He wanted no fight but he was pissed with this vampire for leaving Katherine. He pushed the shoes and purse at him. "She ran out the door," he said with a scowl on his normally happy face. "You are one lucky bastard. Now go and fucking find her or next time she will be mine."

The other vampire turned on his heels and flew out the front door again not looking back. Orlando watched him leave then pulling leggy back snugly to his side walked out onto the dance floor.

Something woke me in the middle of the night. Reaching across to find Nick I felt only an empty space. Nick was no longer in bed with me. Sitting up in bed I listened for a sound that might indicate where he was. He wasn't in the bathroom. I got out of bed and walked quietly out into the living room.

A fire burned in the fireplace but Nick was nowhere to be seen. Then I heard a sound, a gentle strum of a guitar string. The sound had come from the office and I saw that a light was on inside. The door was slightly ajar and I pushed it open a bit more. Nick was sitting on the edge of his oversized chair, softly strumming a guitar.

I stood in the doorway quietly just watching for a moment. I had never heard him play before, though I'd seen the guitar on the stand in his office. The music was simple, but very pretty. Not a song I recognized.

Nick must have heard me because he suddenly stopped and turned to face me. "I'm sorry; I didn't mean to wake you."

"Please don't stop," I said moving closer. "It's very nice. I didn't know you played the guitar." Nick wrapped an arm around my hips, pulling me close.

"I play several instruments. The guitar and piano are my favorites."

"Mine too," I admitted, "although I prefer the electric guitar." Nick smiled up at me.

"I like that too, but this one I can play without the amp."

He sat the guitar down in its stand, moving me between his legs. My fingers stroked through his hair and he nuzzled between my breasts.

"I couldn't sleep so I thought I'd try to work for a while." He explained. "Then I couldn't focus on that either. I called and spoke with Stephan about your ability to transfigure. We decided to move the dinner to his home so that we can have some privacy. Dean can ride with us; just have him pack an overnight bag."

"Oh!" I couldn't imagine what we would need more privacy for.

"Stephan would like to see what all you can transfigure into." He said, answering my unspoken question. "This is very unusual. I've only ever heard of it and no one I know has ever seen it first-hand. You just seem to be bending all the rules." He said playfully.

"It's only one thing I countered."

"Yes, one very big and important thing. And your uterus and ovaries is another very big and important thing."

I was shocked. "You told Stephan about my ovaries?" I asked feeling a little embarrassed. I knew this was all new and exciting to them, but I just felt like my same old self – mostly. I didn't necessarily want my body up for group discussion.

"I'm sorry," Nick said sensing my unease. "This is more for my peace of mind, I know. I just don't want to take any chances when it comes to you."

I sighed, "Then I won't complain since you put it like that." My fingers raked gently down his chest through the hair there stopping at the gold necklace he wore.

I had seen him wearing it a few times before but had never really looked at it. Stopping now I did so. Hanging from the rope chain was an intricately carved pendant. I couldn't tell what it was so I leaned to take a closer look.

"It's only half there." Nick stated talking about the pendant. "It has two parts that fit together." He looked pensive for a moment. "I lost the other half long ago. This one belonged to my mother. The one I lost had been my fathers."

I wondered briefly if the necklace was connected to Adrianna but dismissed the thought immediately. *I can't keep getting jealous over a woman that died a hundred and fifty years ago.* Nick took the necklace off and placed it around my neck.

"Oh, no – you don't have to do that Nick; it was your mother's. You should keep it."

"I want you to have it. It's not the original chain, just the pendant." He kissed it then pressed it into my chest.

"Thank you, I'll take good care of it."

Rising to his feet he pulled me close and kissed me.

"I know you will. Let's go back to bed."

The sun was shining through the curtains when I woke the next morning. Glancing at the clock I saw it was almost nine. Nick was still asleep and I lay watching him for a while.

I beamed. *He loves me!* I didn't want to wake him but I had an overpowering urge to run my fingers through the hair on his chest, down his happy trail then to… Oh, I just couldn't get enough of this beautiful man.

Just thinking about the night before stirred emotions deep within me. Muscles clenched sending pulses of heavenly pleasure through my groin. My eyes blurred momentarily as my pupils dilated in response. I closed my eyes against my desire. Nick needed to sleep. I would go fix us some breakfast.

Nick ambled into the kitchen just as I was taking the last piece of bacon off the stove. Walking up behind me he planted a kiss on my neck that sent shivers up and down my spine.

God I love this man! We ate together at the breakfast bar then I rose to clean up the dishes. I wanted to talk to Nick about the house and other items Angie had left me. Obviously I wasn't in a bind for cash, but the weight of everything that needed to be done was resting heavily on my shoulders and I had little time to deal with it on my days off.

"You know you can quit your job," Nick was saying. "It's not like we need the money and right now you just have a lot on your plate." I considered his words.

"You may be right but as much money as Angie left me it won't last forever. I'll have to work again sometime."

"Possibly, but you should pace yourself. You will always be able to work but you will burn out if you don't take breaks. Besides, I have enough money for the both of us and I would really like for us to do some traveling."

I raised an eyebrow at him. I knew that he only worked when he wanted to but I'd never given much thought about his money.

"Yes," he said, "I'm worth a fortune, but I've never cared to live extravagantly. I like doing things with my hands so I buy old houses and remodel them. Some of them I sell, some I keep for myself. Nick looked thoughtful. "We could buy a nice piece of property and build a new house. I want you to have whatever you want."

"Thank you," I said kissing him on the cheek, "For now I'm happy to live here as long as I'm with you."

We continued to discuss Angie's house. "Real-estate is always a good investment. You could always rent it, and then sell once the market picks back up. Or we could live there if you like the newer, larger house."

"No, I'm not very neighborly. I prefer the larger yard and privacy to the gated communities. I think renting it is a good idea. I still don't know what to do with the rest."

"Go through and take out anything you want to keep, and then have an estate sale. I can help you with that." I sighed, relieved that I finally had a plan.

Over the next few days I thought about what Nick had said. I really didn't need the income from my job but I did need some time off. I had been afraid if I took off too long I would forget my skills but Nick had reminded me that I could do anything.

I didn't have to be a nurse. I could pick from any of a hundred things I had ever wanted to do instead. Time was now limitless for me and I could go back to school a hundred times over if I wanted. I could reinvent myself however I saw fit. When I got tired or bored I could quit and start all over again.

At the end of the week I put in my notice, taking my last two weeks in vacation. When I left the hospital Friday I wouldn't be coming back.

I had spoken with Dean during the week and he had made arrangements to be off the entire weekend for our trip to Stephan's. I was excited about seeing Stephan again and enjoying the freedom of not having to rush back for work. I was in the mood to celebrate.

Nick met me at the door with a huge grin on his face. He couldn't believe I had actually quit my job. He had bought a bottle of champagne. Popping the cork he poured us each a flute then added a drop from the tiny flask of wolf bane.

Lifting his glass he proposed a toast. "To London, Paris, the whole of Europe, and anywhere else my baby wants to go!" We clinked glasses and drank. I was so happy I was giddy. We would get through my divorce and the holidays and Angie's house then Nick and I would be off to see the world.

We left the following morning around ten. Dean had decided to follow us in his truck. He seemed a little nervous and I grinned. If it was me and I was going to stay the night with a group of vampires I'd probably want my own set of wheels too. I knew Dean had nothing to fear from any of us. Stephan kept a supply of human blood should we have a crisis.

We arrived at Stephan's shortly after one. It was like coming home for the holidays. I had missed the big house, the place of my re-birth. I had missed my daily sword lessons, my walks about the grounds, and the wealth of information that Stephan supplied. It was good to be home.

Stephan greeted us at the front door. He smiled, eyes twinkling giving us both hugs and greeted Dean warmly. "Congratulations you two," He said to Nick and me as he showed us into the house. Nick had updated him on our status earlier.

Our rooms were upstairs at each end of the hall. Nick and I would be sharing a room. I was glad it wasn't the one without windows.

Sara served lunch out on the back patio, shadows already growing in the October afternoon. The temperature still remained a bit warm as was common until late October into November at times. Some of the leaves had started turning fall colors though.

Stephan had thought of me and had a tray of sushi waiting. We sat enjoying each other's company and catching up for a while.

Stephan turned to me. "So what is this I hear about you transfiguring into a wolf?"

Dean sat up taking note, his eyes wide. This was new information for him. I blushed. I recounted the story, leaving out the part about Nick leaving me, as much as I could remember. Stephan looked thoughtful.

"I have heard of the ancients being able to transfigure at will. According to legend, they could assume any form they desired. Of course, I have never seen or heard of anyone in recent history – Not until now."

"All I know," I started, "is that I was afraid and I was thinking I needed to run faster that my two legs could carry me. I wasn't even thinking about a wolf. It just happened." Nick spoke up.

"Will she be able to do this again? Will she have to be afraid?"

"She has the ability," Stephan said, "she should be able to change at will, though it may take some practice – which we will work on. I am curious to find out how."

"What do you mean?" I asked not understanding.

"How is it that you have the power when your creator Orlando, nor any above him, have it? What makes you so different? Answering these questions could help answer many others."

Dean spoke up. "Maybe it was the way she got the blood. She didn't drink it like others. Her body was never drained of her own blood. It was injected directly into her bloodstream, bypassing digestion. Maybe something was made bio available that wouldn't have been otherwise. From what I saw in the lab, whatever it was completely replicated itself in her blood."

"You may have a point there," Stephan acknowledged. "It could also be that she had receptors on her blood cells that Orlando did not have. More likely it is a combination of the two variables."

"So you think that it required the direct injection and certain receptors in Kat's blood?" Dean asked. "That does make sense."

"Would I pass this trait down then?" I asked. "Suppose someone got my blood. If my blood were to replicate itself in someone else then they would also have my abilities?"

"If our theory is correct then yes," Stephan said. "Or if you were to have a child." Dean's head swung around.

"Is that even possible?"

"We know that Kat's transformation has been much different so far. She still has, according to Doctor Lee, a healthy uterus and ovaries that could support a fetus."

So there it was all out in the open – The three men talking about my parts. I would have been embarrassed if it weren't so funny. I laughed.

"But," Nick continued, "My sperm are dead."

"Correction," I countered, "just weak according to Doctor Lee." It was Dean's turn to laugh now. He had been learning about in vitro fertilization at school.

"Bro," he said slapping his knee, "it's just a matter of time." Nick looked at Dean in astonishment, and then a wicked light lit in his eyes. *Oh shit! I didn't see that one coming, but then maybe, with Nick, it wouldn't be a bad idea.*

Stephan stood up from the table and motioned for me to go to him. "Katherine," he said. "I want you to close your eyes and remember what you were feeling when you transfigured. Let's see if you can do it again tonight."

"No pressure here," I laughed nervously.

"Just relax," he said "relax and remember."

Doing as he said I closed my eyes, inhaling deeply then slowly let my breath out. In my mind's eye I saw the bar Nick and I were seated at the small round table. I concentrated trying to relive the fear I felt with the first pangs of arousal and the look I'd seen on Nick's face. Nothing happened.

286

I wasn't sure if I could really do this and I hated that I had an audience. I breathed again and tried to block out the fact that everyone was watching me expectantly. I pushed deeper, trying to connect with the desire I had to get away from Orlando. Still nothing happened. I tried to reach the depth of fear and panic I had felt at that time, hoping it would trigger the desired response.

"Breath Katherine," Stephan was saying. I hadn't realized I was holding my breath. Simply telling myself to change didn't work either.

I pushed even further into my memory, my mind conjuring up the fear I felt when Nick had left. The total and utter rejection and the fear that I'd lost him. Like an actor getting into a role I made myself relive that moment, made myself feel the pain and tears began to fall down my face. Feelings of wanting to run away and hide overwhelmed me.

I heard as the small group around me sucked in air making gasping sounds. When I opened my eyes I was on all fours again looking up at the group around the table. The looks on the faces around me was pure shock.

"That's very good Katherine." Stephan said. He moved closer and patted me on the head. I moved toward Nick and regretted it instantly as I walked right out of my clothes.

I tried my voice but nothing came out other than a whimpering noise. I looked at Nick then pawed at the clothes on the ground. He seemed to understand and came to pick them up. I could change back and have my hands but didn't want to re-appear naked in front of Stephan and Dean.

I followed Nick around the corner. As soon as I was out of sight from the others I was standing upright again on human legs. Tears still stained my cheeks, my eyes red rimmed. Nick came to me then holding me tight.

"I'm sorry baby; I should have never left you there." He was reliving it all over again too. I held him close and for the first time I realized my greatest fear had not been that of Orlando. My greatest fear had been of losing Nick.

Quickly I pulled my jeans and shirt back on and returned with Nick to where our little group sat. Stephan looked up as I took a seat.

"We will continue practicing this while you're here. It may come in very handy one day. You should be able to change at will without giving it much thought."

"What about other forms?" Dean was asking. "Will she be able to assume any other forms?"

"We will discover that along the way." Stephan said in his usual easy manner. "It may take some time but time is not something we are short on."

Nick grinned, so big his face almost split into. Holding up a small vial he waved it back and forth. "Maybe what she need's is to have her inhibitions lowered. Maybe we all do." He said holding the wolf bane.

On cue, Sara appeared with a tray of assorted wine. I selected a nice white wine from the tray. Stephan had excellent taste and I was sure anything would be good. Nick poured a small amount in each of the glasses.

"I'm not sure what kind of effects this has on humans." He said to Dean. "It may do nothing at all or it might intensify the alcohol. It's not poisonous in this dosage though." Dean held up his glass.

"I'll try it once."

Even Stephan took a glass. "It's been a while since I had any of this."

Before long we were all laughing as Stephan recalled stories from his youth. It was still hard for me to grasp the length of time the man had lived on earth. Dean's interest was piqued and he sat on the edge of his seat listening to every word. The wolf bane definitely intensified the alcohol effects for humans. Dean was slurring after only one glass.

We moved indoors when Sara announced dinner. I was really hungry again and I guess everyone else was too. We all quit talking for a while and focused on the awesome meal spread before us.

We sat up talking and drinking late into the night. Poor Dean had passed out on the couch and I found a blanket to cover him with. I was pleased that he had gotten over his nervousness and he seemed to have enjoyed himself in our company.

When Nick and I retired to bed he snuggled up close behind me. I loved feeling his breath on my neck, loved having his arms wrapped around me. Most of all I loved falling asleep knowing that he loved me

SIXTEEN

I woke early and made my way downstairs to find Dean and Stephan in the parlor sitting around a small table, stern looks on their faces. I was afraid they might be in an argument but as I approached Dean looked up and smiled. I was relieved.

They had been in deep discussion about something Stephan had drawn out on a piece of paper. From the looks of the drawing it had to do with DNA.

"I'm learning a lot in school," Dean was saying, "but there is so much more I'd like to look at and they just won't allow us to use their equipment for anything but school work.

I have a lab at my house, but to buy the equipment I would need would cost a small fortune. There's just so much I could do. I think I could really make some headway on some of this."

"From what you're describing to me I think you could too." Stephan was saying.

I was interested. Dean was incredibly smart and I knew it. Nick had now joined us and was standing behind be gently kneading my shoulders.

"What is it you are working on," I asked curiously. Stephan spoke up.

"We would like to analyze your DNA more closely and compare it to mine and Nick's. See if we can find out what makes you different."

"Wouldn't you need more specimens to compare me to?"

"Possibly," Dean said, "but for now what we have would be a good start."

"And you think that you'll be able to figure this out?"

"Yes, I believe that I could. It would help if I had some of your pre-vampire DNA too."

"I'm sure you could find some at my old house. How much are you talking about for equipment?"

"Oh wow, off the top of my head I would guess a quarter mil, maybe more than that. I've never priced the equipment and I'd need to figure out what all I'd really need."

I thought about it for a minute. "I think I could give you that much to get started. If you need more I could do a bit more. Will you have the time you need though? With work and school, it doesn't leave much time."

"I have a thought," Stephan was saying to Dean, "Suppose I front you the money. You and I could be partners per se. I would supply the money and support, you could supply the knowledge. I would put you on my payroll.

This is incredibly important to me and I really want to be involved. I could match what you're making in the hospital and your only job would be what you now consider your hobby."

Dean whistled. "That is a very tempting offer, almost too good to be true."

"Believe me it is true. As you can see my house is very extensive and there is ample space for a lab. You could move in to one of the rooms if you like. You would be able to finish school and make your own work schedule."

Dean thought of all the projects he had put away for a later time. An opportunity like this didn't happen often. It might never come around to him again. It didn't take long for him to make his decision. "I'll do it!" he said to Stephan. Stephan smiled and the two men shook hands.

"Let us scout out a suitable space for the lab. I have several rooms in the back that I want you to see first."

Sara had put together a pile of scrambled eggs and French toast made from fruit filled bread. I had a slice with some eggs and a large cup of coffee. The bread practically melted in my mouth it was so good.

Dean was talking animatedly when he came to the breakfast table. His excitement was palpable. They had settled on using a large room near the back of the house that had access to the basement.

Dean would move into one of the spare rooms and rent out his house. They would take the next several weeks procuring the equipment and getting it set up in the room. He ate quickly then went off to find Stephan again.

After breakfast Nick pulled me off to the side. "Let's get out of here for a while," he smiled, "we can go exploring, maybe play a game of hide and seek." I wasn't sure exactly what he had planned but it sounded like fun just to be running through our old stomping grounds. He led me out the back and into the brush. I smiled when we came to the cave where we'd first made love.

"Take off your clothes," he said as we ducked into the clearing inside. I raised an eyebrow at him. "I want to play a game of hide and seek. You can hide or seek first, whatever you want, but I want you to try to transfigure to do it." I was a little disappointed that this wasn't a romantic outing, but it seemed like a good idea.

"I'll seek first. I'll give you a thirty-second head start." Nick could cover a lot of ground in only ten seconds but I would still be able to find him easily with just my vampire instincts. Thirty seconds would put some real distance between us. Nick smiled and kissed me then took off.

I counted thirty seconds and started after him. Not wanting to run around naked I only removed my shoes. I would try to leave my clothes nearby if I could change at all.

I picked up his scent easily but he had crossed his own trail several times and his scent became confusing. I needed a better nose to track with. It was so easy. I was instantly a beautiful gray wolf again.

Shaking the clothing off of me I pulled them into a small pile then returned to my hunt. I sniffed around on the ground for a moment and when I was sure I had the most recent scent, took off following it.

After several miles Nick's scent dead ended at a tree. I ran around it expanding my circle each time until I found where he'd hit the ground again then took off following.

I lost him again when he crossed a stream. Crossing to the other side I was unable to find his scent again. He must have stayed in the water, but which way did he go. I needed a better vantage point. Maybe being up in a tree would help. Without thought I transformed into a huge raven, black as onyx.

Amazed with my newfound ability I wanted to test my limitations. How many different forms could I assume? Where they all pre-determined by my DNA? I had given no thought to what I wanted to be, it had just happened.

Moving to the edge of the water where I could see my reflection I willed myself to be a falcon, rather than a raven. The change was instantaneous as black feathers were replaced by brown and gray ones. So I did have some control at least.

Now that I knew I could choose my form I wondered if I was limited to only living things or if I could become an inanimate object such as a stone. I willed myself to be a large gray rock but nothing happened.

I attempted to change to a small plant and still nothing happened. In the meantime Nick was getting further and further ahead of me. I had spent too much time playing and needed to catch up. I could experiment more, later.

Flapping my wings I took to the air. Circling once again I was able to make out Nick's foot prints in the stream bed. He was heading due north. I flew through the trees staying low until the trees fell away to wide open prairie. His tracks exited the stream and headed south.

I stayed in the air until the ground was too rocky and no tracks were visible. He was upwind of me and climbing up into the hills. Appropriately I became a mountain goat and followed until he was within sight.

He had stopped for a moment surveying the area. A small cave opening lay just ahead. I was still downwind from him so he probably had not picked up my scent.

Wanting to surprise him I returned to my falcon form and sailed into the air. I climbed higher until I was directly overhead then plummeted from the sky, dropping onto a rock just in front of him. He looked surprised, uncertain. Watching him I edged closer then hopped up onto his arm.

His mouth fell open. "Kat," he said in astonishment. The next moment I was standing against him, his arm around me.

"Tag," I said, "you're it!" His eyes sparked as he looked at my naked body in the autumn sun.

"Either way you look at it, I still win!"

Riding on his shoulder as a falcon we made our way back to the cave where I'd left my clothes. As soon as we arrived I flew down and changed back to my human form. It was now late afternoon and the sun was sinking behind the hills. A fog had begun to settle in as the temperature dropped. I watched for a moment. Something about the fog was so comforting and peaceful; it called to me. I sighed and gathered my clothes quickly, dressing for the hike back to the house.

"What's the hurry?" Nick asked pulling me close. "I kind of like you without your clothes on."

"Hmmm," I giggled, his stubble tickling my neck. Turning to face him I wrapped my arms around his neck. "I like getting naked with you too, but we don't have a blanket this time and it would be very uncomfortable without one. I was thinking more of a hot bath and our nice bed back at the house."

Nick's eyes flamed. "I like that idea! Guess the hiding portion of this exercise can wait till another time." I finished dressing quickly and we headed out into the fog.

The game of hide and seek had definitely helped me out in the transfiguration department. It no longer took concentration to assume a new form. I simply thought about what I wanted to be and it happened.

It now happened so quickly it was as though I'd been doing it my entire life. The trick would be to figure out the clothing situation. I wondered if I might be able to transfigure back into a human with clothes on. Next time I would try and see what happened.

Arriving back at the house we made our way upstairs. Dean and Stephan were down in the cellar again, no doubt discussing plans for the lab. Nick started a bath for us. I was looking forward to soaking in the hot water.

Transfiguration took a lot of energy as I was using muscles in a way I normally wouldn't. Once again my triceps were sore and aching from all the running and flying. Stepping into the tub I slid down into the soothing warmth.

Nick soon joined me and began to rub the knots out of my arms and shoulders. I leaned back into his chest enjoying his touch. He slowly worked his way down my arms to the backs of my hands then entwining his fingers between mine, wrapped his arms and mine across my chest. His mouth was on my neck kissing and licking down to my shoulders.

I moaned as chills ran up my spine, desire pooling deep in my belly. Releasing my hands he grabbed some body wash and began to wash me. His hands slid across my body lubricated by the soap, stopping on my breast; pulling at my nipples. I arched my body, pushing my breast into his hands, feeling the thickness of his arousal against my backside. He wanted me and I wanted him.

Turning to face him I returned the favor and began to wash him. Softly I stroked his chest, abdomen then slipped below the water to his erection. His lips parted slightly as I took him in my hands and began to move up and down along his thick length.

His eyes remained fixed on mine, dark and filled with desire. He pulled me to him, his mouth claiming mine. My lips parted as his tongue pushed into my mouth, tasting, exploring.

His fingers were on me now, parting the tender folds of my sex, his thumb on my clitoris, pushing, circling while two fingers slipped inside. "Oh baby – you're so ready for me so fast." He said as he started moving his fingers, searching for my pleasure spot. I tilted my pelvis, pushing my sex into his hand, moaning as he found it.

He pushed back from me. "Let's finish this in the bedroom." With bated breath I acquiesced, rising from the water. As I stepped from the tub Nick wrapped me in a large towel and began to dry me. A towel was wrapped around his hips but water still dripped down his chest and arms.

As he finished drying me I took the towel and went to work on his chest. The air was cold after the hot bath and my nipples beaded in response, drawing up tight. Nick noticed and was quick with his warm mouth and expert tongue, sucking, and pulling, elongating them.

Lifting me in his arms he carried me to the bed, my legs wrapped around his waist, fingers fisting in his hair. I was more than ready for him. I wanted him inside me – Now.

Gently he lowered me onto the bed, my legs still wrapped around his waist pulling him closer. His hands on my knees he pushed them apart as he buried his head at the apex of my thighs.

Again he inserted two fingers into my sex as he sucked and licked on my clit. My hips tilted and pushed against him responding to the intense desire building stronger in my groin.

Sliding one arm under my back he lifted and moved me further into the bed climbing up with me. Then he was sinking into me, slowly filling and stretching me with his hard thick length. The fullness was exquisite and I threw my head back moaning, savoring as his entire length filled me.

Nick moaned my name as I tightened around him, and then slowly, gently began to move pushing deep with each stroke. My hips rocked with his rhythm and I tightened against him with each stroke. I was building inside, ready to explode around him. "Come on baby, give it to me." He growled. His words pushed me over the edge and I called out his name as I came around him.

My body was writhing with aftershocks of the orgasm when Nick found the vein on my neck and bit sending me reeling again as he came inside me. He collapsed then on top of me and turned to his side taking me with him, exposing his neck to me. I bit and felt his body convulse as he continued to pour out within me.

We drank deeply from each other as we lie still entangled, still connected, our bonds growing stronger, deeper. I loved this man, more than I had ever loved anyone. He was part of me and I was part of him, inseparable in my heart.

We joined Stephan and Dean for dinner that evening out on the back patio. The fog had grown a bit denser as night fell. Stephan was excited to hear about my accomplishments for the day.

"Well done, Katherine." He said smiling. "This day has been quite extraordinary; perhaps we will soon uncover some of the mysteries I've contemplated for a few centuries now. Tell me, do you feel comfortable with your changes?"

I pondered his question for a moment. I felt confident with what I already knew and felt that I had made good progress today but still wanted to explore my abilities.

"So far it has been easier than I expected it to be, but there are still some aspects I'd like to try."

"What else," Nick asked joining the conversation.

"Today I discovered at least two things that I can't transfigure into and I'd like to know what my limitations are. I was unable to become either plant or an inanimate object so I just wonder if I'm limited to being animal.

Plus there is the fact that I lose my clothing when I change. I was wondering how I might be able to get around the whole naked thing."

Nick smiled wickedly. "I kinda like the whole naked thing."

I rolled my eyes at the sniggers that went around the table. "I'm sure you do but it really is an inconvenience for me. Moving from animal to animal is easy enough but if I really need to be human it puts me at a disadvantage."

"What you did today worked pretty well." Nick was saying of leaving my clothes in a pile.

"But that will only work if I can get back to my clothes. In an emergency it won't work. I was thinking more…"

Explaining what I wanted to do was difficult since I wasn't sure how it would really work. I just felt that if I could become something covered in hair then why not something covered in leather. After all it was animal. The best way to find out was to try. "Well something like this."

Instantly I became the gray wolf again and hopped down from my chair leaving my clothing behind. I moved away from the table where everyone could see me.

It was now or never. If this didn't work the way I wanted – well Nick would get more of the *naked thing,* but then so would Stephan and Dean. Worst case I would be terribly embarrassed.

I decided to take my chances. Holding my breath I changed back and quickly looked down to assess the situation. I breathed a sigh, letting out my breath. It had worked. I wasn't naked but covered completely in a black leather suit.

The leather seemed to be part of my own skin molded snugly, revealing every curve of my body. I even had a pair of boots that came up to my knees. Nick and Dean sat speechless with their mouths open. Stephan appeared to be jotting notes on a small piece of paper.

"Holy hell," Dean interjected his eyes big as saucers. You look like you stepped right out of the pages of a comic book I used to read."

"Well," I said to Nick, "what do you think?"

He was grinning, so big his face almost split into. "It's not naked, but it's just as good!"

Back in the bedroom Nick and I closely inspected the suit. My suspicions were confirmed, it was not removable. Once again I transfigured, this time back to my naked form. "I like this version better," Nick said. "It's much softer."

SEVENTEEN

Over the next few weeks Nick and I boxed up Angie's belongings that I didn't want and donated them to her favorite charity. It was a lot of stuff and the attendant there was overjoyed.

The furnishing and appliances I moved to my house. I was able to fill every room with good quality furniture, most of it brand new. I also restocked my cabinets with pots, pans, dishes and small appliances.

Everything Dan had taken from me I was able to replace with a much nicer, more expensive version. He had really done me a favor since I now had a place to put a lot of Angie's things. It made me feel good to be able to keep some of her personal effects around, like she was still with me in a way.

Even though I wasn't living in the house I wasn't going to sell it. I loved the wooded property and knew someday I would return to it.

Once her house was empty and cleaned up I put it on the market for lease. With any luck I would have a renter before Christmas. I sold David's old Audi and my car without any problem, two more items checked off my mental to-do list. I was now ready to face the coming Holidays.

Callie called. She would be out of school for the Thanksgiving holidays and planned to come into town. She would be bringing someone with her – a boy that she wanted me to meet. She sounded a little nervous and a lot excited as she asked if it were ok for the two of them to stay with Nick and me.

I frowned. This was the first time that Callie had mentioned a boy before although it shouldn't surprise me. She was, after all, almost twenty one years old. Surely she had had sex by now. I must have just been oblivious, but then she had been living with her dad for a while.

"Sure," I said, "we have an extra room here or if you need more privacy you can stay at the old house."

"No mom, that's fine. I'd like to stay there and spend some time with you."

I was a little shocked but glad she wanted to spend time with me. Maybe she was finally getting over being so angry with me.

I went to make sure the spare bedroom had linens and made a list of a few items I wanted to get for it. Nick was working on another case so he would be busy for a while. I decided to go shopping for the needed items. I sent Nick a quick text and headed out the door.

I decided to drive into Houston to one of the larger malls. It had been a while since I'd really been shopping and I might find something new to wear while I was out. Finding a spot in a parking garage I made my way across the street.

The mall was packed and it wasn't even Thanksgiving yet. I made a mental note to do any shopping before then. I hated fighting crowds.

I went into several boutiques before finding anything I liked that fit well. After making my choices I went hunting for the linens I needed. This was much easier than shopping for clothes. Satisfied with my purchases I headed home.

I had stopped at a traffic light when I spotted a sign on a store in a strip center. That name sounded familiar. *Where have I heard of that before?* I quickly changed lanes and pulled into the parking lot. This was definitely not the nicer part of town. Getting out I locked my doors then headed into the jewelry store.

The clerk eyed me suspiciously when I walked in. I was here on a mission but unsure how I was going to accomplish it.

"Can I help you with anything?" the clerk asked with a tone that didn't match his expression.

"Umm, I'm just looking." I replied.

"For rings, necklaces, or watches?" the clerk inquired.

"Oh, I'll know it when I see it." The clerk was getting on my nerves already. I caught a sudden movement out of the corner of my eye. Another man had stepped out of the back office. My eyes met his and held for a moment. This was why I was here. This was who I wanted to talk to. Elijah Keet.

I took in the man's appearance. It was unnerving how much he looked like Nick, only older but not by much. He had the same brown eyes and chin and his facial hair even grew the same as Nick's. He was taller than he looked on the TV and was nicely built.

He smiled, "Have you been helped?" The clerk started sputtering but I cut him off.

"Actually I am here to see you." I had no clue what I was going to say to the man but he was here in front of me. He had to be Nick's offspring – the resemblance was too strong not to be.

"Is that a fact?" he said looking amused. "What can I help you with?" I started walking toward him, wondering what I was going to say. I had a picture of Nick. Maybe I should show him the picture.

My heart was beating out of my chest. He is going to think I'm crazy. There was no part of what I had to tell him that was even remotely believable. I was now standing directly in front of him.

I looked up to meet his gaze but he was looking at my chest, eyes wide in amazement. He stood staring for a moment then found his voice, his hand moving to my neck.

"That is a very interesting pendant." He said lifting it in his fingers, examining it. "Do you mind if I ask where you got it?" Emboldened by some unseen force I took a deep breath.

"It was a gift," I said, "From your great, great, great, grandfather." His eyes measured me as he weighed my words. At long last he spoke.

"If you are referring to whom I believe you are, then you will need to add one more "Great" in that line. Come, I have something I think you will find interesting."

Taking my hand he pulled me toward the front door. "I'll be back soon," he said waving to the clerk. He turned to me. "It's just a few blocks down the street. Do you mind?" I was a little uncomfortable but only because he looked so much like Nick and the fact that he was holding my hand.

I nodded. He hit a button on his key fob and the horn honked on a silver Mercedes in the lot. He opened the door for me and I climbed inside. He got in on the driver's side and started the car up, pulling out of the parking lot.

"So you are acquainted with Nicolas Cristo?" he asked me. I was taken aback that he knew Nick's name.

"Yes," I nodded. His mouth set in a grim line as he accelerated down the street, turning sharply into the drive of a large home set on a tiny lot. He got out and came around to my side, opening the door for me. Taking my hand once again he pulled me toward the house.

"My family has been waiting for this day for almost two centuries," He said. "Though I never believed it would come to pass in my day. I wasn't even sure it was real." He chuckled to himself. "But we are a family steeped in tradition and superstitions and so I have waited believing. Now here you are, at last!"

We had moved up the steps and he had flung open the front door. "Please come in. I have so much to share with you." Elijah pointed to a leather couch in a sitting area. "Please have a seat and I will be with you momentarily."

I sat waiting nervously as he disappeared up the wide stairway to the second floor. Moments passed and he returned carrying a large box which he placed on the coffee table in front of me. Opening the box he removed a large, ancient family bible, a box of photos and another smaller box.

"This bible," he started, "belonged to my great, great, great, great grandmother – Adrianna Wheeler. She married Ethan Keet, a good man, and the man whose name I bear. But she always contended that her only son was the son of her true love – Nicolas Cristo.

She kept this bible and passed it down to her children with instructions that it should be handed down to each generation and that the genealogy should be recorded in it. She made it clear that someday we would find Nicolas Cristo and we were to give him all of this." He waved his hands gesturing to everything on the table.

He opened the bible. On the first pages were her name and Nick's name, below that was the name Nicolas Keet.

"Elijah explained, "Adrianna kept this bible separate from the family bible her husband owned. She wanted her child to know who his real birth father was and hoped they would meet but unfortunately that never happened."

Elijah held up a finger. "This is what specifically I wanted you to see." He opened the small box and produced a golden chain with a pendant on it. The pendant was intricately carved, like the one Nick had given me. When he held it up against mine they fit together perfectly. "It seems that this has finally come home."

"Mr. Keet," I asked, "Would you like to come with me and meet Nick?" He smiled at me, lines furrowing his face.

"I have waited almost fifty years to do just that. I would love to meet him!"

It was almost six o'clock when I arrived back home. Nick looked up when I entered and I could tell he'd been worried. I smiled broadly at him "Wait till you see what I've brought for you." I said as I brought Elijah into the house, box in tow.

Nick's expression went from confusion to astonishment in an instant. Elijah looked at Nick with reverence as he shook his hand and I must say that Nick looked equally awed. The two were so similar in physical appearance and stature that they could have been twin brothers.

Opening the box, Elijah took out the bible telling Nick the story he'd told me earlier. Nick was beside himself as he read the names at the front of the bible that formed the family tree, his fingers tracing over them.

His son had been named Nicoli, after him but carried the name of Keet, his stepfather. Nicoli's eldest son was Fane. Fane's eldest was Alexandru, his eldest Benjamin. The oldest son of Benjamin died at a young age so the bible was passed to the second son, Nathaniel, who was Elijah's father.

Elijah went on to tell us that Ethan Keet had been a good man and had loved Nicoli as his own. He had known that Adrianna was with child when they wed but married her without hesitation.

He had known she would likely never love him the way he wanted her to, but he loved her. He did his best to care for her until the day he died. Adrianna bore four daughters to Keet but had no sons by him.

Adrianna had ingrained in young Nicoli that he was the son of a very special man that would one day find him. She taught him that he must always look for his father as long as he lived and teach his children to do the same. The bible had been passed down through each generation. After almost two hundred years it had finally found its way to Nick.

Elijah produced pictures as well. There was one of Nicoli as an infant with his mother and then one of him as a young man. I looked on as Nick lingered over each photo. *Adrianna had been a very pretty young woman, much younger than me.*

Again I was forced to fight back the sting of jealousy as he looked at her photo. Nicoli was an attractive young man as well but looked more like his mother than Nick.

Nick had tears in his eyes as he looked at the pictures. Pictures of the son he never knew and a few of his grandchildren. My heart ached for him. To have lost so much – how could you ever get over that? Yet here before him was one of his grandchildren. They had succeeded in finding him after all these years. There was no doubt in my mind how much Adrianna had loved him.

The last item to be given to Nick was the necklace and pendant. Removing the necklace from around my neck he snapped the two pendants together. For the first time I could see the full picture. When put together they formed an intricate pattern of symbols; two hands clasped surrounded by the infinity, the Celtic endless knot, and all encircled by Ouroboros. It was symbolic for endless love between the two wearers.

In a gesture filled with emotion, Nick kissed the now complete symbol then separated the pieces, placing the one back on my neck and the other on himself. In that moment I knew how much he loved me. I knew I would do anything for this man.

As Elijah rose to leave the two men hugged then he turned and hugged me as well. "I'm so glad you stopped in today. This is indeed one of the most notable days of my life." I was glad I stopped too; Glad for Nick – that he finally knew about his family.

Nick was quiet for a long time after Elijah left, looking over the photos and bible. After a long moment he broke the silence.

"Thank you," he said "this was the best gift anyone could have ever given me." His eyes were filled with emotion and I went to him wanting to comfort him.

"Are you alright?" I asked, growing concerned that I may have just caused him more pain.

"Yes – seeing these pictures tonight has made me realize how much better off I am." He paused, searching for the right words. "I lost a love and had wondered about a child, but I did not have to watch them die.

Adrianna's parents were right. Our union would have been nothing but pain. For her it would have been aging while I stayed forever in my current state. For me it would have been watching her and Nicoli die while I was forced to live on and on."

His words made me think of Angie and for the first time since her death I felt comforted that I had allowed her to die. But they also made me think of Callie.

I never wanted to survive my child but now it seemed unavoidable. I quickly pushed the thought out of my mind. I would go crazy if I dwelt on it.

Nick took my hand and pulled me down into his lap. With sudden urgency his hands were in my hair and around my waist pulling me tight against him, his face against my neck as he inhaled deeply. Pulling back he gazed into my eyes, searching – longing.

At long last he closed his eyes and kissed me deeply. "I'm just so glad the fates saw fit to let me find you." I ran the back of my hand down his cheek. This man was so dear to me. I didn't want to think of life without him – ever.

"I'm glad you found me too." I said pulling his head down to mine.

Dean sat back in his chair and looked around the room pleased with his accomplishments. In the past three weeks he and Stephan had converted the large room into a real lab.

Two walls were now lined with stainless steel counter tops complete with a sink on one side. There was a large island in the middle with bar height stools and two compound microscopes side by side. Drawers were filled with petri dishes, tubes, pipettes, flasks, and slides.

There was a Bunsen burner, a centrifuge, a refrigerator, and an autoclave. Along one wall were small wire cages that would hold the lab rats. His desk sat in a corner facing the room.

A large open area stared at him from the back wall. This was where the final piece of equipment would go – A huge console that would take up most of the back wall and was capable of DNA sequencing. This had cost Stephan a small fortune and the room had been rewired to accommodate it. It was slated for delivery in a week. With any luck it would be on time.

Rising from his chair he strode out of the room and down the stairs into the cellar. Actually this was only one of the cellars under the huge house but it was adequate for his needs. The walls had been painted white and new bright fluorescents had been installed as well as stainless cabinets.

This was a secure room. There were cages down here too, but these were small boxes constructed of steel with only tiny air holes and reinforced hinges and doors. The walls, floor and ceiling down here were all made of cinderblock and the doors were steel.

Tucked away nicely into a cove in the corner was the small refrigerator from the closet in his house. Opening the fridge he took out a tray containing blood tubes. He looked at them wistfully for a moment then returned them to the shelf in the fridge. *Soon I will start on that project.*

He glanced around the room again then went back upstairs. There was nothing more he could do here until the console arrived. His few belongings, which consisted of a laptop, a score of books and his clothes had already been brought over and were now in the room he would be staying in.

His house had been rented almost immediately so that was not a concern. School would be done mostly online except for one day a week when he had lab. The drive was not too bad and after this semester he could transfer to a college that was nearby.

He hated that there was nothing to do. It gave him too much time to think about other things. He preferred to stay busy so that he didn't dwell on the fact that love had passes him by more than once.

Of course he was still young and he still had time but would he ever meet another girl quite like Kat? He should have made a move years ago but now she was with Nick and by all accounts very happy to be with him. Nick was a good guy too, not an ass like Dan.

Dean sighed. He would – he knew – always love Kat. He just hoped that someday it wouldn't be as hard to be near her as it was now. In the meantime he would do whatever he could to help her in any way.

He glanced at the time. Ten a.m., Stephan would probably still be practicing with those swords of his. Maybe he would take him up on a lesson or two. He smiled at the thought and turned to find Stephan.

EIGHTEEN

Fall had arrived in full force as a cool front pushed into the area behind a line of thunderstorms. The rain had no sooner stopped when the cool, dry, north wind blew thru evaporating the water off the ground and sucking the moisture out of the air.

Leaves were falling out of trees covering every inch of ground. The sky was steel gray now and everything seemed to reflect the gray all around. Even the grass, still green, had a blue/gray tinge.

No matter how many lights were on in the house it still seemed too dark and too yellow. I was tempted to put up Christmas lights early to add a touch of color.

Despite the dreariness this was still one of my favorite times of the year. I loved the cool, blessedly dry air; the smell of wood smoke from people burning leaves; and the hustle of holiday shopping.

I was glad the front had made it through.
Tomorrow was Thanksgiving Day and it was so un-
holiday like when it was ninety degrees outside.

Callie and her friend, who now had a name, Abel
would be arriving this afternoon. I was really excited to
see her. She had been so angry with me when she left she
wouldn't even visit for the holidays.

I took the last pie out of the oven, one less thing to
do tomorrow. Even my dressing was ready in the fridge,
waiting to be popped into the oven. I went over my mental
list. Honey baked ham, chicken and dressing, almond
blanched green beans, candied yams, fruit salad, and dirty
rice. And for desert; four pies; pumpkin, pecan, chocolate
and coconut cream and a chocolate pound cake.

I shook my head. I always made too many pies but
this was the only time of year I really baked and there was
nothing I like for breakfast better than a piece of cold pie.
Besides Dean and Stephan would be joining us as well.
Nick had invited Elijah but he had previous plans to go to
Ohio where his children lived.

At two o'clock the doorbell rang and I fairly ran to
open it. Callie and her young man were waiting anxiously.

She had grown up so much I just couldn't believe it. I pulled her to me hugging her and she seemed to relax. I waved Abel inside and he moved into the house. I pulled back holding her at arm's length.

"I can't believe you've grown another inch or two." I said smiling "And so grown up looking." She smiled back.

"Geez mom, I look pretty much the same. You're the one who looks different. How much weight have you lost anyway?"

"Not much really, just toned up a bit." Nick joined us in the doorway and I introduced him. Callie's mouth fell open when she saw him. "Come on in and I'll show you were to put your stuff."

Abel shifted, "I need to bring in the luggage."

"I'll help you." Nick said following him out the door.

Callie eyed me. "Where did you find him? He is totally hot mom – and you look pretty good yourself! I guess getting rid of Dan was a good thing."

I laughed, "Things did work out quite nicely. Your young man, Abel, is a nice looking boy."

Callie rolled her eyes, "I'm not so sure he's *my* young man, but yes he is nice to look at." We had a good laugh then. Nick and Abel came in with the luggage and I led the way to the guest room. I was glad I'd bought new linens as I showed them into the room. Nick and I left them to get situated.

"She looks very much like you." Nick said of Callie.

"You think?" I thought she resembled me but I also saw a lot of her father in her, especially in her expressions.

"Yes, I think. She is a beautiful young woman." He said, kissing the top of my head. I nuzzled my face against his chest. I loved being in his arms.

We all walked down to the pier and looked out at the water. Like everything else it was bleak and gray reaching far to the horizon. The wind had kicked up the waves, churning the water causing small blasts of spray to fly up and sprinkle us with salty water.

A few gulls hovered and dipped down nearby, begging for a snack. Nick was showing Abel the boat and

Callie and I walked back to the house to get out of the wind.

"So tell me about Abel." I said wanting to catch up on what I'd missed in her absence.

"Well," she started, "we met at school. We were in a class together and started hanging out afterward, spending a lot of time together."

"And," I asked raising an eyebrow.

She frowned. "He's a really nice guy and we get along pretty well, but I just don't think we have enough in common to be more than friends. When we met I was taking my pre-reqs for the nursing program, now that I've been in school for a while I've discovered I'm really more interested in forensics. He is just not interested – which would be fine, but there's just not a lot to talk about anymore. After you told me about Dan......it really made me think. I don't want a relationship like that." *Oh, this was news.*

"So are you changing your major then?" I thought about what this meant. She had taken a year and a half off after high school and started the following spring semester. Two years into a four year degree and switching gears – but it's best that she do what she really wants.

"So how far back will this put you in school?" I wondered aloud.

"Only two semesters, there are only a few more classes I need, most of the others carried over. I could probably cram them into one semester but I really want to make good grades. There is a lot of chemistry and math involved."

"The truth is I'm not sure I have time for a relationship anyway. Chemistry doesn't come easy for me and I really, really want this. I want to succeed. I need someone that can be supportive and understanding if I have anyone at all."

"Sounds like you know what you want. You shouldn't settle for less, and you're right – you need commonalities. Just don't keep him hanging if you're really not that into him."

"I'm not. I was hoping by coming with me maybe he would see how much we've both changed. Plus I didn't want to break up with him right before the holiday. He is a good friend and I do care about his feelings."

I tucked a hair behind her ear. I was so proud of her. She really had grown up and I knew she would be fine. Thinking of the chemistry and DNA stuff reminded me that Dean would be here tomorrow. "There is someone I want to introduce you to, a good friend of mine. He'll be here tomorrow for dinner and he is awesome at chemistry."

We spent the rest of the day just catching up on the past two years. Nick started a fire in the fireplace and opened a bottle of wine, secretly slipping a drop of wolf bane into mine and his glasses. I sliced some cheese and a summer sausage and put it out with some crackers, grapes and some smoked salmon for a light dinner. We would be eating pretty much all day tomorrow.

I was just putting the rolls into the oven when Dean and Stephan arrived. I gave them each a hug and a quick kiss on the cheek then brought them into the living room where everyone was gathered. Pouring a glass of wine I joined them while I waited for the rolls to cook.

"Dean," I said "you've never met my daughter Callie before have you?"

Dean looked up, his eyes transfixed on Callie. After a moment he found his voice and shook his head. "No, no I have not. For a moment there I was seeing you all over again fifteen years ago." He stood up and shook Callie's hand, his eyes never leaving her face, "nice to meet you." Abel shot him a dirty look. Callie smiled shyly.

"Callie is changing her major." I said again to Dean. "She is interested in forensics and wants to get into that field. It seems she needs some help with her chemistry though and I thought maybe you could give her some pointers."

"Sure I'd love to." Dean said, "Do you Skype?" He asked Callie.

"Yes," Callie nodded.

"Great, I'll give you my email and we can chat that way. Forensics is a great field."

"Do you know a lot about it?"

"Some, I'm doing a lot of work with DNA right now."

Callie's eyes lit up like Christmas and soon the two of them were deep in conversation. Abel looked put out but never attempted to join in.

The timer went off and I took the rolls out of the oven. Nick helped me put the food on the bar and we made a sort of buffet line, carrying our plates to the table.

The food was good but having Callie there made it taste so much better. I was glad that Dean and Stephan had made it down too. This was my new family and I loved being with them all.

After dinner we all sat around the table talking and drinking wine. Callie cut into the pecan pie. "Umm," she said, "my favorite."

"There's Ice cream in the freezer if you want some." After that everyone decided it was time for desert.

We sat in the living room talking well into the night. I noticed that Callie and Dean had no problem finding a subject to talk about. In fact their conversation flowed from one topic to the next without missing a beat.

I suggested to Stephan and Dean that they stay the night and drive home in the morning and both agreed it was a good idea. Stephan took the room where I first stayed and Dean volunteered to crash on the couch. I brought out a pillow and some blankets for Dean then made my way to bed.

Nick came into the bedroom as I was changing into my night shirt and shorts. We lay talking for a while about the day and I mentioned something about Dean. Nick grew quiet for a minute then leaned up on an elbow.

"You do realize that he is in love with you?"

"Who," I asked, confused by his statement.

"Dean."

"What? No I don't think… What makes you say that?" My curiosity piqued I leaned up on an elbow so that we were facing each other.

"The way he looked at you the day I followed you to the hospital. And the way he looks at you every time he sees you." His face crinkled into a scowl, "looks like he's got it pretty bad."

I thought for a moment. "That doesn't seem to bother you."

"You've never given me a reason for it to bother me, I know you love me. And Dean – you were right, he is a good guy. I won't have any problem from him." Then he chuckled, "but Abel might." I grinned; the thought had crossed my mind. I changed the subject.

"So Mr. Cristo, you know I love you?" I asked trailing my fingers down his chest and belly along his happy trail.

"That I do Ms. Armand." I frowned.

"Ugg, I don't like that name anymore." My fingers are caressing his muscular arms.

"What would you like me to call you?" His thumb is tracing my lower lip.

"Hmm, baby will do." Nick laughed. My fingers are running down his side.

"Okay baby. I think I can do that." He says as his knuckles smooth my cheek.

"Can you do something else?" My hand moves back to his chest, stopping over his heart.

"What else?" His fingers trace down my neck then shoulder.

"Make love to me – all night." His hand now is in my hair, holding my head as he rolls over on top of me, covering me. "Oh yea baby," he growls "I can do that." Then his mouth claims mine.

After lunch the next day our four guests began preparing for their journeys home, loading luggage back into their cars. Abel had been even quieter today and a little withdrawn. I glanced at Callie and she just shrugged her shoulders, rolling her eyes, not knowing the reason for his mood.

When Abel slipped out to load his duffle into the car Dean slipped Callie his email information. Not wanting to make the situation any tenser he had waited until Able wouldn't see. Discreetly Callie slipped the paper into a pocket of her jeans.

Callie hugged me before she left. "I wish I could stay longer but Abel wants to get back and spend some time with his family."

"I understand," I said hope in my voice, "maybe Christmas?"

"Definitely, I'll plan for a longer stay then – drive my own car."

"That will be great." I hugged her again. "Be careful driving home."

"We will mom." She turned to Nick and to my surprise, hugged him tightly. "Take care of my mom." She whispered in his ear.

Nick hugged her back. "Will do," he whispered back.

Dean and Stephan both said their goodbyes and Dean quickly added, "Come see the lab, it's up and running."

"We will," I replied hugging both men, Nick shaking hands. It had been a good two days. Seeing Callie again, no longer angry at me, was the best part. As Dean and Stephan pulled out of the drive Nick and I walked arm and arm back inside.

Later that afternoon I received a text from Callie.

Home safe. Had a good time …. Abel broke up with me on way home. ;-)

Quickly I sent a text back noting the smiley.

Glad ur back safe and that things worked out ok. C U @ xmas. Love u

Her smiley face told me everything. She didn't have to be the bad guy after all. I was glad things had worked out for her.

NINETEEN

The knot in the pit of my stomach twisted, tightening as I walked up the steps that led to the courthouse. Muscles in my shoulders and up the back of my neck were tensing and I felt a headache coming on. I swallowed trying hard to push down the lump that was forming in my throat.

My court date had finally arrived but now that I was here I wanted it to be over and done with. This was going to be a battle and I knew it. I hoped I was strong enough to get through it.

Nick reached over and took my hand, giving me a reassuring smile. We had met with Dorian a couple of times in the past week to go over details. Dan's attorney had been in contact with him trying to negotiate a settlement. Dan wanted half of my retirement along with everything he'd already taken. I was surprised that he wasn't fighting for my house too but maybe his attorney had advised against it.

Dorian had not yet let them know that we knew about the money and the length of Dan's affair. If Dan had any idea he would postpone this for as long as he could. As backed up as the court system was it could drag out for years and I wanted this over ASAP. Right now he was feeling confident that he would win and was ready to go in front of the judge to do it. Dorian had smiled. "That is where we will get him."

The docket was to be heard in Reichert's court. With any luck none of the cases ahead of us would drag out. I was third on the list.

I let out the breath I'd been holding and walked through the glass door of the building. Nick stayed at my side and I was glad for the moral support. The knot in my stomach was now accompanied by a hundred flittering butterflies. Seeing the line of people waiting to walk through the security metal detectors made it even worse.

The very atmosphere inside was intimidating. The guards all looked so serious, or maybe just bored. My heart rate had kicked up a notch and my breathing was much faster. I tried to calm my nerves by taking long, slow, deep breaths but it didn't seem to help much. My palms were sweating now and I had nothing to wipe my hands on.

It was my turn now and the guard handed me a plastic bucket while he recited his canned phrase. "Purses and cell phones in the bucket. Please empty your pockets and place the contents into the bucket. If you have on a belt you may want to remove that as well."

I placed my purse and phone in the bucket. The guard must have seen the apprehension in my face and felt sorry for me. He suddenly smiled at me as he told me to walk through the metal detector.

His smile made me feel just the slightest bit better and I let out another breath when I passed through without a problem. Nick was right behind me and once we collected our belongings he took my hand and led me to the bank of elevators.

Entering the elevator Nick pressed the button for the third floor and we took a spot in the back as people poured in after us. I stared into the backs of six or seven other people.

It was a motley crew in front of me. Some were dressed in expensive suites while others wore sagging pants and stocking hats. A few dressed just casually.

I was glad I'd gone shopping for a new skirt and top. I wore a black pencil skirt that hit just above my knees and a white, fitted, button down blouse with long sleeves. Nick was wearing a pair of dark gray casual slacks, a white shirt tucked in but no tie. He was so handsome in anything but he looked really good now.

My free hand moved automatically to the pendant hanging around my neck, rubbing it between my thumb and forefingers. Nick caught my glance and squeezed my other hand before lifting it to his lips and gently kissing my fingers.

The elevator pinged as it came to a stop on the second floor. Everyone exited except for Nick and me. No one else got on with us. The door shut and a moment later we began to move up again.

This was probably the slowest elevator I'd ever been on in my life. My apprehension was building again with each passing second. When the door finally opened on the third floor I let out another breath. Nick pulled me aside. Holding me in his gaze he gently squeezed my shoulders.

"Breath baby," he urged me. "Everything is going to be ok. No matter what happens in here, we have each other." He planted a chaste kiss on my lips and I was so glad he was with me. He was right. Nothing else really mattered. For the first time this morning I began to relax.

Dorian met us just around the corner. We were almost an hour early so we went into a small room to discuss last minute details. Dorian made a few additional notes then we made our way into the courtroom and took our seats.

There was a low murmur of voices as attorneys and clients whispered back and forth. Dan and his attorney showed up with the harpy in tow and sat across on the other side of the room.

His attorney approached Dorian and the two of them walked a distance away talking quietly. Momentarily he returned and sat next to me. Leaning over he whispered. "She is still trying to get us to settle now and is getting a little nervous that we won't. I think she is figuring out we have something up our sleeve." He said looking very pleased with himself.

I was worried again. Suppose they leave and reschedule? I really don't want to drag this out. *I do have a life – yes, an awesome life now with Nick. To hell with it, what if they do reschedule? I can wait indefinitely and I'm not going to worry about it.* I suddenly felt one hundred percent better.

I squeezed Nick's hand and smiled. Giving me a knowing wink he put his arm across the bench behind my back, moving his thumb back and forth across my shoulder.

An officer of the court appeared from a side door. "All rise for the Honorable Judge Reichert." Everyone stood. A thin, white haired man walked up to the bench and took a seat not even looking across the room. He appeared to be in his seventies and I wondered curiously how long he had really lived.

The judge looked at his docket list studying it then after a long moment looked up. His eyes moved unseeingly out across the crowd and as I watched him I noticed an almost imperceptible twitch of his nose, followed by a

346

slight shift of his eyes. *He's smelling the room.* I wondered suddenly what he was capable of identifying with his scent. Has he done this so long that he can judge with his nose?

My thoughts wandered briefly to my expendable list I'd started in the hospital. When I left I had only acquired four names. Surprisingly enough most people where generally decent people. Even the drug addicts, for the most part, really didn't want to be addicted.

I pulled my thoughts back to the present situation. Judge Reichert was still looking around the room. Then his eyes were on mine and I saw the twitch of his nose again and his eyes visibly dilated, turning almost solid black.

He knows – knows that I'm a vampire, but what else did he just learn about me? His response was only momentarily and no one but another vampire would have noticed. The next instant his eyes appeared lazy, even unseeing again.

The first case went on for about an hour and due to the fact that there were children involved the judge ordered mediation. He also appointed an ad litem to represent the children. Luckily the next case was brief as both parties were in agreement and no children were involved. The judge singed the papers and the parties left the room.

My gut constricted again when my case number was called. Dorian and the other attorney approached the bench. They seemed to be in a heated discussion and the judge looked on with his seeming lazy disinterest. I wondered if I was going to have to take the stand. I hoped not, my stomach was once again filled with butterflies and knots.

After several moments the judge waved Dan's attorney off. When she turned around she was seething and she glared at Dan. *Uhh huh! She just found out about the money. He didn't tell even her and she's pissed. She is gonna look like a fool at the end of this one!*

Inside I was gloating. *Way to go Dan, now no-one is on your side!!* She walked back to where he was sitting and whispered in his ear. I almost laughed out loud at the expression on his face.

His mouth almost hit the floor and all of the blood drained from his face. I could almost hear it as small beads of sweat popped up on his forehead. The harpy noticed it too and she looked at him, fear now lining her face.

His attorney had somehow regained her composure as she turned to face the judge again. Dorian stayed near the bench and Judge Reichert flipped through a stack of papers. He was skimming, not reading everything and his face remained expressionless.

It took him several minutes to flip through the stack, then picking it up he tapped the bottom lightly on his podium to neaten it, laying it to the side once it was done.

Looking at Dan he told him to approach the bench. I wondered if he was going to have to take the stand. Dan and his attorney rose and walked forward. I tuned in my hearing toward them, wanting to hear everything. Judge Reichert was grave and no nonsense as he began to speak.

"You have come into my court today seeking a divorce from your wife and requesting a significant amount of compensation citing that you were emotionally and sexually deprived during the course of your eight years of marriage." *Oh, this was news. Dorian had not told me that-* "However, the evidence brought before me today would suggest otherwise. In fact it is apparent that you were involved in an extramarital affair for the entire length of your marriage while you let your wife support you.

And while she was supporting you, paying the bills you were rat holing monies away." I couldn't believe he had just said "rat holing" I almost laughed. "A rather large sum of money for the express intention of using it to start your new life with your lover. I am also told that after you left, while your wife was deathly ill and under someone else care, you returned to the house and removed just about everything that wasn't tied down."

Dan looked shocked. He probably hadn't even known that I had been – ill. He left before it happened and when he did see me again I was fine. At this point it didn't matter. The judge was making a great argument and I was not going to object.

Judge Reichert continued. "I am a fair man and have always been a fair man, but when I come across a scoundrel like you, a man that takes advantage of others good will and reciprocates with evil, well that just riles me.

The fact that you represented yourself as the victim makes it even more distasteful. As far as I'm concerned you never even tried to make your marriage work and because you were getting sexual gratification elsewhere, I would believe that it was probably your wife that has been both sexually and emotionally deprived these years. There is evidence to suggest you were the one who cared nothing for her or the marriage."

"I am not willing to give you a single penny of her retirement. You should have your own fund. As for the money that you were saving – you owe her half of that." I thought Dan was going to pass out and I heard the harpy gasp, then start to sob. *Bitch!*

But the judge was not finished. "You owe her half because you either had it or were saving it while you were married to her and still are married to her. But also I feel that some compensation is due her for supporting you all those years and for the belongings you removed from the home while she was ill.

According to this bank statement that I have before me you accumulated two hundred and fifty six thousand dollars. I don't really care at this point how much you had before you married. You have done this woman nothing but wrong and I will not tolerate this kind of maliciousness in my court.

I believe it is more than fair that you keep twenty percent and your wife gets eighty percent. However if you think this unfair and want me to put your wife on the stand so that I can hear her testimony I will oblige. But be warned, you may lose the entire amount if that happens. I will however grant you the divorce if that is what your wife wishes."

Wow! I truly couldn't believe what had just happened. For a fleeting moment I almost felt sorry for Dan, but I pushed those feeling aside quickly. Dan had brought this on himself. He was the one who had gotten greedy.

This was retribution for all of those years he'd taken from me, giving nothing in return. I had given to him freely from every resource I had; my time; my money; my soul and he had taken and taken draining everything and storing up for him and the harpy. No I would not pity him.

Dan stood before Judge Reichert speechless, his face contorted in disbelief and maybe agony. The harpy was crying louder now. The judge looked out at her but said nothing.

Dan's attorney was talking to him, reasoning when suddenly Dan turned and stormed out of the courtroom, cursing as he left. The harpy jumped to her feet quickly following him, looking bewildered.

Judge Reichert, still showing no sign of emotion said, "I'll take that as an agreement to my set terms." Then without hesitation struck his gavel and handed the stack of paperwork back to Dorian.

The officer of the court called the next case as Dorian made his way back toward me. With his head he motioned Nick and I toward the exit. I was reeling. Was that it? Was it over? What had actually happened?

Without hesitation I followed him out the door, Nick right behind me. As soon as we were out of the room Nick grabbed me, kissing me. "Congratulations Ms. No-Longer-Armand!" he said with a face splitting grin. Dorian turned and smiled pulling us a bit further down the corridor.

At the end of the hall I saw Dan and the harpy having a heated discussion. The harpy turned suddenly with a sour look on her face and stormed to the elevators. Dan walked slowly behind, sulking, not looking in my direction.

"What just happened in there?" I asked turning my attention back to Nick and Dorian.

Dorian laughed, "We won!" he said emphatically.

Then it finally hit me, my eyes widening as the meaning of Nicks words registered in my brain. "I'm divorced now?" I asked, suddenly realizing that was the only thing I really cared about.

"Yes," Dorian said, "I have the document signed and will take it down and have it filed immediately. It will take them a few days but they will send you a certified copy in the mail, but yes, you are officially free as of ten minutes ago."

I couldn't contain my joy. "Yes!" I said jumping up and down, pumping my fist in the hallway. Grabbing Nick I kissed him again feeling exuberant as my new found freedom washed over me.

All of the tension from the previous months slowly slipped away and I felt my body truly relaxing. I had not realized how tense I'd been. This was over. It was finally over – and we had won!

Nick wrapped his arm around my waist as we strolled into the restaurant. We had spent the rest of the day on the seawall relaxing. Nick had produced the small vial of wolf bane earlier when we stopped for drinks. His eyes had twinkled as he pulled it from his pocket. "I knew you would win but either way you would be divorced and I was ready to celebrate."

He had also packed us a change of clothes. I marveled at his fore site. It was a balmy day for mid-December – not unusual for the area at all. Tomorrow it might be thirty degrees, but today we were wearing shorts and flip -flops.

I was ready to celebrate too. It had never occurred to me that court would happen the way it did. I was still trying to get my head around it. Dorian had explained that it would take a while, maybe a month for the orders to be signed as far as the money part was concerned and then it would be pulled from Dan's account and sent to me.

Honestly I wasn't concerned with the money. It was the liberation I felt that kept me on a mental high for the rest of the day. I had sent Callie a brief text, promising more detail later then turned my phone off.

I wrapped my arm around Nick's waist and he tightened his grip on me. I loved this man and he loved me. His words from earlier came back to me. *No matter what happens we have each other. Yes, I have him and I would go thru hell to be with him for the rest of my life.* The thought warmed me and I leaned my head against his shoulder, a feeling of pure bliss enveloping me.

The black SUV drove slowly by the clinic where Doctor Lee worked. Lee was the writer of an article that appeared in the latest periodical that circulated among the vampire population. She had in fact written many articles for the journal but this one was particularly interesting. It described a young woman who had made the transition from human to vampire with her reproductive organs intact. It stood to reason that the young woman was a patient of Doctor Lee.

The call had been made and instructions had been received. The team would return after hours and enter the facility. Medical records would have to be accessed. The voice on the other end of the line wanted to know every detail of the patient.

There was a growing excitement in his voice. Was she the one he had been looking and waiting for all these years? He hung up the phone and his fingers rubbed along his chin. Slowly a smile spread across his face. Soon enough he would know.

TWENTY

Dean carefully measured and weighed the white rat making note of changes in the physical appearance as well. The rat had almost doubled its size in the past week and was now on a diet that consisted mainly of blood.

This was one of his personal experiments that he was conducting on the side in the basement lab. The DNA research in the main lab was going well and with each new piece of information he obtained he applied it to his experiments down here.

Having gotten the measurements he carefully placed the rat back into the steel box with tiny holes. The rat did not seem to be aggressive once it had fed, but he didn't want to take unnecessary risks.

Securing the lock, he recorded his information in the computer. He had obtained a new DNA sample that he would analyze tomorrow to compare to the original sample taken from the rat.

This was the fourth rat that he had worked with. The first one had begun violently thrashing about the cage within forty-eight hours of injection then died, succumbing to an intense fever. The second was the same except that it was only thirty-five hours before the thrashing had begun. The third rat began at eighteen hours.

With each successive rat he had made slight modifications to the serum based on the changes he identified in the DNA. This fourth rat had started the thrashing in less than six hours.

In the hours following, Dean had suspended it in a cooling bath he had made from an aluminum pan and a small pump to circulate the water. The rat had survived the fever and appeared to be thriving as long as blood was supplied.

Daily DNA samples were taken to track any changes noted. So far this rat had stopped showing changes after five days, four of which it remained in the cooling pan.

When it came to Dean's personal projects he had full autonomy. Stephan allowed him to conduct whatever experiment he wished as long as he was making progress on the work upstairs. Dean felt that the two projects were inter-related and he was continually gleaning new information from both projects.

With Kat's permission he had scoured her old house looking for a source that could supply him with her DNA – pre – vampire state. Finding an old hair brush under her bathroom sink he painstakingly removed each individual hair until he found one with an actual follicle attached.

He was ecstatic when he'd been able to extract a DNA sample from the hair. This allowed him to see and identify the changes that had occurred within Kat's DNA strand. For now he was attempting to identify and map out her new DNA sample. This was a tedious project and required a lot of rats.

Opting to work with no more than six rats at a time in the main lab, he had begun DNA modification, specific to the changes found in Kat's sample. Careful monitoring would be required to note the changes that occurred.

He looked at his watch, for now it was time to take a break. He thought awkwardly about that. Since when did he take breaks in his studies, especially when he was on the verge of a major breakthrough?

The answer to his question was a bit unsettling. He took breaks every night at this time because Callie would be contacting him on Skype. They would chat for hours; usually it started with a question in chemistry then turned into everything else until late in the evening.

Truthfully Callie had gotten the whole chemistry thing after just a few lessons. She was an incredibly smart young woman with all the beauty of her mother.

Dean frowned at the thought. He had loved her mother for years and had let her slip through his fingers more than once. Was this why he was now willing to take breaks from his work? He was actually letting someone into his very private life, exposing a little more every time he chatted with her.

Did he really want to go there? Part of him screamed no, stay away. Another part of him knew that he would be there every night, waiting for that familiar ping on his computer, at least until Callie, like her mother, fell in love with someone. Then he would fade forever into the background again watching in case she ever needed his help.

Dean sighed, feeling a bit defeated. He couldn't pursue Callie, just as he couldn't pursue her mother. What did he have to offer a girl like her?

Putting away a few pipettes and a box of slides, Dean made his way upstairs to the kitchen. Sara had made dinner over an hour ago, and as part of her new routine had set aside a covered plate for him. He was never on time for dinner, always finding one more thing to do in the lab.

As he removed the gold colored cover the aroma from the food made his mouth water. It was still warm. Sara had made prime rib – medium rare, with roasted potatoes and asparagus.

He had a few minutes before Callie would be on Skype so he sat at the bar to eat. That way he wouldn't have to pack his dirty dishes back down from his room later. Taking a bite he closed his eyes. Man that woman could cook!

Finishing his dinner he put the plate in the sink and headed upstairs with a glass of wine. He had never been a wine person before, preferring beer, but spending the last eight weeks with Stephan he had acquired a taste for the stuff.

Of course it could be the fact that he'd never had any good wine until he came to stay here. Stephan had an extensive wine cellar and impeccable taste. One area of the cellar was devoted strictly to collection. From what he could see Stephan would have to enlarge that area soon, having collected almost five hundred bottles, adding a new bottle each year.

Wine wasn't the only thing that was new to Dean. He had taken up sword play, as he referred to it, three times a week in the morning with Stephan. The old vampire was incredibly fit and he usually kicked Dean's ass, but Dean was getting better with each lesson. He was getting a bit trimmer around the waist too; due to the cardio and all the twisting he was doing swinging the sword.

True to his word Stephan had taken an active part in the lab. When the console had been delivered both men had taken a three day training class on how to operate it. Under Dean's tutelage he was learning how to prepare slides for various items. He also made sure that Dean had whatever he needed for the project.

When his first paycheck had been deposited Dean went to Stephan. It was more than he expected and wanted to be honest. Stephan simply waived him off saying he had raised him to a fair wage for the work he was doing.

Reaching the top of the stairs he turned and made his way down the hall to his room. As he entered he heard the familiar ping from his computer. His steps quickened, making his way to the desk. All of his thoughts about work melted away as he slid into the chair in front of the computer monitor.

Christmas holidays were just around the corner and I wanted to check on my house and tidy the yard again. Today was dreary and gray and a heavy mist had settled over the area making everything wet. The grass had stopped growing for the season but now leaves littered the yard and my pond lilies needed to be cut back for the winter.

I worked around the yard all morning spreading a lawn feeder after the leaves were picked up. One of my old neighbors came by to chit chat so we stood talking in the front yard for a long while.

When she mentioned that today was an early release day at school I decided to finish up and get to the store before it was filled to overflowing with families shopping for the holidays. Picking up the pace I hurried around the yard using up the rest of the fertilizer and began picking up lawn tools.

A few houses down some kids were getting home from school, while a man walked his dog down the street. Elsewhere a young mother attempted to load her young child into the family vehicle, and a jogger ran by listening to his iPod.

No one seemed to notice as the black SUV drove slowly by. In fact no one had noticed its presence in the neighborhood at all over the past few weeks. Had they paid attention they would have noticed the darkly tinted windows that were too dark to see through and the fact that it drove by almost every day.

Today, like every other day, the vehicle moved through, scanning the house at 3015 Pineloch. Inside the SUV someone made a phone call. "Sir the target has returned to her home. Are we to bring her in?" The voice on the other end of the line responded. "Not yet, but I want to track her every move. I don't want her getting away from us." "Yes sir," The man obeyed, "Juliet out." He hung up the phone then spoke into a small microphone.

The man with the iPod suddenly changed directions and made his way to the Acura parked at the end of the drive at 3015 Pineloch. Stopping behind the car he bent over with his hands on his knees as if resting.

Scanning the area to make sure he wasn't being observed he quickly placed a small object under the bumper then resumed his jog.

Turning onto the next street the jogger was approached by the black SUV. A side door was thrown open and the man scrambled inside and pulled the door shut as the vehicle drove out of the neighborhood.

Pushing the corner of the suitcase down I managed to get it zipped the rest of the way. I was finished packing for our trip to Stephan's. We would be spending the holidays at his house and Callie would be joining us there.

The arrangement had worked out perfectly as it was a much shorter drive for Callie. Stephan had some interesting news he wanted to share with us on the progress of his and Dean's studies.

Nick took the luggage out to the jeep to load it. We had planned to take the Acura but with the threat of bad weather the jeep seemed a better idea. Already the temperature was dropping and icy drizzle was falling from the sky.

I loved road trips during this time of year. Bundling up in the car with the heater on and dashing out into the freezing cold to snag a cup of hot chocolate or coffee at gas stations along the way. It didn't matter that our destination was only five hours away; I was still excited about the trip.

Throwing our winter jackets in the back seat I climbed in ready for the drive. Nick had the heat on full blast in an attempt to clear the windshield. He climbed into the driver's seat smiling and rubbing his hands together.

"Ready?" he asked excitement in his eyes. All of the Christmas gifts were stowed away in the back with the luggage. Quickly I went over my mental list checking off items. Even if I had forgotten something Stephan had pretty much anything we would need.

"Ready!" I grinned.

Nick put the car in gear then reached over for my hand squeezing it. "This will be our first Christmas together." I smiled remembering what I'd gotten for him. It was still two days till Christmas and the anticipation was killing me. I hoped he liked what I'd gotten for him.

As we drove further north the temperature plunged and the drizzle turned to sleet. The roads became icy and we passed several cars that had slid off the road into the ditch.

I was glad we were in the jeep and that Nick was driving. He was driving slower now but still confidently pushed on. Occasionally I would feel the change in the surface of the road as we moved across a patch of ice but the tires on the jeep kept good traction throughout.

After three hours we were less than half way there. The weather has slowed us considerably so we stopped to stretch our legs and grab something hot to drink. The jeep was covered in tiny icicles and the wheels each had an ice starburst formed around the hub from the spinning motion throwing the freezing rain out as we drove.

Nick walked around the vehicle knocking off the ice from the wheels and bumpers. He stopped for a moment looking at something that was frozen in the ice from the rear bumper, then deciding it wasn't important, tossed it aside into the ditch.

A few miles further down the rain stopped and the roads cleared and we were able to make better time. Fewer cars were on the road now and we took advantage of the open highway. When we finally pulled into Stephan's drive we were less than an hour behind schedule.

It was even colder here but dry and surprisingly the cold really didn't bother me like I'd expected it to. It was much more welcome than the hot humidity of summer. As we unloaded the jeep our breath made little puffs of steam in the cold air.

Inside Stephan had set up a huge tree in the parlor right in front of the windows. He seemed pleased with it as he showed Nick and I were to put the gifts. "I haven't had a tree in a very long time. It's been centuries since I've had anyone to share the holidays with."

His statement made me wonder about his life before and what loves he'd left behind when he was turned. It gave me a bit of insight into the more private side of this vampire I'd grown so close to.

Leaving our gifts under the tree we made our way upstairs with our luggage then returned to the main living area where we sat around the fire that burned in the huge fireplace.

Dean came up out of the basement surprised that we'd made it on schedule. He came over kissing me on the cheek then shook nick's hand, slapping him on the back.

"I'm going to the kitchen for some wine. Anyone else want some?"

"Yes." We all nodded. I started to get up to help him but he motioned for me to stay put.

"I've got it. I'll be right back." He walked off then in the direction of the kitchen and reappeared a few minutes later holding four wine glasses between the fingers of one hand and a bottle of chardonnay in the other. Placing the glasses on a corner table he retrieved a corkscrew from his back pocket and proceeded to open the wine, pouring each of us a glass.

"Did Stephan show you the lab yet?" He asked as he handed us the wine.

"No, we just got here a few minutes ago." I said taking a sip. The wine was cool and refreshing. "That's very good Dean, I thought you were more of a beer person."

"I was but Stephan's got me hooked on wine now. Come on I'll show y'all the lab."

We all followed him down the hall to the back of the house. I could tell he was excited because he was talking the entire way. Stopping outside the door he pulled a card from his pocket and swiped it through a card reader then punched in some numbers on a key pad to gain access. Nick and I were impressed.

"Stephan and I just thought we should have a little bit of security with all the expensive equipment and the testing we're doing." He explained. He swung open the door and motioned us in.

The room was nothing like I remembered it. It seemed bigger and was now full of equipment. Everything had a sterile, clinical look from the stark white walls to the stainless steel counters. Rows of fluorescent lights illuminated the entire room. There were rows of cages along one wall containing white rats.

Dean was talking a hundred miles an hour about the security, the fire containment system that Stephan had installed and the data backup that was in place. I walked around the room looking at his microscopes and Bunsen burner, finally stopping in front of the cages. Dean was animatedly talking to Nick about his findings.

Something inside one of the cages started moving and I stepped closer to get a better look. A large white rat was scratching around in its cedar shaving and when I approached it hid in the back corner. I tapped on the cage to get the rat's attention, trying to get it to move so I could see it. The rat turned to face where I was tapping the cage, sniffing the air as it cautiously approached.

"Careful Kat," Dean warned, "It bites." I withdrew my hand from the cage just as the rat attempted to bite where my finger had been.

Dean continued talking to Nick, explaining everything about the massive piece of equipment that took up almost the entire back wall. Stephan came to let us know that dinner was ready and we all headed to the main dining room.

A black Suburban pulled into the gas station. The driver scanned the parking lot, examining each car that was there. The signal had not moved from this location for several hours but it was apparent the vehicle was not here. The driver stepped out into the biting, icy wind and pulled his coat tighter around him. From the front seat of the Suburban he withdrew a handheld monitor.

A dot on the screen pulsed in the same spot. Moving toward the store the driver noted he was moving further away from the dot. He turned and looked the other direction. There was nothing there except the gas pumps, now void of cars.

Beyond that was a large ditch and a hundred yards of field that separated the gas station from the two lane highway. He walked in the direction of the pumps then past them to the ditch. His monitor was accurate within inches and he was almost on top of the dot now.

Carefully he stepped onto the frozen embankment of the ditch searching for good footing. He didn't want to go sliding on the ice into the bottom. There was nothing here in the ditch except frozen brown grass and highway trash along with some dirty brown snow. A large chunk of snow and ice caught his eye and he bent to pick it up.

"Goddamn it!" he swore when he saw the transmitter imbedded in the ice chunk. Slamming it onto the cement drive the ice shattered and he stooped to pick up the transmitter. He was proud of himself that the device was still working despite having been encased in ice but still knew the boss was not going to be happy. Once again the target had evaded them and they would have to wait for her to reappear. No, the boss was not going to be happy at all.

Dean had excused himself after dinner returning to the lab and Nick and I sat in the parlor with Stephan. Stephan was very pleased with Dean's work.

"He's very thorough," Stephan was saying. "He looks at things from every angle and asks all the right questions. He has a brilliant mind and I'm glad he's working for me. Already he has answered several of the questions I've been asking for centuries."

"How is the DNA mapping coming along?" I asked interested in Dean's work.

"Slowly, but we are moving forward a little every day. Dean is working on other projects in the basement lab that are significant to the DNA project. He works upstairs most of the day, goes to the basement for a while, eats a late dinner then Skype's with Callie."

This was news. I hadn't heard much from Callie lately so it explained what was occupying her time. "Sounds like you don't see him much."

Stephan shook his head. "Not much unless I go to the lab, which I do daily. But also we meet in the mornings and work with the swords. As Dean puts it – sword play. He's getting quite good at it and I think he is surprised at how much he enjoys it."

I smiled remembering how much I had enjoyed it myself. "I will have to practice with you while I'm here."

"I'd be delighted."

We were suddenly startled by a loud crash coming from down the hall followed by Dean chasing what appeared to be a large white beaver – except it lacked the flattened tail. On second thought I decided maybe it was a nutria.

"Watch out." Dean called to us. "Don't let that thing bite you."

The nutria scurried around the room with mad, red eyes, growling and hissing as it ran from one corner to the other.

"What the hell is that?" Nick asked looking on in astonishment.

Reacting to Nick's voice the nutria turned and charged at him. Nick was on his feet instantly and gave the animal a vicious kick with his booted foot, sending the animal flying across the room. The animal landed in the drapes, hanging by its claws, then scurried up to the top where it ran down the metal rod and jumped to fireplace mantel. Not sure where it was going next I crossed to the other side of the room.

Stephan and Nick were closing in on the animal, trying to corner it. "Don't try to catch it with your hands." Dean was saying. "He is one mean son-of-a-bitch. He'll take your hand off." I noticed that Dean was wearing some thick gloves.

Nick and Stephan held their ground trying to determine how best to capture the animal when it sprung over their heads and landed on the sofa in front of me. Nick was at my side in an instant, prepared to defend me from the animal. It perched on the back of the sofa glaring and snarling at us.

"Get upstairs." Nick commanded. I didn't argue but quickly jumped up and over the railing to the second floor landing. Turning to watch what was happening I saw the animal focus on me and I knew it was going to follow. It crouched low then sprung with its hind legs. I jumped to the side expecting it to land next to me but it never happened.

Dean had appeared just as the animal made its lunge. With sword in hand he swung at the animal slicing it cleanly in half mid-air. The animal fell to the floor with two thuds and blood spread crimson across the travertine tile.

The smell of the blood hit my nostrils immediately sending a shock through me. I looked at Stephan and saw his eyes dilate infinitesimally reacting to the scent of the blood and his back went rigid for a moment. Nick was at my side instantly, watching my face. I was alright and I nodded to acknowledge his concern. But the blood was not ordinary blood. It was vampire.

Dean looked up from the animal still gripping the sword. He was completely unaware of the shockwave that had passed through the room.

"Sorry guys about the mess, I'll get it cleaned up." Leaning against the sofa he gingerly removed his right glove. His hand was covered in blood, dripping off his thumb and index finger from a steadily flowing wound.

It was then that I realized he'd been bitten and I went to assess the wound. Stephan called for Sara and she came quickly with a mop to clean up the floor, placing the rodent in a plastic bag. Stephan instructed her to carry the carcass down to the incinerator to be burned. I took Dean into the kitchen to wash his wound. Nick followed us.

"What kind of rat was that?" Nick asked again.

"Just a regular lab rat," Dean replied, "with a few DNA modifications." I removed Dean's other glove. "It only got my right hand." He was saying. He held up the glove looking at where the animal's incisors had sliced through the fabric.

"What are those gloves made of?" Nick asked.

"Kevlar – and good quality stuff too."

"Shit!" Nick exclaimed "you weren't joking about it taking off a hand."

"It would have had mine if I wasn't wearing the gloves. I was down in the lab trying to get a new DNA sample and I guess he decided he wanted one of mine." He laughed hoarsely.

The bite on Dean's hand went clear through the heel of his thumb and was an inch long. He was hurting pretty badly but he was still able to move it with no problem. I cleaned it as good as I could using some betadine I had in my first aid kit after flushing it with sterile saline. After that I sutured it closed and wrapped it loosely with gauze. "Don't wrap it too tight," he had complained. "I have to be able to drive with it. I'm leaving early to go pick up Callie."

"I thought Callie was driving in." I said hearing this news.

"She was going to but I told her I didn't want her driving in the snow and she was fine with me picking her up."

"So I take it you talk to her often."

"Every day on Skype," he admitted – giving nothing away. Then he added, "I'm tutoring her in chemistry."

"No wonder she doesn't have time to talk to me." I said jokingly. Secretly I wondered about the two of them.

TWENTY-ONE

Dean had gone up to bed for the night but Nick, Stephan and I were restless. The sudden invasion of the scent of fresh blood had us worked up.

No one had mentioned the distinct vampire scent the rat's blood carried. When asked, Dean had implied it was an experiment but he didn't allude to the kind of experiment. If Stephan knew anything about it he didn't mention it and surely he had to know what Dean was working on here in his home. Didn't he?

I felt certain Nick and Stephan would be able to recognize the vampire scent. They had been around a lot longer than me and I had recognized it. Since neither of them said anything about it I pushed it out of my mind. It must not be that important.

Stephan had casually mentioned earlier that he'd noticed quite a few deer and hog tracks nearby. He didn't have to tell anyone that he was suggesting a hunt. It would be a good way to burn off the adrenaline brought on by the rat incident and we could feed as well. It wouldn't be as satisfying as human blood but any fresh blood was better than nothing at all.

At midnight we set out on foot. I had transfigured into my leather suit for the hunt. It was more natural to move in, not to mention easy to clean. Anything we caught was to be brought back for the meat once drained. Nothing would be left to waste. We hunted as a pack cutting a wide circle getting the wind to our faces. It didn't take long to pick up the scent of deer and there was more than one.

We followed the scent for miles keeping a steady pace. The deer could run fast on their four legs and we might need a burst of energy to catch one if it ran. Moving downhill into a small valley the tall grasses and scrub oak started getting thicker and the deer scent got much stronger. They had bedded down for the night in the tall brown grass. We moved cautiously forward, watching. It was a large group of five or six does and a buck.

We were within a few yards of the deer when the wind suddenly changed carrying our scent to them. They bolted, not certain where the threat lie. In their confusion one of the deer ran straight at me then turned at the last possible moment, taking off at a dead run.

I was fast but overshot my mark several times as the deer dodged and turned in its attempt to evade me. I was losing ground and my deer was about to be home free, then I lunged.

The deer's hind legs buckled as I sank claws deep into its hindquarters dragging it down with my weight. In full on predator mode I had changed into a great cat and overcome my prey at the last second.

The deer was down scrambling to regain a foothold, hooves thrashing frantically. Its fear only served to intensify my feral instincts. I was on its back in moments, breaking its neck, stilling its hooves. Then I felt my fangs descend as I sank my teeth into the still throbbing artery along its graceful neck.

Its life's blood flowed freely and I drank long and deep as the warm liquid filled me, satisfying the deepest cravings of my preternatural instincts. Every experience the deer had lived through I was experiencing in my mind.

I was in tune with the deer, acknowledging the life that flowed out of its veins and into my own. As its heart beat slowed, mine increased. As its body cooled, mine burned with the heat of a furnace. I was filled with strength as the deer breathed its last and became limp.

It was then in these last moments that I began to understand the flow of the universe and how we are all connected. This deer would never truly die as long as I was alive because it was now a part of me. I even had its memories. This was a peaceful side of a kill that I had not before experienced. Unlike taking the blood of the humans I'd hunted and witnessing the violence in their lives, here I learned that there was balance.

True, not all humans were violent but my choice was to not hunt the innocent among them. I would never experience the serenity I felt now from human blood. Seeing this for the first time I suddenly realized my role in life, whether I wanted it or not, my place would be to help the human race as only someone immortal could. We were here to guide mankind.

Nick and Stephan had managed to subdue their prey as well. We all fed well and were fully sated when we made the journey back to the big house. By the time the first pink light broke across the horizon three deer hung fully dressed and ready for the packing house. Stephan cut some fresh meat for later then packed the rest in ice. Later that morning a truck arrived to take the meat to process.

I went upstairs to shower. Dean had left earlier to pick up Callie. They would be back at the house by ten barring any delays. Nick joined me in the shower and we took turns washing each other, then went to bed for a nap before Callie arrived. Curling into Nick's arms I lie listening to the rhythm of his breathing until I drifted off to sleep.

My sleep was filled with images that collided and morphed into other images. Images of Callie and bleeding deer; Orlando with his golden chains; Stephan and Dean fighting – swords clanging; giant vampire rats and a pair of eyes so green they appeared to glow in the dark and they were watching us – watching me, like a predator ready to pounce.

TWENTY–TWO

My eyes flew open to the sound of tires on gravel and I knew that Dean and Callie were at the gate. I must have subconsciously been listening for their arrival because usually I tuned out such sounds. If I didn't I would go crazy with everything that I was able to hear rattling around in my head.

Sitting up in bed I realized that Nick was no longer beside me. Hurriedly I got up and dressed, going downstairs to meet them. The green eyes from my dream returned to my thoughts and I had an uneasy feeling but I dismissed it as quickly as it came. Callie was here and this would be our first Christmas together since she'd left to live with her dad.

Walking out the front door I met Callie coming up the steps with a chocolate pound cake in hand. She handed it to me and gave me a kiss on the cheek.

"Thank you," I said smiling. She smiled back at me.

"The kiss is from dad and the cake is from Monica and dad. They both wanted me to tell you and Nick Merry Christmas."

It had been years since I'd seen David – Callie's dad. We had stayed friendly toward each other but when he remarried I did my best to stay away so that things wouldn't be "weird." I didn't want to be the ex-wife that was always around, preferring to only contact him when necessary.

When Callie was fifteen he and Monica had moved due to a job transfer which made it easier to stay away, but harder for Callie. Come to think of it, their move had probably just added to the tense situation with Callie at home.

"How is everyone?" I asked speaking of her dad's family.

"Dad is good. Monica is good. Donny and Danielle are finally starting to act like normal human beings." Donny and Danielle were Callie's half brother and sister; a set of twins that were six years younger than Callie.

"How old are they now?" I asked.

"Just turned fourteen last month," Callie replied.

I smiled again. "Things will get better. At least they have both parents to keep them corralled." The kids weren't bad per se, but still I felt sorry for anyone who had two teenagers living under the same roof at the same time. One was all I could deal with. Sometimes more than I could. Callie must have read my expression because she quickly retorted.

"I wasn't that bad!" she said following me into the house.

The next morning Callie awoke to find Stephan and me dueling in the parlor, being careful not to knock over the Christmas tree. She watched in disbelief as we moved about the room like the characters in an action scene from a movie.

I was a bit rusty after months of non-practice but it came back to me quickly. I was confident not only with the sword but also with what I was able to make my body do. Jumping and flipping in the air to avoid the tip of Stephan's sword while finding my mark on him.

Our duel went on for thirty minutes or more until Stephan backed me into a corner I couldn't get out of. I conceded the victory to him.

"Well done Katherine," he said taking my sword. "Your skill and confidence has grown despite not practicing every day." I smiled at the compliment.

"Where did you learn to do that mom?" Callie asked astonished.

"Stephan taught her." Dean said walking into the room, removing his shirt as he did. "He is also teaching me." Dean's lean body rippled with corded muscle as he moved across the floor to where Stephan stood. He looked damn good and I couldn't help but notice the look of pride in Callie's eyes as she watched his every move.

They had disappeared last night after dinner, I think to the lab, but I wasn't going to go searching. They had been pretty cozy since their arrival and I for one was happy for the two of them. Dean was a good man and I trusted him explicitly and Callie was no longer a little girl but a grown woman.

"Are you here for a challenge?" Stephan asked eyeing Dean with amusement. Dean nodded. "Choose your weapon then." Stephan said motioning toward the table at the far end of the room.

Dean crossed to the table where he chose a pair of twin katanas. I was impressed that Dean would select the katana at all, much less a pair of them and I was curious to see how far he'd come in his training.

This pair of swords was some of Stephan's favorites. He had acquired them on one of his many trips to Japan and often practiced alone with one or both of them. He had leather holsters that could be worn crisscrossed on the wearers back and one that could be worn with the traditional obi sash. I suggested we carry the duel out to the courtyard. Both men agreed.

Nick had gone into town on an errand so it was just Callie and I that followed the two men out to the courtyard. As they led the way I tried to remember how long Dean had lived here – an attempt to gauge where his skill level should be with the swords.

I quickly learned he was much more advanced than what I'd anticipated. He was agile and fast, wielding the twin katanas as if he'd been born to use them. He possessed a grace and form that was not unlike Stephan's own. Stephan had taught him well, but Dean had excelled and the gleam of pride in Stephan's eye for his protégé was unmistakable.

I watched in awe-struck wonder as the two men thrust and parried – Dean using both swords to block and deflect Stephan's advances. Both men were sweating now despite the cold air. It was a clear day and the sun reflecting off their wet bodies mingled with the steam that rose in wisps giving an otherworldly quality to the scene.

Muscles coiled and released in powerful motion as bodies twisted and arms flexed and extended with each strike. A sense of deja-vu filled me with each clang of metal on metal. For a fleeting moment a scene from my dream passed before me then vanished like smoke before my eyes.

For a human, Dean did exceptionally well against Stephan. True Stephan could quickly overpower him if he so desired. In an instant the sword play could become deadly but today was not about power – rather confidence and skill. As I watched Dean I realized he had ample of both.

It came as no small surprise that Dean won the match, besting Stephan with the two katanas crossed at his throat. Stephan smiled and surrendered his sword. Both men had several cuts where the blades had grazed each other and I hoped that Callie wouldn't notice that Stephan's were already healed. Luckily she was too engrossed in the wounds Dean had endured to notice.

Callie hurried Dean off to wash his wounds but I stayed behind with Stephan. I knew he was fine but I wanted to talk to him.

"I'm thoroughly impressed with what you've taught Dean." I said. Stephan once again smiled knowingly.

"He is very teachable and I have immensely enjoyed having him as a student. But he has taught me much as well." He paused a moment reflectively. "For the first time in my very long life I feel like I have a family; You Katherine, and Nicolas and now Dean. He would make a great vampire don't you think?" I smiled and silently nodded my acquiescence then together we walked back inside, arm in arm.

Callie and Dean had disappeared once again then returned bundled up to announce they were going into town to window shop and explore the town. They asked Stephan and I if we wanted to go along but we both declined, Stephan offering information on a few attractions they might find interesting. Once they were gone Stephan retired to his study so I busied myself wrapping a few last minute gifts and hoping Nick would not be too long.

Just as I was finishing the last package Nick walked into the room, a secret smile on his face. I was glad he was back. Even though we spent so much of our time together I still missed him when he was away, even if only for a few hours. In such a short time he had become my world and my life seemingly revolved around this beautiful man.

Seeing the look on my face he closed the distance between us and enfolded me in his arms. I nuzzled my face into his chest breathing deeply of his scent. There was nothing I loved more than the smell of Nick and breathing him in evoked a myriad of memories and emotions. He pulled back and traced his thumb along my lower lip before kissing me gently.

"I everything alright?" he asked.

"Yes," I replied. "I just love being close to you and missed you while you were gone." Nick laughed. "I was only gone a few hours."

"I know." I said standing on my tip toes to kiss him again. "What did you do while you were gone?"

"I can't tell you," He said, his eyes crinkled in a smile. "What did you do?'

I flopped down on the bed and he sat next to me as I told him about the events of the morning. He listened intently as I recounted every detail of the swordfight between Stephan and Dean. When I finished he arched a brow at me.

"Sounds like you were paying pretty close attention to Dean and his muscles." I gasped at his insinuation in mock indignation.

"Uh-huh," I said climbing into his lap straddling him, gazing into the deep brown of his eyes. Everything about this man turned me on and sitting like I was, pressing into him was incredibly arousing.

"They were some pretty fine muscles too." I said walking my fingers up his chest. "Nice pecs. Nice delts. Nice biceps, almost as nice as yours." Reaching down I grabbed the hem of my shirt and pulled it over my head then removed my bra as well. My nipples beaded immediately as the cold air hit them.

"Oh baby," Nick purred as I reached to pull his shirt off and pressed my bare breast into his chest.

"And if you don't believe me you can check right here." I said tipping my head to one side and tapping at the small vein in my neck.

Nick growled; his eyes like melting chocolate, dark and dilated as he bit into the vein. Instantly my cleft saturated, slick within the delicate folds. Nick's erection was pushing against his jeans, hard against my sex as he drank from me. He pulled back, a look of bewilderment in his eyes then returned to my neck to drink again.

We made love slow and gentle and I fed from him as my orgasm exploded through me. I would never get enough of him. Never tire of the feel of his cock inside me or the safety of his arms around me. We lie still until his cock stopped pulsing, emptying completely inside me.

Nick leaned up on one elbow, his other hand gently caressing my arm as we faced each other.

"I saw something just now when I fed from you. Something in your memories," He paused. "I would like you to tell me about it." I nodded waiting for him to continue. "It was a pair of green eyes; Insidious green eyes. What do you remember them from?"

I knew immediately what he was talking about. "I-it was a dream," I stuttered. "A dream I had after our hunt. That is the only place I've ever seen them, but in the dream they were watching us – me. Why do you ask?"

"It's nothing sweet heart," Nick said reassuringly, "I was just wondering." But his eyes still looked concerned and I couldn't shake the feeling that there was more to it than what he'd admitted to.

Later that evening Nick found Stephan alone in his study and approached him about Kat's dream.

"I swear," Nick said, "When I saw the eyes – they had to have been Vladimir's. But how or why would Kat be dreaming about someone she's never seen or ever heard of before?"

"Are you sure it was Vlad?" Stephan asked.

"He's the only vamp in the world I know of with eyes like that. Kat said in her dream the eyes were watching her. I'm just concerned. That's all."

"Well I don't have an answer to your question at this time but I will look into it. In the meantime let me know if anything else comes up."

With that Nick turned and left the study. As soon as Nick left the study Stephan turned to the expansive shelf of books. After looking for several minutes he retrieved the ladder and climbed up to the top shelf. He selected a book that, by the looks of it, was as old as the vampire himself then settled back down at his desk and opened the book....

Christmas Eve dawned freezing cold and raining
but as the day progressed the temperature rose slightly
and by late afternoon it had started snowing. By dinner
time it was black outside and snowing heavily, giant flakes
floating out of the sky on a windless night.

For a while we all sat under the cover of the back
porch and watched as the courtyard transformed into an
ice palace. Icicles hung from the eaves and tree branches
where the rain had frozen earlier in the day and a thick
layer of new snow blanketed everything in luxurious
white, sparkling like diamonds in the lamplight.

We retired to the dining room for dinner then later
to the parlor where we sipped red wine and watched the
fire flicker and dance among the logs in the fireplace.
Sara brought a tray of pie slices out and we all had a piece.
I enjoyed the rest of the evening chatting with Callie, the
first time we'd really talked since she'd gotten in.

I don't know if it was the events of the last few days
or just my overactive mind but when I finally dozed that
night my sleep was once again filled with strange dreams.
The green eyes were back again, but this time there was a
face to go with them.

The eyes were getting closer and a feeling of unease niggled at me in the back of my mind. As one dream melted into the next the worry remained. I felt the need to protect Callie from some unseen threat. Then Nick was there and I knew everything was going to be alright.

Nick lay awake watching Kat as she slept. She was restless, tossing and turning almost immediately after falling asleep. He'd never heard her talk in her sleep before but tonight she was – though most he couldn't make out. He wondered what she was dreaming about as he watched her fists clench, her knuckles turning white and her brow pucker into a tight frown.

He considered waking her but finally just decided to pull her close. Instantly her body relaxed as he pulled her back against his chest, nuzzling his face into her hair and whispering gently to her. His arm draped over her waist and she grabbed is hand and entwined her fingers with his. "I love you Nick," she whispered still asleep.

"I love you too sweetheart," he said wrapping himself around her like ivy then fell asleep.

Dean lay awake staring up at the ceiling. He had come up against a brick wall in his experiments. The death of his latest rat had been a setback but he could duplicate that. So far he had managed to reduce the transformation time down to a couple of hours total but other than being vampire in nature they had none of Kat's special abilities. This frustrated him and he ran his fingers thru his hair. WHY?

This question had been at the forefront of his mind for weeks now. The rats were being injected with Kat's modified DNA blood and they were changing quickly as he'd hoped but why didn't they have her abilities?

He replayed the conversation he'd had with her at the restaurant a thousand times and could never glean any new information from it. He thought about the night at the hospital. He'd heard the story a hundred times – Kat was assessing the patient…..

As a light bulb flickered on in his head Dean sat bolt upright in his bed.

"Of course!" he said to himself aloud, "the Ativan. That must explain it. Kat received vampire blood with a dose of benzodiazepine. It must be in the receptors. The benzo must have blocked certain receptors. Instead of acting on them to create certain characteristics they were left open, unsuppressed!"

He had been looking at this trying to figure out why the blood wasn't making the same changes in the rats when all along it was the blood on certain receptors that was preventing these changes. He flew out of bed and down to the lab. Within minutes he had a new rat and a syringe with Kat's DNA modified blood.

If his theory was right in just a short period of time he would have a vampire rat with all of Kat's abilities. Hopefully it wouldn't turn into a rhino and demolish his lab.

Digging around in his medication store he found a vial of Ativan. Carefully drawing up a small amount into syringe he mixed the two then injected the serum into the rat. Now he just had to wait.

The smell of fresh ground coffee brewing brought me out of my dreams to find Nick entwined around me. He stirred as I attempted to dis-entangle myself from him.

"Merry Christmas baby," he said kissing my hair. I smiled and returned his kiss.

"Merry Christmas to you too."

We dressed and went downstairs to fresh coffee and a huge breakfast that Sara had made. Nick and I had finished eating when Callie came in followed by Dean who looked as if he'd spent the night in the lab. Stephan had eaten before any of us and was, as usual, practicing with his swords in the parlor. After breakfast we all went into the parlor to exchange gifts.

Buying for Callie had been easy. She was still living with her dad and only working part time so there was a lot of stuff she needed for school that I knew her dad couldn't afford with all the other mouths he has to feed.

I bought her a laptop computer and printer for doing her homework on. I knew she was sharing one with the twins up until now and it was time she had one of her own. I had spoken with David and he had agreed that she really needed one for her school. I also bought her a new Droid Razr phone. She loved everything.

Everyone else was difficult to buy for. We all had pretty much anything we needed or wanted so I had to get creative and creativity just isn't one of my strong suites.

Because I knew Dean liked to read I bought him a couple of books from Nick and me. One supposedly written by a vampire called *"To Walk in Shadow"* and one just for fun called *"So now you're a vampire – how to navigate in the world of the undead."* He got a kick out of both of them promising to read them soon.

For Stephan I chose a jeweled globe for his study and a small framed portrait of Nick and me. He beamed when he saw the portrait and I knew it was because it was the first from his new found family.

Nick had been extremely difficult to buy for. Like me, Nick had nothing that he needed and didn't want a lot of anything. I wound up getting him a nice laminated map of the world for his office wall, a travel planning guide and a pair of airline tickets to our first destination, France,

406

in March of the New Year. This was only part of my gift to him, the rest I would give him in private later.

I sat back to watch as everyone opened their gifts. I was surprised to see that Dean had bought Callie a necklace. It was both beautiful and fitting. Made of silver it was a double helix DNA pendant hung from a delicate silver chain.

He had put a bit of thought into his gift to her and was rewarded with a huge hug and squeal of delight when she opened it. I'd never seen Dean look happier than he did at her response to the necklace.

I didn't see anything else after that because Nick surprised me with his gift to me – a ring. Fashioned of Platinum the band was made up of several delicate rope looking strands, entwined around a red, heart shaped stone. Placing it on my finger he told me the ropes were my love and the heart was his that he'd given completely to me. I cried as I kissed him, at a loss for words. He understood.

Later, alone in our room I gave him his other gift. Over the last two months I'd spent a lot of time online and with Elijah making what was now Nick's family tree. It was three feet wide and four feet long. Together Elijah and I had managed to get a picture of almost everyone and we had birth and death dates for each person.

Nick sat and studied each face and the dates before turning to me.

"Thank you Kat," he said pulling me close. "This means so much to me."

"I wouldn't have been able to do it without Elijah. I'm glad I was able to find as many pictures as I did." Nick pulled me into his lap and kissed me.

"Our first Christmas together baby – The best one I've ever had."

TWENTY-THREE

Two days later Stephan met Nick in the study.

"I've been doing a bit of reading since we last spoke," Stephan started, "and it seems that Kat may be having premonitions. Once again this is unfamiliar territory since I've never known anyone else with these abilities. However, according to my resource books, vampires used to possess these powers."

"Premonitions, why would Kat be having premonitions about Vlad? If that's true then we have trouble. He was watching her in her dream. I can't imagine Vlad watching Kat being a good thing."

"Don't get too worried about anything yet. Vlad is a very powerful and influential vampire. Most of us meet him at some time in our lives. If what Kat is seeing is a premonition it could be something years from now.

It is also possible that she collected his image from your own memories without realizing it. Even if it is a premonition it doesn't mean it has to happen, only that the possibility is strong."

"Yea, maybe you're right. So you think I shouldn't say anything to her then?"

"Considering that we have no reason to believe that Vlad even knows about her, or much less is watching her, I don't see any reason to alarm her. In the meantime we should keep our eyes and ears open. If she truly has the ability to see into the future then we'll see evidence of it."

Callie and I had gone into town to catch some after Christmas sales and have some girl time before she went back home. Really I wanted to talk to her alone. We'd only got to talk for a little while Christmas eve and with everyone in the room I felt it wasn't the right time or place.

"So how is your school coming along? I take it Dean is helping you with your chemistry."

"School is great and Dean has been a god-send for the chemistry. I couldn't have gotten through it without help."

"You two are talking a lot I take it. He seemed to know more about your travel plans than I did." Callie was quiet for a minute. I turned so that I could see her face. "Not that I mind. Dean is a great guy Callie. I'm just curious." Callie visibly relaxed as she let out her breath. "So what is going on with you two?"

Callie smiled. "Well, we talk a lot and we seem to have tons to talk about. He helps me with my homework and has helped me to really understand so that I can do most of the work on my own. But we still sit up and talk way into the night almost every night."

"Do you like him?"

"Oh yea – very much. He is smart and totally hot and he just has the best smile ever. Most of the time I think he likes me but… well he hasn't tried to kiss me or even hold my hand since I've been here so I'm not sure anymore. I'm afraid I was reading more into his willingness to tutor me than there really is."

411

"But you skype every night when you're at school?"

"Yes, every night at seven."

"Honey, I have known Dean for a long time and if he is taking time away from his projects to talk to you for hours then trust me he likes you, a lot."

"So you would be ok with our age difference?"

"He's not that much older than you. What maybe seven or eight years?"

"Nine…well almost."

"Age can be a big thing for some people but it doesn't really matter if you have common interests and goals."

"What do I do then to get him to make a move? I mean I have put myself out there so many times with just nothing, but sometimes the electricity is so strong in the air you could power the room with it."

"That strong huh?" I laughed.

"Oh mom, you know what I mean don't you? I can just feel the attraction but then I don't know if he can feel it too or if it's just me."

I laughed. "Yes darling I know what you're talking about." I thought for a moment about Dean and realized that he had loved me for years and never acted on it. I would never tell Callie this however.

"I think that you are right about Dean. He is incredibly smart and attractive but for whatever reason he thinks that you are too good for him so he may never make the first move. Baby girl, you will probably have to make that move and then convince him that only you can decide who is or isn't good enough for you. You'll have to make him understand that you think he is good enough and that is all that matters."

Callie considered what I said then nodded. "I hope you're right mom."

We ate lunch together then made our way back with our purchases. Callie was quiet all the way back to Stephan's and I suspected she was formulating her plan. I smiled to myself. Dean didn't have a chance!

Dean sat at his desk staring off into space. He had come to the lab to get some work done but was too preoccupied to get into it. Callie was going home tomorrow and his thoughts had turned to his conflicting emotions.

The last thing he wanted to do was drive her home in the morning. Not that it was a problem, he just didn't know if he could be that close to her again for that long in the car. He'd gotten close to her. Too close and he knew he had no right.

She was a beautiful, smart young woman with her whole future ahead of her. But right now he was feeling selfish and what he wanted was to claim her for his own. Not that it mattered. What would someone like Callie ever see in a lab rat like himself?

The truth was, he told himself, he had allowed himself to see more into their relationship than what was really there. To Callie he was nothing more than her tutor and friend. It could never be more than that – could it?

He looked at the latest entry in his log book before closing it and putting it away. Any other time he would have been ecstatic. After all he had achieved his goal. The rat could definitely change.

He had realized earlier this week when the rat had been startled that its fur had changed colors, camouflaging itself to blend in with its surroundings. Then at one point when he had tried to extract the rat from its cage it had bristled up with what appeared to be porcupine quills. Try as he might he just couldn't get excited about it.

He breathed out a sigh then pushing himself to his feet locked the lab and left. He headed for the kitchen. Right now he could use a glass of wine or maybe just some milk. Anything that would help him sleep tonight and get him through the next twelve hours.

Walking into the kitchen he opened the fridge and stood staring blankly at the contents. He was so caught up in his thoughts he didn't notice when someone walked up next to him.

"Well, have you made a decision yet?" Dean jumped, taken off guard by the sudden appearance of Callie standing next to him.

"Huh……What?" he asked not understanding the question. Callie was standing next to him wearing nothing but a night shirt that hit her mid-thigh and the light from the refrigerator shone through illuminating her shapely form beneath it. He sucked in a sharp intake of breath at the site.

"Have you decided what you want from the fridge? I was feeling like a snack maybe."

"Oh – yea," he said pulling out a carton of milk. "Thought maybe some milk would help me sleep."

"I'll take a glass of that too. Probably don't need to eat this late. Milk should be ok." She opened a cabinet and took out two glasses and Dean poured them each one. They sat down at the breakfast bar with their glasses of milk.

"Actually I wanted to talk to you. I didn't see you much after dinner." Dean nodded. He had deliberately disappeared. Being near her was just too much tonight. It would be okay again when she was on the other end of a computer chat. At least he hoped.

"Yea I went to the lab to work on some stuff. Didn't get much done though."

"Well I was just wondering what time you wanted to leave tomorrow." She lied.

"Oh – well just whenever you're ready to go. Not in any kind of rush." He quickly threw back his glass of milk. He needed to get away from her before he broke. Getting up he walked to the sink and rinsed his glass then turned running straight into Callie. She was so close he could smell her body wash, feel the heat radiating off of her.

She smiled up at him reaching around him to put her glass in the sink, effectively trapping him against the cabinet. *God she is so beautiful – Does she know how gorgeous she is? And that mouth.*

He shut his eyes. His breathing was laborious and ragged. She was so close and he was incredibly aroused by her nearness. He was fighting the urge to pull her to him with every ounce of strength he had.

Looking up into his hazel eyes she moved even closer. "There's something else I need to know Dean." His eyes snapped back open.

"What else?" he asked trying to hide his increasing discomposure and failing miserably; his voice coming out hoarse in barely a whisper, his mouth instantly dry.

Reaching up to his face she ran her fingers along his cheek down to his chin. His eyes closed against the sensual assault. When he opened them again he saw her standing on tip toes, her mouth moving close to his ear.

"I need to know if you want me the way I want you?"

He knew he should push her away but he couldn't. Every part of him ached for her. Then she kissed him. Her lips were so soft – divine. He couldn't fight. Not anymore. She was there and he wanted her.

Her hands moved around his neck and he responded wrapping his arms around her waist and back, pulling her closer. He groaned as he lost all control, his mouth devouring hers, his tongue licking, exploring.

Her hands were fisting in his hair as his mouth kissed a trail down her neck. She pulled away slightly resting her forehead against his.

"Take me to bed Dean." She implored. Carrying her over to the bar he placed her on a barstool, his eyes searching hers.

"I don't think I can." He started.

"Why not, do you not want me?" She was hurt at his rejection.

"No... that's not it at all."

"Then what is it Dean?"

He sighed and looked at her defeated. "It's just that.........well you are smart and beautiful and I'm..."

"Dean I am smart and I am a grown woman capable of making my decisions. And you are...... well more than I could have ever hoped for. I want to make love to you. I want you to take me to bed."

"Are you sure?" he asked. She pulled him close again and kissed him deeply.

"More sure than I've ever been in my life."

His face lit up with a thousand megawatt smile as he picked her up into his arms and carried her out of the kitchen and up the stairs to his room. He didn't even set her down as he pushed the door shut behind them.

"Are you sure this is what you want?" He asked "Because I know I want this – have wanted it for a while now."

Callie smiled again and stroked his face with her hand. "Yes, I'm sure." He buried his face in her neck trying to regain some control.

"Babe, I sure hope your mom doesn't kill me for this!" Then his mouth found hers once again.......

TWENTY-FOUR

I awoke to the annoying sound of my alarm clock and flipped the switch off before stretching the remaining grogginess from my body, thankful it had interrupted my dream.

This was the third day in a row that I'd had that awful dream and it was starting to concern me. In fact every night since Christmas, if I dreamed at all, he was in it.

Those green eyes and that ruthless expression gave me shivers every time I thought about it. I had decided a few weeks ago that it was probably something to do with my hormones and pushed it out of my mind.

It was two o'clock in the afternoon February twelfth and I was contemplating setting my nap alarm for another hour. I just couldn't get enough sleep these days.

Since arriving back home after Christmas there had been a million things to deal with. A couple had made an irresistible offer on Angie's house so I decided to sell it. It had taken the entire month to close and had just signed the final paperwork yesterday.

In two weeks Nick and I would be flying out to France to start our European tour. I had so much to do to get ready by then. We would be gone for a while so I had to arrange for mail to be picked up and bills to be paid.

Two days from now would be Valentine's Day and I had planned a nice evening out with Nick. I wanted things to be perfect when I shared the news with him. I smiled at the thought and my hand automatically went protectively to my stomach.

But that was two whole days away and right now I had other things to do. Like get out of bed for starters, and then maybe find something to eat. Yes, I was starving and somehow I didn't feel like human food was going to cut it. I needed to feed, which meant a trip to the butcher at the very least.

I glanced at the door and saw Nick there watching me. A smile played on his lips as he sauntered across the room and sat next to me on the bed.

"Hey baby did you get a good nap?" he asked.

"Yes, just not quite long enough." I said stretching again. There was a hint of concern in his eyes at my answer.

"You sure have been tired a lot. Are you feeling okay?"

"Yes, just a bit run down."

"Are you sleeping well at night? I've noticed that you're tossing and turning a lot lately, even today when you were napping."

"Yea it's those dreams." I said trying to brush them aside. Nick looked alarmed.

"What dreams? Are you still dreaming about Vlad? Why didn't you tell me?" Nick had told me about Vlad one night and we had decided I had probably seen him in Nick's memory. Still he had wanted to know if I was still having dreams about him and what they were about. I couldn't very well tell him that I thought it was my hormones and ruin the surprise so I opted to say nothing at all.

"Well, yes." I said sheepishly. Pretty much every night and the same dream the last three days."

"Can you tell me what it's about?" He asked with apparent interest.

"I don't remember every detail. I just remember that he wants me for something. Every time I feel that Callie is in danger and…" I drop my hand to my belly. "He is surrounded by men but only a few of them are vampire. There is always fighting, swords you know and Dean is there, but he is always a vampire in my dream. Now how crazy is that?"

"What else do you remember about the dream Kat?"

"Not much. Sometimes I see Orlando in them. Why?"

"Nothing baby, just curious – that's all."

"Good because I'm starving and I think I'm going to need to feed soon." Nick lifted me to my feet and kissed me, his eyes giving nothing away.

Then let's go take care of that."

Two days later…..

Nick sat in front of his computer working on a small project he'd taken for an old acquaintance. There was very little footwork. Most of his research could be done from his office on the internet. When his phone rang he answered it without looking at the caller ID.

"Hello," he said still staring at his computer.

"Mr. Cristo," said the voice on the other end of the line. Nick stopped what he was doing on the computer. He knew this voice from somewhere but could not place it at the moment.

"Yes, this is Nick," He replied. "How can I help you?"

"It's not what you can do for me but what I can do for you," said the voice. "I need to speak to you about your lady friend and it is of utmost importance."

"I'm listening," Nick said suddenly serious.

"Not on the phone." said the voice. "Meet me in thirty minutes at the bar called Davenport's – you know the place. Come alone. I will be sitting at the bar."

The phone disconnected and Nick was left with an unsettling feeling. Should he even go? Who was that? He racked his brain trying to identify the voice unsuccessfully. What did they need to tell me about Kat, and why do I need to come alone? After a moment's hesitation he got in his car and left. Even if it was nothing, it concerned Kat and he wanted to know about it.

Pulling into the parking lot he noticed there were only other a few others cars in the lot, one of them an expensive sports car. Glancing at his phone he noticed it was barely seven p.m.

He made his way up the stairs into the establishment. He recognized the figure at the bar before he even saw his face. He was instantly angry. What the hell did Orlando need to talk to him about concerning Kat?

He strode over to the bar and stood facing the vampire. Orlando turned on his barstool and smiled. "Ah, my good friend, sit – have a drink." He said motioning to the stool next to him. "Give my friend whatever he wants." He said to the bartender. Nick was not in the mood for socializing.

"What do you need to tell me about Kat?" he asked, cutting to the chase. Orlando studied the vampire for a moment, sizing him up.

"When last I saw you," he began, "you were angry with me then as well, but I did nothing that you couldn't have prevented yourself." Nick knew the vampire was right and it only served to irritate him more. "Sit." The vampire said again.

Reluctantly Nick sat on the stool. The bartender stared, waiting for his order. "Crown and seven," Nick said then tuning to Orlando, "What is this about?" The bartender placed the tumbler on the bar in front of Nick then left.

Orlando turned to face Nick once again. "I have heard from a very reliable source that Vladimir has taken an interest in our dear Katherine."

Nick's head swung up sharply at the mention of Vladimir's name. Sirens were going full blast in his head. He didn't like Orlando's use of the word "OUR" when he referred to Kat, but he dismissed it in light of the more urgent information. The images he'd seen from Kat's dream flooded back into his mind as a feeling of near panic moved thru him. This information was both shocking and alarming.

Vladimir was one of the oldest vampires he knew of. He was the vampire equivalent of a mob boss and his influence was far reaching. And while Nick had never heard of Vlad harming the innocent, the thought that he had his sights set on Kat was disconcerting.

Those who knew who and what he was were too afraid to go against him. He surrounded himself with hired guns and was rich enough to buy anyone or anything he desired. He was a man of action and usually got what he wanted. But how far would he go to get Kat? What was the driving force behind this action?

"Are you sure your source is reliable?" Even as he asked the question he knew it was. Kat's dreams had been telling them for months now to expect it. He had just hoped it wouldn't be so soon. Now as he sat here he understood why Orlando would not talk on the phone and why he insisted Nick come alone.

"Yes, very reliable." Orlando replied.

"Why would he be interested in Kat? He can pretty much buy anyone he wants, why Kat?" Orlando's mouth tightened into a thin line. If what he'd heard was true there was little anyone could do to stop it from happening but he liked Katherine and wanted to give her every advantage.

"Because she can reproduce."

Orlando's words pierced through Nick like a dagger as the implication of his meaning hit home. He slumped on his barstool as if someone had kicked him in the gut.

The information had to be true, how else could have Orlando known that Kat could reproduce? Orlando looked solemnly at Nick. "I'm sorry my friend that the alcohol does nothing for us in these times."

Nick's mind was reeling. He had to protect her somehow. He had to get her far away from Vladimir. Orlando spoke again.

"Change her phone; check her car for tracking devices and your home for wire taps. He has been watching her for some time now and is preparing to make his move. Let me know if there is anything that I can do to help. It will be done."

With that Orlando paid the bartender then pulled a business card from his wallet and passed it to Nick.

"My number for when you need me." Then he was gone.

Nick scrambled back to his car planning out his next move. He had to get Kat to safety but he had to make sure they weren't followed. He thought of Orlando's advice and suddenly went pale. "Shit!" he exclaimed as he remembered the chunk of ice that he'd broken off the bumper on their way to Stephan's.

In his ignorance he'd bought a little time for Kat, realizing now that the plastic he'd seen was actually a transmitter. "Why the fuck didn't I recognize it for what it was back then?"

His tires threw rocks across the parking lot as he spun out onto the main road. He needed to call Stephan but he had to make sure Kat was okay first. He'd get to her first then pickup new phones for both of them.

He was out of the car and busting through the front door of the house before the car stopped rolling. "Kat" he called out, panic in his voice.

I looked up to see Nick bust through the front door like a mad man as I finished folding the last of the towels. The look on his face told me something was terribly wrong. I froze afraid of what news he had for me. Had something happened to Callie or Stephan? He closed the distance between us and had me in his arms.

"Oh thank god," he said against my ear. Then he knelt in front of me, holding my arms as if I were a child as he spoke. "I need you to listen and do exactly what I tell you as fast as possible. We have got to get out of here now.

I will tell you everything as we go but please just trust me." I nodded not able to talk. "Grab a small bag with essentials and your phone but turn it off. Meet me at the Acura in ten minutes." He kissed me again then went to the garage as I ran to the room to grab my stuff.

Nick carefully looked the Acura over until he found the transmitter. Rather than destroy it, he left it in the garage so that it would appear the car had not moved. Checking to make sure there were no other transmitters he then grabbed a few tools and a large metal lock box from behind his workbench and placed the items in the trunk of the car. By the time he had finished I was in the garage waiting.

"Get in and buckle up."

I followed his command immediately without questioning him. He pulled out onto the road without wasting a minute. It was now dark outside and the temperature had dropped several degrees. As soon as we were on the road he began to speak. He was short and to the point but his face was filled with concern.

"The dreams you have been having about Vlad are not dreams at all but premonitions. He has been watching you and now he is ready to make his move. We are getting you out of here to someplace you will be safe until I can figure out what to do." I gasped as what he was saying sank in.

"Callie," I started grabbing my phone from my purse.

"Do not turn that on." He shouted so loud I dropped my phone. "We will stop and get new phones and make necessary calls with them. I can only assume our phones are tapped too. Well throw them away once our contact information is transferred over."

"What do you mean tapped too?" I asked panic rising in my voice. "How long has he been watching me and what does he want me for?"

"There was a transmitter on the car, one on the jeep too at Christmas that broke off in the ice. I just realized what it was today. The house may be wired. I'm not sure. I didn't have time to look."

He pulled out onto the freeway and accelerated, glancing into his rearview mirror. "I have to assume that they will come looking for you at the house and that they can possibly track out phones. Since they were unable to track us to Stephan's I'm hoping they don't know about him. We should be safe there for now."

"But what about Callie; she was always the one in danger in my dreams, not me. I need to talk to her." I insisted.

"I don't think they will try to get Callie yet."

"What do you mean yet?" I almost screamed.

"Look baby," Nick lowered his voice. "I think they will look for you first and try to get you. If they go after Callie it will be to draw you in. I'm hoping we still have some time. I can't risk them finding you. If he gets Callie he won't harm her as long as he believes that you will come for her."

"You didn't tell me what he wants with me." Nick pressed his lips into a thin line. I could tell he didn't want to answer my question. His eyes remained on the road but he reached over and squeezed my hand in his.

"He wants you because you can reproduce. I can only assume he wants you to bare his child." My hand flew immediately to my stomach again. How far would this vampire go to implant his own seed in my uterus?

In all the excitement I had forgotten about my plans for tonight with Nick. My plans to tell him… but now I couldn't. There was too much for him to worry about. He didn't need to worry about this too.

Nick made a quick turn into the cellphone store and be both got out. Luckily we were the only people there and we were quickly upgraded to new phones. As we left the store Nick dropped our two old phones in a trash can outside. He was immediately on the phone with Stephan telling him everything. I listened closely to his conversation. He had not told me about Orlando so this was news to me.

"Have Dean leave immediately to get Callie. She won't be safe, neither will her family if she is with them.

At that very moment six men were climbing out of a boat at the end of the pier. They were dressed entirely in black from head to toe with black paint on their faces. Each man was wearing night vision goggles and was armed with M–16 automatic rifles, equipped with a light on the barrel. No one spoke a word but followed hand signals from the leader of the group.

Stealthily they made their way across the yard then spread out surrounding the house, two men at each entrance, two others watching the windows. At precisely 2100 hours the team entered the dwelling.

Moving swiftly through the house they checked each room before arriving in the master bedroom. The room was empty and the bed still made. A quick sweep of the bathroom and closet confirmed there was no one there.

The leader of the group made a phone call that was answered on a private line. "Sir, Juliet team reporting. The target has vacated the premises." The voice on the other end of the line responded. "Sir, yes sir," said the team leader. "We will wait for further instructions." Hanging up the phone he looked at the group of men. "We are done here. Move out!" He ordered.

My chest constricted at the thought of Callie being hurt. All these weeks of dreaming that Callie was in danger now came back and stuck in me like a knife. Why had I pushed the dreams aside?

I tried to call her but my call went straight to voicemail. I left a message for her to call me. I realized she may not even listen since this was a new number that she would not recognize.

The miles ticked off at a snail's pace. We were driving to Stephan's where Dean would be bringing Callie. He had left already and should be able to get her and get back by the time we arrived.

Nick remained silent but I could see the muscles in his jaw clenching, his eyes intent on the road ahead. This drive was killing me. I almost could have run there faster. *Why didn't I pay attention to those dreams?*

Rehashing what I should have done was only making me more anxious so I decided to figure out how to keep Callie and myself safe once we were back together. I attempted to clear my mind and focus on Callie.

How could I keep her safe? I tried to relax, to stop being so fearful. What would Vlad want with her anyway? I stared out the windshield at the road stretching out before us. Vlad wanted me, not her.

Suddenly the highway fell away before me and I was standing in an enormous room. Actually it was more like a warehouse, huge, with cement floor and corrugated metal walls.

Men were moving around me, probably twenty total but a few of those were vampire. Most were wearing fatigues and I noticed they had gun belts. There was a strange smell in the air and I wondered what it was.

Looking around I could see the first story windows had bars covering the outside. The windows at the second floor lever, however, had no bars. The floor of the facility had large grates in it leading down into the sewer. A series of catwalks spanned the open area of what would be the second floor level and above that was an enclosed third floor.

I watched as a door burst open and Vladimir strode in, flanked by two other vampires. His green eyes were so bright they appeared to be glowing, and the corners of his lips curled up in a smug sneer. There was no mistaking that the fire in his eyes was the result of feeding on human blood – recently.

He walked like a man of great authority, back straight, shoulders square, chin lifted. He was used to giving orders and having them carried out immediately. The men with him were talking fast as they made their way across the large expanse to a room that was nestled in the far corner, next to the metal staircase.

Curiosity called me to see what he was doing here so I followed him to the room and watched as he opened the door. Unlike the rest of the building that was bare concrete and metal, this room had been finished out quite comfortably.

The floor was covered with thick, expensive brown carpet. The walls were textured sheetrock and painted a creamy shade of beige. It was furnished with a solid wood desk, a couple of deep cushioned chairs and a sofa rested against the back wall.

As I stepped further into the room I saw Callie. She was tied to a solid wooden chair in the middle of the room, tears streaming down her cheeks. She was so frightened.

I walked into the room unnoticed. Going to Callie I wrapped my arms around her shoulders and whispered in her ear. "Everything is going to be okay honey. I'm going to get you out of here. Be strong."

"Kat – Kat," Nick was calling to me, shaking my shoulder. My head snapped up to look at him as I gasped in air. "Are you okay over there? You kind of zoned out on me for a few minutes." He continued to look at me with uncertainty.

I nodded. "He already has Callie." I said too calmly. "I have no choice but to play his game."

"Who has Callie?" Nick asked. "Dean?" I shook my head.

"Vladimir has Callie; he's holding her as bait."

When we arrived at the big house Stephan and Dean met us at the front drive. The last hour on the road had been spent on phone calls back and forth. Dean had gone to meet Callie at the campus library but when he'd gotten there she was gone.

He'd found her car with the driver door left open and keys hanging in the ignition. Her purse was in the front seat. Her cell phone was nowhere in the car so he assumed she had it.

Beneath his calm exterior Dean was a frazzled mess. The lines on his face showed just how much he was worrying and he paced constantly inside the house.

We met in the parlor to discuss what had to be done. I was not about to lose my daughter to this monster, nor was I or Nick going to give up my womb to incubate his seed. Somehow I had to protect my tiny bubble too. Absentminded I rubbed my hand protectively across my abdomen.

"We can assume," Stephan was saying, "that Callie will be fine as long as we pretend to meet Vladimir's demands. We must also assume that if he finds out we are trying to deceive him he may kill her. We need to strike

441

smart and strike hard. Once we get Callie back we will have the upper hand."

"What do you expect would happen if I gave in to his demands?" I asked Stephan. I had no intention of doing so but I wanted to know just the same.

"That's out of the question Katherine." Nick stated angrily. I held up my hand to him.

"I just want to know. Please let Stephan talk." I said not backing down. I nodded at Stephan to continue.

"Katherine, the desire to ensure that his bloodline continues, which I assume is the driving force behind Vladimir right now, could cause him to return to his preternatural instincts. In that case you could consider the lion. The dominant male will first eliminate the competition; he then kills all other cubs the female has to drive her to breed again."

"Because he has actually gone this far, I think we must consider the worst. I believe our only option at this time is to fight, and if it comes down to it, kill him before he harms one of you."

"You would not be keeping anyone safe by sacrificing yourself. Either way, Vlad may attempt to kill Nick and Callie. We just have to stop him." I thought my heart would burst out of my chest hearing Stephan put it so bluntly.

"I don't intend to sacrifice myself. I just needed to know what was really at stake." Somehow I needed to find a way to keep both Callie and Nick safe from Vlad. I needed to do this without putting myself in a position that would present an unnecessary risk to my little bubble.

"Yes," Nick agreed but we have no idea what we're up against and there are only three of us and Orlando – maybe a few of his men. There may be a few more friends I can ask for help, but it's a lot to ask friends to go to war with Vlad."

"There are four of us." Dean corrected. "I will be there to fight with you."

"I'm talking about vampires." Nick argued "No offense, but a human man doesn't stand a chance against the vampire. It would be suicide for you to go in and we need you for things other than fighting."

443

"If you think I'm going to sit around and do nothing while Callie is in danger then you have another thing coming." Dean shot back.

"I'm telling you, you can't fight against vampire." Nick insisted.

"He may not have to." I stated. All eyes turned to me. There are probably a total of twenty men there and only six or seven are vampire, including Vladimir. I don't know the location but I can make you a drawing of the layout so that you can plan the strategy. Of course I didn't see the perimeter but maybe when we find out where we can google a satellite image."

"Good thinking Katherine, "Stephan said bringing me a sheet of paper and a pencil. "Include as much detail as possible. Once we know exactly what we're up against we can plan accordingly." I took the paper from Stephan and drew out in as much detail as I remember the layout of building. I included the grates and window and even approximate positions of the overhead catwalks.

Dean huffed in frustration. "This waiting is killing me. Why hasn't he called yet? From this drawing it still looks like you will need me there. There are still too many people to get through"

"We'll do better if we don't have to worry about one of our own." Nick said angrily. Tension was rising in the room and I was afraid a fight would start. "It's bad enough that he's after the woman I love."

"Do you think you are the only one affected by this?" Dean shot back. "You think you're the only one who loves Kat?" I'd never seen Dean so angry before. "Well guess what buddy, I loved Kat for years and still care for her. But right now he has Callie. He has the woman I love and while you're trying to keep Kat safe I'm trying to find a way to make Callie safe again. He has her damn it and I am going with you. And I will be a vampire."

"What the hell do you mean by that?" Nick wanted to know. This is happening now and even if one of us agreed to turn you it would take days, maybe weeks. We don't have that kind of time."

"No," Dean replied quietly, "It will take only a couple of hours and I should have Kat's abilities when it's done. Of course it will probably feel like my body is being torn apart but if my rats can survive it so can I."

445

"I knew it was vampire." I blurted out. Nick and Stephan looked at me with puzzled looks.

"Will someone tell me what the hell is going on?" Nick asked, running his fingers through his hair in exasperation.

"Look," Dean started, "I've been experimenting with Kat's blood, tweaking her DNA to cause the change to occur faster. I've been using lab rats. The rat that got out was a vampire.

I was so close but I couldn't duplicate her abilities. Then finally it dawned on me. While the vampire blood ultimately causes the change, if certain receptors are affected the abilities are inhibited. The Ativan prevented those receptors from receiving vampire blood."

Stephan said beaming.

"I actually have a lab rat that changes colors to camouflage itself and it also can quill up like a porcupine when threatened." Dean admitted.

"But a rat is not a human," Nick argued. "You can't just try this serum on yourself. What if it goes badly wrong?"

"I have to try for Callie." Dean stated adamantly. "I can't just sit back and watch."

"You're willing to become vampire for a possibility?" Nick was just trying to reason with him now. He knew exactly how this change could separate Dean from Callie. "Do you realize what you may have to give up if you become vampire?"

"I realize that if something happens to Callie then I might as well be dead. I can love her from a distance if I have to, lose her to someone else and stand back and watch. But I cannot watch her die. Not now."

"Do you think time will make it easier? Will it be easy to watch her grow old and die while you're still a young man? Nick was angry again and his voice was raised an octave as he spoke.

"I never said it would be easy." Dean screamed back in his face. "I just said I had to do it."

Kneeling down in front of me Dean put his hands on my knees as he looked up into my face. His eyes were pleading when he asked. "Do you think maybe you could see where she is? Use your abilities to locate her and get us a little more information about the place. I know it isn't something you've been controlling but would you try?"

My heart broke looking at him, knowing his heart was breaking for the same reason and for the first time since this whole ordeal started I broke down and cried. I would do anything to help Callie. Anything would be better than sitting around waiting for Vlad to contact me.

"Of course I'll try Dean. I think I'm going to need some privacy though. I really wish I knew how to trigger it."

"Before you start I need you to give me an injection." Nick started to protest again but Dean would have none of it. "You'll probably need to come too. I'll need someone to chain me up in the lab and keep me cool for a while." Then looking at Stephan he said. "I'm going to need some blood too."

We all followed him to the lab but instead of turning in the door he took the stairs to the basement level and unlocked it. I had never toured this one but I noticed it was built with reinforcements. The rat cages were heavy duty with only tiny holes for air instead of the wire cages he had upstairs.

Going behind his desk he opened a panel that revealed a hidden refrigerator. Removing two vials and a syringe he proceeded to draw up the serum mixed with Ativan. He was talking steadily as he worked.

Kat I'll need this injected intra-muscularly but wait until I'm secured to the wall. I expect to become extremely violent for a short time, maybe thirty to forty minutes. I will increase in size and I may even look misshapen for a few minutes. That should correct, but I will be considerably larger than I am now.

Within ten minutes of the injection I will need to have my body temperature lowered. The tub in the corner with ice water should work but if the water starts warming use this." He pointed to a cylinder of gas with a cone nozzle on it. "This is liquid nitrogen. Short, quick bursts will cool the water and me. Please don't turn me into a popsicle. I'll need to be kept cool until my core temperature stabilizes."

He handed a gun to Nick that resembled a check out scanner. "Use this every three minutes after the first thirty minutes have passed. Just aim and squeeze the trigger. It will measure my surface body temperature.

When you have three consecutive readings below one hundred fifteen you can stop cooling. Try to aim at my forehead." Then he looked at Stephan. "Wish me luck!"

Stephan turned immediately and called for Sara to bring ice and lots of it. In a few minutes the tub was filled with ice and pulled into position where water was being added by the hose used for cleaning the lab. Stephan disappeared and returned moments later with a length of heavy chain and two metal cuffs that he attached to an already existing molly bolt in the wall.

Dean removed his shirt and belt then Stephan fastened him into the cuffs. Once settled he nodded his head at me.

"Are you absolutely sure you want to go through with this?" I asked. "You know we will find a way to get her back whether you're a vampire or not." His expression was grave. Leaning over he kissed me on the cheek.

"I'm sure Kat." I'll be fine.

I wasn't so sure though and it must have shown on my face as I hesitated.

"Hey," Dean said. "Don't be like this. Kat you know me better than anyone here. You know I wouldn't do this if I hadn't checked and rechecked everything to make sure it was going to work the way it's supposed to. Have you ever known me to be wrong about something like this?"

"No," I admitted reluctantly. "I know you do your research. I'm just scared."

"Don't be scared." Then he winked at me. "Actually I think I was meant to be a vampire."

Thinking back on my dreams I gave him a slight smile. "You know what? I think so too." Then I gave him the injection and backed away.

The serum started working immediately. I looked on in horror as Dean began thrashing about screaming out in agony. I could hear his bones breaking inside his body as he was literally pulled apart.

Muscle and tendon was tearing away from the bone as his frame expanded in size. I couldn't bear to watch him writhing in agony or hear him screaming in pain but I couldn't leave him either. He needed me, need us – all of us if he was going to survive.

Together we hoisted his burning body into the tub of ice water. Steam rose off the water filling the room like a sauna, the ice in the tub quickly melting in the heat from his body. Sara ran for more ice. Even in the tub he thrashed and screamed, calling out Callie's name in his delirium. My heart ached for him. All of the pain that I'd suffered through over several days, he was experiencing right now in a short amount of time.

The transformation was unbelievable. The metal cuffs that before had allowed his hands to almost slip through were now snug around his wrists. He had gained at least four inches in height and his chest and shoulders, though well-defined before, had become much broader.

He was moaning between screams and the water was once again warming. Taking the cylinder of nitrogen I swept short quick strokes of the gas across the surface of the water and his skin. The fever was raging so high I was becoming concerned that he may not fully recover mentally if he survived the ordeal. Suddenly his face started swelling, pushing his features into a grotesque mask. I gasped in shock.

I gasped, my hand going to my mouth. "Please don't leave him misshapen like this, please." He was no longer thrashing about but his moans and cries continued. I approached him and grabbed hold of one of his hands.

"Callie," he started to say but as pain shot through him his voice escalated into a roar.

"No, Dean It's me, Kat." I said rubbing his hand. I glanced at the time it had been thirty minutes. "Start monitoring his temperature." I told Nick. His hand was almost too hot to hold so I released him for a moment to use the nitrogen again. Once done I returned to his side and took his hand in mine again.

Time suddenly seemed to be crawling. Each time I glanced at the clock only seconds had passed. The thought that he might not live through this began to plague my thought. Ten more minutes past and he still required cooling. Sara brought in more ice and I poured it into the water and onto his chest. His screams were beginning to subside but he continued to moan. He was still incoherent. Gently I bathed his face in cold water. Another ten minutes and Nick announced we could stop cooling him.

I sat next to him and continued to bathe his face. I was relieved to see the swelling start to subside and he looked more like Dean again. Still he was not arousing but he was moving his head when I spoke to him.

Silently I slumped back into the chair I had pulled alongside the tub. Nick knelt beside me and kissed me on the cheek.

"He'll be okay," Nick urged. Tears stung my eyes again.

"If anything happens to him Callie will hate me for giving him that shot – I'll hate myself."

Nick kissed me again. "I'm going up to bring some blood down for when he comes to." I nodded and Nick left.

I sat watching Dean for long moments. He had been a friend for so long and now was willing to give up everything for Callie. He had to come back to us, he just had to. I closed my eyes and breathed a silent prayer to anyone that might be listening. *Please, please, please just let him wake up. Let him be alright.*

He was breathing peacefully now and I watched the rise and fall of his incredibly muscled chest. I thought of Callie and our last talk about him. The look in her eyes as she spoke of him…

The room suddenly fell away and I was in a car. Not just any a car, a silver Jaguar XK convertible but the roof was up at the moment. Vladimir was driving, talking on the phone.

"I think we'll give her a little longer to worry and then make the call. She'll be more ready to co-operate if her nerves are fried. I'll be there in five."

We rode on a short distance. I saw mile markers but no street signs. Turning onto an unpaved road I saw a large building surrounded by a tall cyclone fence with barbed wire at the top. A sign above the front entrance displayed the name *Abel Construction Limited.* A guard shack with a gate operator stood just outside the front entrance.

Vladimir barely slowed the car before the gate opened allowing him entrance. A few security cameras where perched on the roof of the building. There were no other guards in the yard that I could see. Beyond the fence was a twenty foot deep ditch where the storm drain emptied into.

I was just about to follow him inside when a hand grabbed my shoulder and brought me back to the present. Sweat was beaded on my forehead and my shirt was soaked. Nick and Stephan were kneeling on either side of me. Dean remained slumped over in the tub, his eyes closed.

"Abel Construction," I said still gasping for air. "The sign on the building…. Abel Construction Limited."

"We can google it." Nick said pulling me into his arms. "We'll find it."

"You won't have to." Stephan said pulling himself upright. "I know the place."

TWENTY-FIVE

Vladimir Dimitru strode into the building with purpose. The fact was everything he did in life had a purpose. Tonight was no different. He had fought in and lived through more wars than he cared to remember. He had seen the rise and fall of nations, the construction of pyramids, and witnessed as time changed vast lush meadows into desert wasteland.

He had lived countless years on this earth through countless eras and had not survived on mere luck. He had learned that each step he took must be carefully planned out, each move given careful consideration. Thus he had moved forward through life, amassing fortunes, building his empire around him through meticulously plotting his next move, his next course of action.

What he was doing in this building tonight was part of that planning; an idea he had formulated centuries ago. Now finally after a millennium he was on the threshold of seeing his greatest ambition come to fruition; his desire to father a vampire child.

It was not for inability to produce viable sperm. He was one of the ancients – his reproductive abilities remained intact as well as other abilities that vampires of these times did not possess. Nor was it for lack of finding a willing woman. Vladimir was ancient blood forever imprisoned in the attractive, virile body of a thirty-year old; the epitome of Adonis.

He had mastered the skill of his calling powers. Human and vampire women alike found him altogether irresistible, more than willing to bed him and carry his child. The problem seemed to be finding one with a viable womb that was strong enough to support a baby vampire.

He had searched for what seemed an eternity to find just that. His search had led him into the bed of many mortal women but their bodies had proven too weak to sustain the life growing within them. Each time the embryo drained the life out of them before tearing apart the very womb that incubated them. None of his children had lived.

Except for sexual gratification, fucking a vampire woman was of no purpose. Their uteruses could not support life – until Katherine. He had watched Katherine, as he did with all new converts, looking for that one woman who would defy the laws of vampire nature. After all this time he had finally found her and he was not going to let her go.

Vladimir knew enough from the intel he'd been given that she had already chosen a mate. She would not willingly give herself to Vladimir at first. That was why he needed the girl. The girl would insure her cooperation, at least for a little while. It wouldn't take him long to seduce her with his call, after that she would beg him to take her.

The mate would have to die. There would be no end to the fighting until he was dead. It did not matter that he won Katherine over. The mate would never stop trying to take her back. Not that he'd blame him. If it were his mate he'd not stop until one of them were dead.

Vladimir's thoughts turned to Callie. Once he had what he wanted from Katherine what would he do with the girl? His gut told him he should eliminate her so that Katherine would have only one child to nurture. He didn't want another taking her focus. But what if she refused to nurture his offspring if he harmed the girl? Suppose she injured herself to end the pregnancy? No he would need to keep her alive and well for future insurance.

Maybe he would turn her as well. If she was like her mother perhaps she too could carry a child for him. He somehow doubted that. She was pleasing to look at and at another time in his life he would have bedded her just for the pleasure but not now. Now his sole focus was producing an heir; a true flesh of his flesh heir to carry on his legacy.

He had seen some of the other vamps looking at the girl as if they would eat her alive. *Fucking cocksuckers! Thinking with their cocks.* He would put Rathe in charge of the girl. Rathe was loyal and would make sure his orders were carried out if it cost him his life. If left to their own devices the men would surely succumb to the temptation in front of them unless he intervened.

Stopping at the door he paused for a minute before opening it and stepping into the room. The girl was still tied to the chair in the same spot she'd been in earlier. Her eyes were red and swollen make-up smeared from the flood of tears she'd cried since being taken.

Fury surged through him. *Goddamn it! Can they not follow fucking instructions? She was to be released in the room and given access to the bathroom and the sofa in the room.* He crossed to her without even speaking and broke the ropes that had her bound.

As soon as Callie was freed from the ropes she sprang to her feet that were now numb from sitting in the chair so long. Her hopes of dashing out the door shattered as her weak legs gave out beneath her and she crashed toward the floor.

She would have fallen on her face had the man not caught her and hauled her up against his chest. She could feel the hardness of his chest as he locked her into the vice that were his arms. Her body chilled against the coolness that radiated from beneath his shirt. Looking up her eyes locked with his impossibly green ones that seemed to be glowing at the moment.

The man, Vlad, she thought she'd heard someone call him, made a Tsk tsk sound with his tongue.

"There's no use trying to escape." He said into her ear. "I am much stronger and much faster and you'll only hurt yourself if you try." The tears welled up in her eyes and spilled down her cheeks once again.

"What do you want from me? Why have you brought me here? Please let me go." she pleaded, her voice breaking between sobs.

"Shhhh– shhh, now," he said in the most consoling voice he could muster, his hand stroking up and down her back. He had decided it would be better to win her over rather than have her scared and hysterical the whole time. He was all about business and this would help with the acquisition he was proposing.

Callie's back stiffened beneath his touch and she tried to pull away from him. It was no use. He held her captive against his chest, his powerful arms unyielding. Vladimir was irritated the girl was still resisting him. He'd never had a human woman resist him ever. He'd expected her to be an easy victory paving the way for another easy win with her mother.

"Please, please let me go." She begged again.

"I can't do that just yet," he said. "I still need you."

"What do you need me for?" she asked, "I really have nothing you could want. My family has no money for a ransom."

Vladimir laughed. "I don't need any money. I need your mother and I want you to help me get her." Callie froze when she realized that her purpose was to be a bargaining tool for this man.

"What do you want with my mother?" She demanded, fear wrapping its icy fingers around her heart. She knew her mom would not hesitate to do anything he asked to keep her safe. She couldn't imagine what it was he wanted her mother for but whatever it was couldn't be good. She couldn't let him hurt her mom. "Please, whatever it is you want with her. Please just leave her alone. Use me instead."

Vladimir felt as the fight left the girl and released his grip. He hated having to use her like this. He had never pretended to be a saint but still, terrorizing women was a trait he abhorred in other vampires.

He knew he had acted too rashly sending his men to bring in the girl. This was yet another dent in his armor of self-control. This desire to sire a child was affecting him, causing him to think irrationally, varying from the plan. He had panicked when Kat had suddenly vanished without a trace.

His desire to have a child was not the only thing affecting him. This girl was getting under his skin as well. Her innocent beauty - her bravery called to him on a baser level.

Lowering her to the floor he turned her to face him. Taking her face in his hand he turned her head, exposing the creamy flesh of her neck and the throbbing pulse just below the surface. He closed his eyes as he lowered his face to her neck, his nose almost touching as he inhaled deeply.

Callie shut her eyes tight, steeling her nerves. "*I can do this for mom*" she chanted the mantra to herself.

"So brave and so beautiful," Vlad whispered in her ear. "And I am very tempted to take you up on your offer, but I've tried with human women and they are not strong enough to carry my seed to fruition. That is why I... need your mother."

Callie's head snapped around at his words. His eyes were still closed and his mouth partially opened revealing the fangs that had descended. She bolted back away from him but the distance between them was closed instantly by Vlad. She had never seen anyone move so fast in her life and it scared her even more.

Vlad was frustrated now. She had tempted him and he had stupidly given in allowing his fangs to descend. Even now his cock was throbbing painfully against the zipper of his pants. Grabbing her Vlad flung her to the sofa a little more forcefully than he'd meant to. Like lightning he was on his knees next to her, pinning her down as she struggled to get free.

"Going back on your offer so soon?" he asked her with an angry glare. "Just moments ago you were willing to do anything for your mother. Now – what happened? Did my fangs frighten you?"

Callie stilled beneath him. He was right. What was she willing to sacrifice for her mom?

"Yes," she answered truthfully. "You frighten me. What are you and what do you mean about human women. My mom is human."

Vladimir shook his head attempting to dispel his arousal before he did something stupid. Fucking this girl for pleasure was not part of the plan. Still her offer was tempting. If he did turn her and IF she was able to conceive then he'd no longer even need the mother.

He would have a consenting partner. One he would no doubt enjoy fucking and avoid a small war in the process. Vladimir liked it when things remained neat and uncomplicated. Fighting among vampires always got messy.

"It seems to me that your mother has been keeping a secret from you. She is no longer human. She is vampire – like me, but unlike other vampire women she is still able to conceive. I need her to carry my child."

"My mother is nothing like you. You're a monster."

Vlad growled at her. "If I were a monster I'd have fucked you already and would be feasting from that delectable neck of yours. Then I'd let the others have their turn with you instead of protecting you from them. Now what about your offer?"

"I thought you said a human couldn't do it."

"I could turn you first."

"And if I'm not like mom…..If I can't…?"

"Then I will still need Katherine."

Callie considered her options. If there was even a small chance that she could keep her mom from harm she had to take it. "If you will leave my mom alone then I will do whatever you ask."

The vampire growled against her ear, his cock swelling once again in anticipation of what was coming. "Don't worry baby," he whispered as he turned her head to expose her beautiful neck. "I'll make this just as good for you."

Callie shut her eyes tight against her fear. Her heart pounded in her chest and her body tensed bracing for the bite that would change her world. *I love you Dean – please forgive me for what I'm doing. Please understand.*

Nick looked at Dean, still reclined in the water then back to me. "Let's get him out of the water then we can work on a plan for bringing Callie home."

Dean shifted his head just slightly without opening his eyes. "Don't even think about going without me," he said; his voice a hoarse whisper. I was at his side in an instant, relief flooding through me at hearing his voice again.

"How are you feeling?" I asked as Nick removed the shackles from his wrists.

"Like I've been hit by a truck," he said attempting to open his eyes. "And I'm parched. You got anything to drink." Nick and I helped him out of the tub. He was shaking violently and was unable to stand on his own. We lowered him into the chair and Nick offered him a unit of blood which he gulped greedily.

I called for Sara to bring some blankets and together Nick and I got him out of his wet pants and wrapped up in the blankets. After a second unit of blood he was able to open his eyes and the shaking subsided. I was concerned from all the sounds of breaking bones and tearing flesh that he wasn't completely healed but he seemed to be fine. He was able to move his arms and legs normally without pain.

"I won't be doing that again anytime soon." He announced as we helped him to his feet.

"I should hope not. I don't think I could watch it again." I told him. "You had me scared there for quite a while. We'll get you upstairs and I'll find you something to wear." I said knowing that he would no longer fit his own clothes.

"I'm ok now," he said turning loose of our arms. "I can make it."

I didn't want to let him go but he insisted and was able to make it to the top of the stairs before stopping for a breath. Because my recovery from the transformation had taken days I was less than optimistic that Dean would recover any faster, but he soon proved me wrong.

I found some of Nicks jog pants and shirt and brought them to him. He put them on and after another unit of blood was moving about normally.

Gathering in Stephan's study he drew up a diagram of the warehouse where Vlad was keeping Callie. Based on the information I gave him he was able to place the security cameras and possible ways into the facility without being seen.

I went over everything I'd seen in as much detail as possible. I knew Callie was afraid and wanted to get to her as soon as possible. I also wanted our plan to work so I forced myself to sit still and pay attention to Stephan. I could tell that Dean was also anxious.

Nick had contacted Orlando and he had promised himself and three other men to assist. We would meet up with him a few miles from the warehouse and discuss the plan. For the moment Stephan suggested we use them to prevent anyone else from coming in on us once we were inside.

"It will be to our advantage if we strike before he contacts us. That way we have the element of surprise. I suggest we stake the place out and see who comes and goes. The upper story windows will be a good entrance point.

I would like to get someone inside through the drainage pipes to secure Callie before the rest of us come in. Of course we won't know how large the openings really are until someone attempts them."

"I can go in." I volunteered. "I'll be able to make myself as small as I need to, to get through. If it is large enough I can bring Callie back out the same way. There was a drain just outside the room she is being kept in."

"Yes Katherine, I was going to suggest that since you may be the only one of us able to get through." Stephan replied.

Nick voiced his disapproval. "I don't like the idea of Kat going in there alone and I don't want her going in first." He said speaking to the room but looking at me. "It just isn't safe. His ultimate goal is getting you. I don't want to take that chance." I squeezed his hand.

"I know Nick but it's our best option." I responded. "I will do everything in my power to stay safe and keep Callie safe as well." Once again my hand fluttered protectively to my stomach. This time the action did not go unnoticed. Stephan saw it and arched an eyebrow at me. Our eyes met for a moment and a slight shake of my head warned him not to say anything.

Dean, who had been sitting silently, looking contemplative suddenly, spoke up. "I might be able to do it." He stated. "I should have all the abilities Kat has; I should be able to change too."

Stephan nodded and Nick suddenly looked hopeful. "That would definitely increase our odds if another of us had her abilities."

"No time like the present to figure it out." Dean exhaled and looked at me, "any suggestions?"

I took him aside while Nick and Stephan worked out a few more details. We sat toe to toe in a couple of chairs I'd moved together. "Just focus on what you need at the moment. To be able to fly, to be smaller, etc. Like this." I shut my eyes for just a second and thought of my suit, changing instantly at will. "Now you try it."

Dean shut his eyes, his brow furrowed into deep creases, his fists clenched tightly on his knees. I closed my eyes again too for a minute, mostly to give him some privacy. Then I heard it.

"Oh shit Kat, come on – how do you do this?" I looked up thinking Dean was talking to me only to see his eyes still tightly shut in concentration. I started to speak to him then stopped when I heard it again. *"I was hoping this would be easy. I need it to happen now."*

Dean's mouth was not moving but it was clearly his voice in my head. I felt certain he was unaware that I could hear what he was thinking. I wondered if he would also be able to hear me as well.

Instead of answering with my voice I decided to reach out to him. Focusing on his face I thought the words *"Dean, can you hear me? Look at me."* Instantly he looked up at me.

"I'm sorry Kat were you saying something to me?" He asked.

I had an idea. "Close your eyes again and just listen this time." He did as I said and I reached out to him again, this time seeing inside his mind. *"Like this,"* I told him.

Guiding him like this was easier than trying to explain the process.

As our minds came together he suddenly understood. One second I was looking at Dean, the next I was staring at one of his large lab rats peeking out of Nicks jogging pants. A second later Dean stood before me again. He flushed as he realized he was now naked before me and I turned around so he could get his clothes back on.

"That is the major setback of transfiguring." I told him over my shoulder. I couldn't help the silly grin on my face. A second later a loud crash filled the room as a very flustered Dean fell onto the coffee table in his panic to get some pants back on. I turned around and helped him to his feet.

"I'll have to remember that." He said grinning at me. "What was that you did just now?" He asked me looking a little more than puzzled.

"I'm not really sure myself." I explained. "I had closed my eyes and thought you were talking to me. When I opened my eyes I still heard your voice but your mouth wasn't moving. I thought that if I could hear your thoughts maybe you could hear mine."

"It felt like you were inside my head just now."

"I think maybe I was. I was trying to show you, rather than tell you how to transfigure."

"Well it worked."

"Can you do it on your own now?"

"I think so. Let's see." The next moment Dean was standing before me in his own leather suit, complete with a crisscrossing holster for the twin katanas on his back. His suit, like mine was skin tight revealing every muscle in his body.

He had always been pretty well toned but now he looked incredible. *Look out Captain America!* I made him turn around for me and whistled when I saw his tight tush.

He looked down at himself then back up at me, a face splitting grin now in place. "Now you're not the only one who gets to dress like a comic book hero."

I laughed. "Just don't make me look at you naked again." I teased.

The light banter helped to ease the tension we were both feeling and put us in a better frame of mind. However the sense of urgency still remained pushing us toward action. Nick and Stephan appeared moments later. They had heard the crash and wanted to make sure everything was okay. Dean turned to face them as they entered the room.

"We're ready to get this done." He stated. Nicked eyed him in the suit.

"Good," he said nodding his head. "So are we. Let's go."

Nick had opened his metal lock box revealing an assortment of knives and guns. He was now wearing a shoulder holster that suspended a large knife for easy access with his right hand, a Glock on his left hip and another knife strapped to his right thigh.

"The guns are for the humans, the knives for the vampires. You have to sever their head to kill them." Then handing me a gun he said, "Take this. They will be shooting at you. Shoot back." I nodded and strapped it on then went for my sword. I noticed that Stephan had his sword and a knife.

We left in two separate cars. Nick and I in one and Stephan and Dean, complete with his twin katanas, in the other. We would meet Orlando and his group just after dark.

Our rendezvous spot was an empty field about five miles from the warehouse. Orlando and his entourage arrived in a Range Rover pulling up next to the other two vehicles.

My last meeting with him had not gone well at all and I was apprehensive to say the least about this meeting. To my relief I was no longer drawn to him, the pull utterly eradicated by Nick's mark on me. I wasn't sure how he would respond to me either and was unprepared when he greeted me much like a family member, pulling me into a hug and kissing me on both cheeks.

"Katherine it is good to see you doing so well." He announced as he pulled me close. I have to admit there was a certain sense that I did belong to him, even if not romantically. He was my sire – so to speak.

He made quick introductions to the men he'd brought with him then Stephan pulled out the drawings of the facility. Everyone gathered around the trunk of Stephan's car as he outlined the plan.

We would go in on foot through the surrounding woods. Dean and I would attempt entry through the drainage system while Stephan and Nick went over the fence through the upper story windows. Orlando and his men would form a perimeter and hopefully prevent anyone from coming or going.

With any luck the security would be minimal as they should not be expecting us. I hoped for a quick get in and get out but the closer we got the more nervous I became.

I turned to Orlando before we left. "Thank you for coming and helping us." I said.

"Katherine it is the least I can do. I feel somewhat responsible that you are even in this position. Although I hope that we do not have to cross Vladimir tonight. It is never a good thing to make an enemy of him."

"He's that bad then?" I asked, afraid my fears were about to be confirmed.

Orlando looked thoughtfully before responding. "No my dear, it isn't that he is so bad, just very determined and very powerful. He usually gets exactly what he wants. It just seems that he wants what he shouldn't right now."

I pondered his words as we made our way to the warehouse. As scared as I was right now for Callie I just couldn't bring myself to feel the anger I should have felt. In the grand scheme of things it seemed that Vladimir's humanity was pushing through the vampire exterior. He wanted what we all wanted at one time or another – to have a child.

I'd been there before. I knew how bad the longing could get. True I hadn't resorted to kidnapping but I wasn't in the same position as him. I could have become pregnant again; I simply chose to deny myself the gratification because of my circumstances. But what if I'd been incapable of conceiving? What would I have done for a child?

I thought of Nick and his recent discovery that he'd fathered a son and how happy he'd been just knowing that. I thought of Angie and David and there frozen assets – the hope that must have been there; the idea that someday they would have another child together.

Dean nudged my shoulder. "We're here." He whispered at my ear. The pipes draining into the ditch were fifty feet ahead. Nick and Stephan were approaching from the other side. Orlando and his men were staying out of sight at the moment. I glanced at the front gate before entering the pipe. The guard shack was empty.

The pipes were huge, not quite large enough to stand upright in but at least I wasn't crawling – yet. Dean was just ahead of me. A loud crash echoing through the pipes caused us both to flatten against the wall. I looked over at Dean amazed to see he had changed to the color and texture of the concrete pipe he was leaning against.

"Wow, can you sprout the porcupine quills too?"

"Huh?" he asked. I nodded at him and he brought his hands up before his face to examine them.

"This is awesome!" He said in a whisper. As soon as he pulled away from the side of the pipe he returned to his natural color.

We came to a junction where the pipe ran off to the right and left. Looking left in the distance it appeared that the pipe opened up even larger. We stayed right believing this would bring us closer to the room where Callie was being kept.

Shortly the pipe got smaller, and as I had dreaded, was crawling on my elbows. I hoped they didn't get any smaller. After a few minutes the pipes turned up and we were forced to jump up to the grate. Jumping wasn't the problem; it was knocking the grate off and making a huge noise to alert anyone close by.

Dean went first. He jumped so hard that he was able to grab the grate and carry it with him far above the opening landing with the grace and stealth of a cat. Once he was sure no-one was around he motioned me up. I was at his side a second later.

We had surfaced in another part of the building. Replacing the grate we started making our way to the room. We were in a section that I had not seen in my vision. This area had several small offices along a narrow hall. Following the hall we came to the open area. Across to our left was the room where Callie would be.

A movement overhead brought my attention to the catwalk where I saw Nick watching quietly. Stephan was silently making his way across with the stealth and balance of a cat. There seemed to be no one else here. I'd not seen or heard a guard any of Vladimir's men.

We crossed the open space so fast a human could not have seen us if they'd been looking, pausing at the door to listen before entering. Something was wrong. The room was too quiet. I opened the door and Dean burst inside. I followed on his heels only to find that my suspicions had been right. Callie was not here.

She had been here though. I could smell her but I smelled something else. Vladimir had been here with her. I could smell his arousal and I knew Dean could too. The look on his face and the deep growl that escaped his throat told me he recognized the scent for what it was. The muscles in his jaw clenched tight.

"If he has hurt her…" he cut off, closing his eyes.

"Let's just find her," I encouraged.

"Do you think she is still here?"

I took a deep inhale of the air around me. I could still smell her, faintly. "She's here – somewhere." But there were other scents. "We're not alone anymore. They know we're here."

We stepped back into the warehouse to warn the others. We'd walked into a trap. Then the bullets started flying. Dean leapt into action locating the source of the bullets and putting one of the gunmen out of commission.

Stephan was on the ground immediately. In a stunning display of speed and precision he used his sword to deflect the bullets, sending them flying back in the direction they came from.

Nick remained on the catwalk using his vantage point to cover the two men on the ground. With lightning speed he moved from one target to the next, his bullet finding its mark with deadly accuracy.

The sound of glass shattering announced the arrival of Orlando and his men, crashing through the second story windows just moments after the shooting started. The vampires broke through the meager human defenses with little effort.

Vladimir's men had to have been here all along and I wondered how they'd masked their scent. I scanned the room. I didn't see Vlad but I knew he had to be here. Callie was still here and he would not go far. He would stay nearby to ensure he didn't lose his bargaining tool.

The only warning I got was a flicker out of the corner of my eye then he was there. His men were drawing the fire from the rest of our group, keeping them distracted while he got to me.

That split second warning had allowed me just enough time to step to the side, effectively evading his grasp. He had lost the element of surprise and I was now prepared for his affront, sword drawn and at the ready.

The game had changed to my advantage. I was no longer the pursued by the pursuer, a turn Vladimir had not expected. I was determined not to allow his escape. He had my daughter and I wanted her back.

Around us the fight went on but we barely noticed. The humans had been taken out quickly but the vamps were still fighting. It was hand to hand combat now, vampire pitted against vampire in a desperate struggle.

Everything was at stake for me. Any loss would be more than I could endure. I had to end this quickly. I could not bear the loss of any that were with me. Not when it was for me alone that they were here.

"You surprise me Katherine," Vlad was saying to me. "I didn't expect so much fight from you."

"Where is my daughter?" I asked ignoring his statement.

"You want her – come get her."

I knew he was attempting to lead me away from the group but I had no choice but to follow. He was, as best as I could tell, unarmed. It was evident he did not want to hurt me. He could have picked up any number of fallen weapons to use to subdue me had he wanted to.

Returning my sword to its sheath, I tracked his movements and followed. He was allowing no time for an attack, simply leading the chase. I pursued him around the warehouse from floor to ceiling, uncertain of what I'd do once I caught him.

Finally he jumped to the floor again next to one of the drainage grates. What happened next surprised even me, as he suddenly transformed into a rolling vapor and slid off into the underground pipes.

"Two can play at this game." I said under my breath. He believed me unable to follow, unaware that I also could transform. He was in for yet another surprise. I removed the grate and jumped off into the darkness.

I took a moment once I landed to see which direction he went. I caught a faint hint of mist to my right. The pipes were small and I had no time to waste crawling. I discarded the gun and transformed into a large rat. Sword in tow I scurried down the long length of pipe.

I followed the vapor until the pipe opened up into a large cavern. Jumping down I transformed back. Unsheathing my sword I moved cautiously forward. He was here somewhere in the shadows. He could be anywhere lurking.

"Katherine."

The voice came from right behind me, startling me. I turned swiftly, stabbing blindly as I did. My sword hit its mark sinking deep into his chest. I instantly felt remorse. Hurting him had never been my plan. Despite what he'd done to get me here he'd not tried to harm me in any way.

He staggered backward, a look of surprise on his face. He was wounded badly. He could heal but it would take some time. Staggering forward grasping his chest he moved toward a door on the far side of the chamber. In shock I followed, staying back a short distance.

Inside the room he stumbled against a makeshift bed. I looked on in horror as I realized Callie was lying there limply. He knelt beside the bed, leaning heavily against it, stroking her face affectionately. It was then I stopped to listen and could hear her pulse. It was thready and weak but still there, her breathing barely audible.

"Isn't she beautiful?" He asked as if talking to an old friend, his fingers, covered with his blood, gently stroking her face and hair. I looked at my daughter laid out across the bed, motionless and pale she looked like a porcelain doll. I noticed the puncture wounds on the side of her neck and my heart flipped again.

"Did you turn her then?" I asked.

"No." he replied still stroking her hair. "I wanted to and she had been willing….if it would keep you safe." His voice was growing weak. "I fed from her…saw that I would never have her heart. I had thought that wouldn't matter but…it did.

I couldn't change her…knowing she might not be able to bear the children she desires. I saw it in her blood." Vladimir was losing a lot of blood and the scent of it was hauntingly familiar. He was growing weaker by the minute. But his blood, it was almost as if…

I moved quickly toward him. "Will you finish me off then?" He asked – almost a plea. I shook my head, throwing my sword aside. I grabbed his arms pushing back the sleeves revealing his right wrist then his left. And I saw it. There on his left wrist was a scar faded with time so that no one but a vampire would recognize it but it was there.

Still I had to be sure. I ripped open his shirt exposing his wound. It was bleeding far worse than I had imagined. I sensed him quiver. He thought I would end him by draining his blood, but that was not my intention. Lowering my mouth to his chest I tasted his blood then bit deeper and drank freely, gathering his memories as I did. My suspicions were confirmed. I knew what I had to do.

Kneeling beside him I offered him my wrist. "Take this and feed, you need your strength to heal." He looked at me in astonishment as I offered my arm.

"Why would…?"

I shoved my arm out to him again. We didn't have a lot of time. The others would be looking for me soon I was sure.

"Just take it and feed." He didn't question me again but took my arm. I felt his fangs pierce the flesh and the blood leave my body as he nursed my arm. Startled he looked up at me and I knew he understood why. He'd seen my memories, knew what I knew to be the truth.

After a few minutes he leaned back against the bed breathing hard. His chest wound was starting to close. A noise at the door drew my attention as Dean entered; he seemed to be favoring his left leg. The blood drained from his face when he saw Callie on the bed.

"Is she….?"

"She's alive but weak; we need to get her out of her. Can you take her to the surface?" He collapsed next to her on the makeshift bed, pulling her up close against his chest, speaking softly to her, covering her face with gentle kisses. Callie barely opened her eyes and seeing Dean attempted a weak smile.

"You came." She said – her voice barely a low whisper. "I'm so sorry Dean."

"Shhhh," He said covering her mouth with his. "I'm taking you away from here." He glanced over at me with a strange look on his face.

"I'll be along soon." I assured him and I watched as he carried Callie out of the room.

I looked back to Vladimir. "Are you strong enough to get out of here?" His chest wound had completely closed now and he was breathing more steadily.

"I think I'll be able to soon enough." He stated still watching my every move. I looked at his handsome face and strong body. There was much more to this man Vladimir. I was fortunate to get a glimpse. It was a small glimpse, but it had revealed truths. One of those truths was that I owed him much more than I had just done for him.

He had a story to tell and I wanted to know what it was. I knew we didn't have time tonight but Vladimir had not seen the last of me. I placed my hand on his chest feeling the slow steady beat of his heart. His eyes met mine once again.

"Thank you Katherine," he said earnestly. I nodded in response.

"Katherine!" Nick's voice boomed down the pipes and I knew he would be here soon looking for me.

I turned to Vlad. "Are you ready?" He was attempting to stand when Nick rushed through the door, his face filled with fear then anger when he saw Vlad. I stood between the two men.

"I'm here Nick and I'm fine. We are all fine."

"Move out of my way." He said moving toward me with determination, a knife ready in his hand. I knew Vlad was still weak and Nick was going to kill him.

"Nick don't, you can't do this." I pleaded.

"Give me one good reason why I shouldn't he yelled. He's threatened you, kidnapped Callie and now Stephan is injured because of him." I felt sick.

"Is it bad?" I asked

"Bad enough," He barked. "He'll live but this was all so senseless, all those humans dead because of him." I held my ground. Vlad was now standing behind me.

"He's right Katherine; he has a right to want to kill me."

"NO." I stated emphatically. "The killing stops here." Then turning to look at Nick, "You can't kill him Nick. He is the one that turned you. It was him that pulled you away from the bear and fed you from his arm. It's his blood that runs in your veins now."

Nick's face turned ashen as he stared in disbelief. "What he did to Callie wasn't right but it was understandable. If nothing else I owe him. I owe him one for saving you for me."

I watched as the anger fled from Nick's face and he lowered his arms. After all these years he was face to face with his creator. Finally after a long moment he breathed out a sigh.

"Come on Kat, let's go home." I walked into his arms and held him as he closed them around me.

Leaving the room I turned and looked at Vladimir *"You haven't seen the last of me."* His eyes flickered infinitesimally revealing his surprise, then immediately I heard his reply. *"I'll be looking forward to it Katherine – take care of the child.* Then he was gone.

TWENTY-SIX

Two days later………

Taking a break from my trip planning I wandered down to the back patio. In another week Nick and I would be flying out for our extended European trip.

I watched as Callie and Dean walked hand in hand about the grounds at Stephan's. Dean had hardly left her side since her return, hovering over her making sure she was okay.

Vlad had fed on her draining a lot of blood and leaving her weak, but with some IV fluids and iron rich foods she was back to her normal self and was tired of everyone fussing over her.

I thought back to the night at the warehouse. Stephan had been wounded but not severely although it did take him a few hours to recover. He complained that we were all making a mountain out of a molehill – his words verbatim – about his injuries. He assured us all he'd endured far worse many times over and the bullet hole and stab wounds were nothing to worry about.

Nick had suffered only superficial wounds that were healed by the time he reached me in the tunnels. Dean had a nasty gash across his left shoulder he sustained when a bullet grazed him and a deep cut just above his left hip from a blade wielded by one of Vladimir's vamps.

Orlando and his men were uninjured except for some cuts they sustained when crashing through the glass panes. They had stayed with us through the night, in case there was a surprise attack.

All in all four humans were killed that night and the rest fled when they realized they were fighting vampires. Six of Vladimir's men were vampire. Dean killed one of them, severing his head with the twin katanas. Stephan had killed another. The others had retreated suddenly as if called off from the fight.

I'd sat with Callie through the night, force feeding her broths and anything she would eat. The next morning we'd had a long talk. She asked me about my being a vampire so I'd told her the entire story, as best as I could remember, even about my first meeting with Orlando

I could tell she had something she wanted to say but she looked conflicted.

"So when you come together and share blood you can see everything about the person?" she asked.

"Pretty much, yes," I stated.

"And if Dean were to take my blood he would be able to see all about me?"

I nodded. Callie started to cry then. I hugged her close.

"What's wrong?" I asked

"It's just that when I was with Vladimir and he was going to turn me." She lowered her voice to a whisper. "Mom, I really wanted him and I don't know why. I love Dean, but I wanted to be with Vladimir. I don't want to hurt Dean. I'm afraid if he finds out…..he'll stop loving me."

"First of all, from what Vlad told me, he saw that you were in love with Dean and I'm sure Dean would see the same thing. But if it worries you maybe you should talk to Dean about it. Be open and honest about it."

"Secondly, one of the abilities that vampires have is our calling power. It pretty much makes us irresistible when we want to be, once we learn to use it. It's how we attract prey when we need to feed and unfortunately can be used for other things." Callie looked relieved.

"I'll talk to Dean." She stated simply.

I was pulled back to the present by Nick's arms snaking around my waist, pulling me tight against his chest. There was one more talk I needed to have – I had put it off long enough. I turned in his arms to face him. He rested his forehead against mine kissing me lightly on the nose.

"You sure are quiet today. What have you been thinking about?" My hand went to his face, caressing it with my fingertips. Reaching up he covered my hand with his and placed a kiss in the center of my palm. I closed my eyes and inhaled deeply taking in his scent that I loved so much to be near.

"I'm thinking about the man I fell in love with. Thinking about how my life has changed since he found me…" I paused looking up at Nick through my lashes. "Thinking about what a wonderful father I know he's going to be." I waited a moment letting what I had just said sink in. He jerked his head back suddenly looking at me eyes wide with surprise.

"What…." "Do you mean…" "Are you saying…?" I nodded my head slowly, a wide grin spreading across my face. Then right there on the patio Nick knelt before me and placed his ear to my stomach. He stilled as he listened intently, not even breathing then slowly a smile spread across his face. When he looked up at me his face was beaming.

"I can hear it, our baby's heartbeat." Jumping to his feet he pulled me into his arms and swung me around before putting me down again, kissing me. When he pulled away his expression had changed to one of awe and reverence.

"We're having a baby." He said the smile bursting forth again. Then he had me over his shoulder running through the house shouting to anyone that was listening. "We're having a baby."

Buried in his study Stephan looked up listening intently for a moment then smiled shaking his head. "I knew she was special."

Out on the backside of the property Dean was telling Callie about the koi in the pond when he stopped mid-sentence then threw his head back laughing.

"What? What's so funny?" Callie asked.

"Your mom just gave Nick the news." He said still smiling.

"News of what?" she asked exasperated.

Dean grinned widely and kissed Callie on the nose. "That you're going to be a big sister!"

Two years later...

The woman stopped for a moment in front of the narrow wrought iron gate to check the numbers of the apartment against the address she had written down. This was the place. Pushing the gate open she made her way down the short path and up the stairs to the front door where she stopped once again, drying her sweaty palms on the front of her wool skirt.

She didn't really want to be here. She hated having to talk to strangers but she had promised Kat. She would do anything for her...

Gathering her wits about her she timidly reached up and knocked on the door. She waited what seemed an eternity before the door opened up to her revealing a tall, older man with balding hair. He looked down at her over his large, crooked nose; squinting his eyes into a frown.

"Can I Help you Ma'am?" He asked with a distinct British accent.

The woman responded nervously. "Oui monsieur, pardon my intrusion, but I am looking to speak with Monsieur Dimitru. Is he in?"

"The master is in but with guests at this time. Is he expecting you?" The butler asked.

"Non monsieur, my apologies, I am here on an errand to deliver a post. Madame Katherine asked me to see to it."

The butler showed the woman into the large foyer, instructing her to wait. Obediently she stayed right where he left her, only shifting her eyes about to take in the magnificent old home.

The butler stepped into the large dining area where several men were seated at a long wooden table, discussing business over breakfast. Approaching the man at the head of the table he bent and whispered something in his ear. The man's eyes widened momentarily as he listened to the butler.

"Excuse me gentlemen," He said pushing his chair back from the table. "I have a matter that needs to be tended to. I will only be a moment. Please continue without me."

Vladimir Dimitru stepped out of the dining room heading to the front foyer. He looked tired. His shoulders not quite as straight as before and his eyes lacked the luster they once held, but he was intrigued by the nature of this unscheduled visit.

He could see the woman far before he reached her. She was tall and willowy with long auburn hair and hazel, almond shaped eyes. Her full red lips were a stark contrast to her milky white skin.

She was nervously fidgeting with an envelope, sliding her thumb and forefinger over the crease of the flap. As Vladimir approached she peeked up shyly through her thick black lashes.

Vladimir extended his hand to her, introducing himself. She nodded slightly.

"And you are?"

"Ah, forgive me monsieur. I am Angelique Aube. Thank you for seeing me Monsieur Dimitru, I am sorry for the intrusion to your day. My Madame, Katherine, requested I deliver this to you." She said handing him the envelope.

He took the envelope from her noting her French accent. Opening the envelope he removed several pages of paper. Motioning to a couple of chairs along the wall he nodded.

"Please … asseyez-vous s'il vous plait, j'en ai pour deux minute."

She nodded, "Oui, merci." She said going to sit in one of the chairs. He watched her as she moved away from him. *Very graceful,* he noted

Vladimir unfolded the paper and began to read.

Vladimir,

I have recently heard that you are now residing near London which is why I am writing you.

My time here has come to an end and I must return to the states where family is waiting.

During my stay her I met a lovely young woman that you have now met if this letter has found you. For reasons that are too many to contain in this post I became quite close to her. So you will understand that when she was struck by a tragedy I could not allow her to die.

She is my one and only convert.

Sadly, I must leave her behind and being that she is so new I had hoped to find her a new charge. She has no other family to whom she can turn. Perhaps there is a way that you might find to employ her.

As my convert I am truly proud of her. She is quite like me. She possesses qualities that, I must say, are rare – yes quite rare indeed. I believe her to be capable of any task that you might put before her. I leave it to you–

My apologies that I have not yet made my visit to you as I had promised when last we met. I have not forgotten, nor have I forgotten the truths I learned that night.

Forever in your debt,

Katherine Cristo–

Vlad shook his head in frustration. Just what did she expect him to do? He wasn't a charity organization. Taking a new vampire under his wing would take more energy than he had right now. *Things were just so different since....that night.*

He was tired and his head was starting to hurt. He had business to attend to. *Guests waiting on him in the other room for fuck's sake!* Running his hands through his hair he started to fold up the note, mentally reciting her request – when it struck him.

He opened the letter once more and quickly skimmed over it again.

"She is my convert..." "Quite like myself...."
"Qualities that are rare...." "Capable of any task...." "I have not forgotten...."

Vladimir stood in utter shock. He now fully understood the real reason Katherine had sent her to him. Not in a million years would he have expected this. He barely even believed that it was happening now.

He turned his attention back the girl sitting quietly by the door and for the first time really looked at her. She was enchanting...beautiful... and according to Katherine, worthy to be loved for many reasons.

Slowly he folded the papers and placed them inside his breast pocket. A smile began at the curve of his mouth and slowly spread across his face until it lit in his eyes, bringing back the glow that used to reside there. The change to his countenance was immediate as the tired look vanished and his shoulders squared back once again.

Not too long ago he'd had a dream but somehow had lost sight of it. Now it looked as if that dream might become a reality…..

Fastening my lap belt I settled into my seat. We were aboard a private jet that Nick had chartered to take us back to the states, preparing to take off from Heathrow Airport. In just a matter of hours I would be back home. Callie and Dean would be meeting us. I couldn't wait to see them again. We'd been gone two years.

Nick handed Charlie – our thriving, rambunctious, toddler– over to me while he buckled himself into his seat. Charlie was sleeping now. With any luck he'd stay that way for a while. I lifted his chunky fingers to my mouth and kissed them, enjoying a quiet moment with him asleep.

I was glad we had chartered the jet. The trip would be so much easier with room to move around in where the baby could play. I had dreaded the thought of trying to contain him in my lap for that many hours on a regular plane. That and the fact that he'd recently acquired the nasty habit of biting (no clue where he'd gotten that from) and I was afraid he'd bite the other passengers.

Before we'd left the states, Doctor Lee had told me to seek out an OB/Gyn that was a good friend of hers living in London. Doctor Brown had met with me and monitored my progress, and when we decided to stay in Europe, delivered Charlie.

After takeoff Nick lifted the baby from my lap so that I could rest. It would be so good to get home. I closed my tired eyes for a few moments.

I recognized the voice the moment I heard it say my name.

"*Katherine.*"

Opening my eyes I expected to see Vladimir standing in front of me, but there was no-one.

"*Katherine.*" The voice said again. "*Thank you.*"

I closed my eyes and smiled to myself. "*You're very welcome!*"

Thank you for reading Bloodline Immersed In You. I hope you enjoyed it as much as I enjoyed writing it.

I am looking forward to my next book to be released in the spring of 2013 and possibly a sequel to Bloodline sometime after that.

I'd like to hear what you think about the book. You can leave feedback by reviewing my book on amazon.com Check out my website @ www.ardeanpublications.com